THE GUILD CODEX: SPELLBOUND / EIGHT

DAMNED SOULS
AND A SANGRIA

ANNETTE MARIE

dark owl
fantasy

Damned Souls and a Sangria
The Guild Codex: Spellbound / Book Eight

Dark Owl Fantasy Inc.
PO Box 88106, Rabbit Hill Post Office
Edmonton, AB, Canada T6R 0M5
www.darkowlfantasy.com

Cover Copyright © 2020 by Annette Ahner
Cover and Book Interior by Midnight Whimsy Designs
www.midnightwhimsydesigns.com

Editing by Elizabeth Darkley
arrowheadediting.wordpress.com

ISBN 978-1-988153-53-7

MORE BOOKS BY ANNETTE MARIE

STEEL & STONE UNIVERSE

Steel & Stone Series

Chase the Dark

Bind the Soul

Yield the Night

Reap the Shadows

Unleash the Storm

Steel & Stone

Spell Weaver Trilogy

The Night Realm

The Shadow Weave

The Blood Curse

OTHER WORKS

Red Winter Trilogy

Red Winter

Dark Tempest

Immortal Fire

THE GUILD CODEX

♠

CLASSES OF MAGIC

Spiritalis

Psychica

Arcana

Demonica

Elementaria

MYTHIC

A person with magical ability

MPD / MAGIPOL

The organization that regulates mythics and their activities

ROGUE

A mythic living in violation of MPD laws

DAMNED SOULS
AND A SANGRIA

I

I'D NEVER SEEN the Crow and Hammer this packed yet this silent.

Fifty-one members sat around the pub tables or on stools at the bar, and every face was turned toward the east wall. For some, a fearful shadow lurked in their eyes—the non-combat mythics. In others, a bright spark of expectation—the adrenaline-loving fighters. And in a few, a cautious worry—the wiser, older members who knew this wasn't normal.

This wasn't just a meeting. It wasn't just a job.

Like the rest of my guild, my gaze was fixed on Darius, who stood facing the men and women for whom he'd created a home.

"Thank you for coming on such short notice." His somber words carried across the room. "We have an urgent matter to discuss that will affect every member of this guild."

Bracing my elbows on my knees, I searched for a hint of his usual quiet amusement. I couldn't find any.

"Many of you are familiar with the incident eight years ago known as the 'Enright extermination,' where eleven demon mages were discovered in Oregon and wiped out by the Keys of Solomon. The Enright demon mages were part of a larger organization called the Court of the Red Queen. For lack of a better term, it is a cult—a demon-worshipping cult.

"Just over a week ago, an investigation undertaken by several of our members uncovered more." His gaze swept across the room. "The Court of the Red Queen survived the Enright extermination and has been active for the last eight years. Furthermore, the cult has now taken up residence in Vancouver."

A buzzing whisper sputtered through the room but fell silent as he continued.

"This group is extremely dangerous. Not only are they adept at hiding in plain sight, but their members include summoners and contractors with no regard for MPD regulations. And as demonstrated in Oregon, they know how to create demon mages. If the cult is in Vancouver, that means, in all likelihood, there are demon mages in Vancouver too."

I expected another wave of whispers, but no one so much as cleared their throat. I understood why.

Demon mages were the most universally feared type of mythic. A human possessed by a demon, with access to the demon's magic and a high probability of slipping into violent madness—yeah, they were nightmare fuel of the worst kind.

An unbound demon was more destructive, possessing greater magic on top of beastly strength and a nearly unkillable body, but demon mages were more feared because their danger was hidden behind a human face. You could spend years in the company of a demon mage and unless he drew on his demonic power, you'd never know.

My gaze slid to the mythic sitting on the stool beside mine. Ezra watched Darius with his usual poker face.

"After a week of careful investigation," the GM continued, "we've identified eight suspected cultists. Though we haven't uncovered their stronghold yet, we suspect their numbers are much higher, and an unknown percentage of them could be demon mages.

"Tomorrow morning, I'll submit our investigation to the MPD, at which point their agents will take the lead. Multiple guilds will be involved—including, most likely, non-local demon hunters like the Keys of Solomon. But Vancouver isn't a remote location like Enright, where the casualties of the battle were limited to cultists and guild combatants."

My hands curled into fists. Cultist casualties … including Ezra's parents. It turned out the Keys of Solomon hadn't murdered innocent families at Enright, but between their excessively anti-demon members who'd tried to kill Ezra and their unexpectedly pro-demon members who'd tried to kill me, I wasn't a fan.

"The Crow and Hammer has called Vancouver home for over fifty years." Darius's gaze speared each guild member, one after another, as he spoke. "And we will allow neither a demon cult nor an outside guild seeking bounties and glory to destroy it. Protecting our city will require every single one of you, whether you're a psychic, alchemist, scholar, apprentice, or combat mythic who'll step onto the battlefield.

"To defeat demons and demon mages, we need weapons. We need artifacts. We need potions. We need to analyze the cult's past activities, their possible resources, and effective strategies for killing demons. Everyone here can contribute their time, energy, resourcefulness, and unique talents."

He flipped open his folder. "We have prepared teams, which our officers will lead. We won't demand anyone enter combat if they prefer not to, but we expect you to support your guildmates in every way you can while we face our most dangerous mission in decades.

"Our first team, led by first officer Girard, will source and build an arsenal of weapons, artifacts, and alchemy to use against the cult. Our second team, led by Tabitha, will gather and analyze past research, combat technique, and case studies involving demons and demon mages. Our third team, led by Felix, will handle non-magical supply logistics and communications.

"And our fourth team"—a corner of Darius's mouth lifted— "will be led by our newly promoted fourth officer, Aaron Sinclair."

A beat of surprised silence rang through the room, then cheers and applause erupted at top volume as everyone turned toward the copper-haired pyromage sitting on my other side. He grinned and waved, and I laughed at the uncharacteristic self-consciousness in his expression.

"Aaron," Darius called over the noise, "will oversee combat training, which will incorporate strategies and weaponry provided by the other teams."

Clapping enthusiastically, I looked past Aaron to the spot beside him, eager to know what a certain dark-haired, cool-headed electramage thought of this. The sight of his empty stool punched me in the gut. Aaron had finally gotten his promotion, and thanks to Makiko, Kai wasn't here to congratulate him.

"My role," Darius said, "will be overseeing the officers and coordinating with other Vancouver guilds. Tomorrow, I will visit Odin's Eye, the Pandora Knights, the Grand Grimoire, and the SeaDevils to speak with their GMs. Together, we will protect our city. Time is of the essence."

Darius summarized our next steps, then read off the assigned members of every team. I was assigned to Felix's team. Ezra—and pretty much every combat mythic, which was almost half the guild—was assigned to Aaron's team.

I hoped Darius had let Felix know that I wouldn't be available to help. Protecting Vancouver from the Court of the Red Queen was high on my to-do list, but my top priority was saving Ezra from his soul-binding contract with Eterran. After that, we could help our guild take down the cult—and their leaders, Xanthe and Xever. The mentalist who'd lured Ezra's family into the cult and the summoner who'd turned him into a demon mage both deserved to be roasted on an open-flame spit.

As the meeting ended and conversations broke out across the room, I whirled toward Aaron.

"Um, a *promotion?*" I smacked his shoulder. "Why didn't you tell me?"

"It only happened yesterday." He smirked. "But I'd have kept it a secret anyway, just to see the look on your face when Darius announced it."

"Congrats, man," Ezra said, leaning around me. "Knew it'd happen sooner or later." His expression turned thoughtful. "Kai owes me fifty bucks."

"For what?" Aaron asked suspiciously.

"I bet him you'd become an officer before you turned thirty."

"*Thirty?*"

"But Kai figured it'd take you another five to ten years to *really* get a knack for thinking before you light things on fire."

Aaron snorted, and as Ezra grinned in response, my diaphragm cartwheeled across my stomach.

You'd think, after eight months of exposure to Ezra's grins, I'd be desensitized by now, but I was going through a process here. Namely, the Ezra I'd gotten to know over those past eight months was changing—evolving, or … maybe awakening?

As though sensing my thoughts, his mismatched gaze turned to me. My stomach did another round of acrobatics.

"Aaron!"

Laetitia swept over, followed by half of Aaron's team.

"So you're an officer now, eh?" The tall hydromage gave him a flinty once-over—probably remembering a few past incidents that, somehow, had all ended with Aaron drenched in water—then cracked her knuckles. "What's the plan for training?"

"Step one is forming teams with the right balance of strengths and weaknesses for combat against contractors and demon mages," Aaron answered. "We'll focus on defense first, then practice the most efficient ways to kill them so we don't exhaust ourselves and our magic."

"What, you can't just incinerate demons with your unstoppable fire?" Cearra, my least favorite blond apprentice sorceress, muttered.

Andrew shot the younger woman a quelling look. "We'll want to inflict as much damage as possible, and fire is a good option. We could ask the alchemists to make us firebombs."

"And some nasty-ass smoke bombs," Gwen added with her usual sprinkling of vulgarity. "Blind the bastards so the demons can't spit us like damn pigs."

"But *we* need to be able to see what we're doing," Darren countered. "Bleeding them out would be better. We should be planning the easiest ways to slit some veins."

Aaron held up a hand, calling for silence, and everyone obeyed instantly—but before he could speak, another voice trickled in from the back of the group.

"Those tactics … they probably won't work."

The gathered mythics looked around in confusion, searching for the source of the light alto voice, then parted to reveal the young woman standing behind them, so petite she'd been invisible.

Robin Page blinked owlishly as everyone looked at her.

"What do *you* know?" Darren asked, keeping his sneering tone subtle enough that no one would call him out for it—no one except me.

I angrily opened my mouth—

"I'm a demon contractor." Robin nudged her glasses up her nose. "But I'm sure your experiences are valid too, Darren."

I choked back a laugh as the sorcerer clenched his teeth.

Robin turned to Aaron. "Fire can burn legally contracted demons, but at least one cult demon is so loosely contracted that he can wield his magic. Fire could make him stronger."

"Stronger?" Aaron repeated blankly.

"Demons can convert heat into magic. To burn them, you'd have to apply heat faster than the demon can absorb it." She tapped her chin thoughtfully. "Alistair can do it, but I'm not sure about regular fire."

I stared at her. Everyone else was also staring or scanning the pub for the volcanomage in question.

"Cold can only kill a badly injured demon." Robin tucked her hair behind her ear. "Bleeding them out won't work very well, either. Their blood is thick and clots quickly. Even deep wounds stop bleeding within a couple minutes."

"How are we supposed to kill them, then?" Darren snapped.

"Hmm." Robin thought for a moment. "Vampire saliva?"

Several of us exchanged confused looks.

"If you inject demons with a large dose of vampire saliva," she added, "they collapse."

Aaron rubbed the back of his neck. "How much is a 'large' dose?"

"Um. About like … a couple of tablespoons?"

Cameron raked a hand through his hair in frustration. "Where are we supposed to get that much vampire saliva?"

"We can barely find *one* vampire lately." Darren shook his head. "Their numbers dropped off a cliff after the December surge."

"We'll look into vamp spit," Aaron said, "but as always with demons, our best bet is taking out the contractors, and that'll be our focus. Thanks for the tips, Robin."

She smiled, and as Aaron asked who had experience fighting contractors, I inched through the group to Robin's side.

"Can we talk?" I whispered.

At her nod, I linked our arms and steered her away from the cluster of combat mythics. Everyone else in the pub had grouped up as well, beginning the early preparations for one of the guild's most perilous operations ever.

My gaze drifted across them as I passed—the alchemists, Sin's silvery purple hair among them, had joined Ramsey,

Lyndon, and Weldon, who were all well-versed in artifacts. Other familiar faces filled the room, and tightness spread through my chest. Was it asking too much to pit this guild of misfits against the Court of the Red Queen?

"Tori?"

I realized I was just standing there with my arm hooked through Robin's. Refocusing, I veered into a dim, quiet corner and released her arm. "Any updates?"

She didn't have to ask what I was talking about. "Not yet. We're working on it."

An entire week had passed since we'd given her the cult grimoire so she could find a way to save Ezra. How long did it take to read a tome of complex spells written in a dead language?

Okay, maybe my expectations weren't entirely fair.

"It isn't a simple process," she added in a whisper. "I know you're impatient, Tori, but as far as I can tell, unmaking a demon mage has never been done before."

"I get that." I checked once more that no one was anywhere near close enough to overhear us. "It's just that Ezra doesn't have much time left."

Though he seemed stable enough, his new cooperation with Eterran had me worried. We were gambling everything on the cult grimoire, and if Robin couldn't find answers in time, all our struggles would be for nothing. Our only other option was the demonic amulet, but having witnessed the horrific death of one demon mage while under its influence, none of us were willing to experiment with its mysterious powers.

"We found the demon mage ritual in the grimoire." Robin fidgeted with the hem of her sweater. "It's a complex set of spells. We thought the host body acted like an infernus, but looking at the rituals, it seems more like a summoning circle. Once a demon is inside a summoning circle, the only way to get him out is to destroy the circle or move him while he's inside an infernus."

"So ... what? Ezra needs to swallow an infernus?"

Her eyes popped at the suggestion. "Uh, no. The infernus would need to breach Ezra's essence, not just his body."

"His soul," I muttered. "That ex-summoner we talked to said some people believe the demon is inside the human's soul."

She nodded. "And that's the problem. But there must be some way ... I'll keep trying, and Zylas will help too."

I wanted to ask a thousand more questions—like how her demon was helping and why she was in an illegal contract with him—but this wasn't the time or place for that discussion.

She adjusted the chain around her neck, the infernus hidden under her sweater. "I don't know what it will look like yet, but saving Ezra will involve some sort of ritual. We'll need a private location where we can set up a Demonica circle. Can you find one for us?"

I straightened my spine. "Yeah, I can do that."

"If it has an existing circle, that would save us some time."

"Leave it to me."

With a quick farewell, she hurried off to find Amalia, leaving me alone in the dim corner of the pub with my mind spinning. I couldn't help with the grimoire, but now I had a job: to secure a secret location to perform the ritual that would unmake a demon mage, and all the better if it included a premade Demonica circle.

If only I had the slightest clue where to start looking.

2

SMACKING MY FIST into my palm with determination, I turned around, intending to rejoin Ezra and Aaron at the bar—and walked right into someone. I bounced off and caught myself on the back of a chair. My collision victim recovered with a slightly more graceful bobble.

I blinked at her. "Hey, Sabrina. Where'd you come from?"

"Just over there?" She canted her head toward Felix's team, smiling wanly.

My spine-tingling diviner radar pinged. Sabrina's pale blond hair was pinned back in a messy ponytail, and her makeup consisted of eyeliner, mascara, and maybe lip gloss—which, since she usually looked ready for a photoshoot, suggested something was off. Combine that with her pale complexion and the way her eyebrows were scrunched worriedly even as she smiled, and I was instantly concerned.

The last time I'd seen her looking this distraught, she'd snuck into the guild during an unbound-demon lockdown to tell my fortune. Not only had she predicted that Ezra, Aaron, and Kai would leave me—and possibly die—but she'd also predicted that I could change their fates with one crucial decision.

"How are you doing?" she began, her attempt at a conversational tone ruined by the intent way she stared into my face. "Have you talked to Ezra?"

Her question sounded innocuous, but it was a topic I avoided at all costs—i.e., *feelings*. The last time we'd had a serious chat, she'd warned me to open up to Ezra before it was too late.

"Yeah," I admitted reluctantly. "I told him I love him. Er ... well, I texted him."

"You *texted* him?"

"What's with the scandalized tone? He didn't seem to mind. And we talked on the phone too."

"So are you two a couple now?"

"Uh ... no. Not ... um ... it's complicated. There's this ... uh ..." As I trailed off, something about her expression sent a new prickle down my spine. "Sabrina, do you know something?"

Her face paled more than the unhealthy pallor she already had going on. "No! I mean, I—the cards are ... never specific, but ... sometimes I can see ... things," she finished uncertainly.

What "things" had she "seen," exactly? I didn't want to fish for information in case I gave her answers she didn't have.

"I was thinking ... maybe ..." She twisted her hands together. "I could do a reading for you?"

She'd just given me a way better reason than usual to say no. I couldn't have her guessing Ezra's secrets. "Uh, maybe another time, Sabrina."

"Oh." She wilted. "Okay. I understand. I'll … I'll get back to my team."

Guilt poked holes in my gut as she turned away, and I was almost too distracted by my own worries to notice her reach up to her face. I rushed after her and caught her wrist, tugging her toward me.

The tear she'd been about to wipe away ran down her cheek.

"Shit, Sabrina." I searched her face more closely. "What's wrong?"

"Nothing." When I didn't budge, waiting for a real answer, she squirmed. "It's just the cards … I know you don't like fortune-telling, so I've been trying to ignore it, but I've been having these dreams and I just—but it's fine! You don't have to do a reading with me."

She forced a smile, her brave face weakened by her quivering lips.

Damn it.

I tended to think of magic as something mythics could control—mages and their elemental powers, sorcerers and their carefully constructed spells, alchemists and their purpose-built potions—but I'd seen enough to realize that not all magic was like that. Whatever mysterious force powered Sabrina's divination magic existed outside her, and she was merely the conduit.

I snugged my arm around her narrow shoulders, pulled her to the far corner of the bar, and guided her to a stool.

"Do your cards have another message for me?" I slid onto the seat beside her. "It's not your fault, but I hate how it's always bad news."

"Whatever is coming will happen anyway, though," she pointed out. "The cards might help you prepare. That's what they're for—to bring understanding so when the challenges reach you, you're ready for them."

She was right. The cards weren't the cause of the trouble. They were an early warning, and I'd be a fool to ignore anything that might help me—and everyone else—survive whatever was coming.

"Okay." I steeled myself. "Let's do this."

She assessed me, a shimmer of tears clinging to her eyelashes, then reached into her purse. Withdrawing her deck, she unwrapped it from its black silk cloth. The gold pattern on the backs of the cards flashed as she shuffled at top speed, and after a minute, she stacked the deck neatly and offered it to me.

I began to shuffle. The cards slid across my palms, their edges pressing into my fingertips. The feel of the cards pushed away everything else. The packed pub faded from my awareness. The noisy conversations muted to a distant rumble. My eyes were closed, but I didn't remember closing them.

"What's in your heart, Tori?" Sabrina's whisper floated to my ears, blending with the rustle of the cards that had consumed my attention. "Focus on that. Let it fill you."

What was in my heart? The answer was simple, easy: Ezra. My mind swirled with thoughts of him, of the cult that had changed his life, of his past and his uncertain future, of Eterran and their blending spirits, of how to save him before it was too late.

Warm, soft hands enclosed mine, the deck between my palms. Sabrina guided the cards down onto the table.

"Cut the deck."

Eyes still closed, I cut the deck.

"Draw cards. As many as you want."

I slid the first card off, and it disappeared from under my fingers as she took it. I slid off another, then another. Two more. When I touched the deck again, I felt no need to draw more cards.

"Open your eyes, Tori."

I opened them—and the light, noise, and bustle of the pub hit me like a slap to the face. I blinked rapidly, disoriented as though waking from a trance. Weird. I'd never spaced out like that during a reading before.

Sabrina had laid the five cards on the table between us, arranged in the shape of a plus sign. "This is a relationship cross spread. Your heart is consumed by someone—by your relationship with him."

I couldn't argue with that. We both knew I was obsessed with Ezra.

When I didn't protest, she nodded. "Then let's begin. The first card represents you, Tori."

She lifted the card on the right side of the spread, but as she turned it over, it slipped from her fingers. The card landed on one pointed corner, spun in a faltering circle, and fell face-up, perpendicular to the rest of the spread.

The ink illustration depicted a nude woman, a wreath of flowers in her hair, holding the jaws of a lion. Beneath it was a single word: *Strength*.

"It's sideways," Sabrina observed.

"Well, yeah. Because you dropped it."

"There are no accidents during a reading." She studied the lion-wrangling woman. "Upright, this card means courage, compassion, and self-confidence, but reversed, it means weakness, inadequacy, and self-doubt. I think the sideways card means your two sides are at war with each other, Tori."

My mind immediately jumped to my combat belt in my locker downstairs, its pouches empty of magic.

"Now we look at the person who's consuming your future." She flipped the card on the opposite side of the cross, revealing a familiar horned fiend holding a naked man and woman in chains. "The Devil."

Lovely. The Devil had appeared in the reading that had preceded the Keys of Solomon attack last Halloween, our flight from the city, and Ezra's near death.

"Again," I growled. "Why is the deck telling me the same thing twice?"

"It's not. Look." She twirled her finger above it. "This time, the card is reversed. Instead of being chained, the subject is breaking free. The reversal means freedom, release, and restoring control."

I darted a glance toward the demon mage at the other end of the room. "Okay, what next?"

"The foundation of your relationship." She turned the card at the top of the cross. On it was a wheel surrounded by four beings: an angel, an eagle, a bull, and a lion. "The Wheel of Fortune."

"And what does that mean?"

She gazed at the card, her eyes distant. "Destiny ... opportunity ... where does the difference lie? Forces outside human control, the ever-turning wheel of change."

"Huh?"

Her gaze focused. "It means fate, chance, and change. Those are what brought you two together. You are each other's catalyst for change."

I wrapped my arms around myself, suppressing a shiver.

"The next card … your present." She turned the card to reveal the Lovers—a naked man and woman, passionately intertwined.

"Whoa, whoa." My cheeks heated. "Your cards are jumping the gun, here. I'm not—"

"It isn't literal, Tori," Sabrina interrupted, an amused twinkle softening the worry in her eyes. "The Lovers suggest a harmonic balance, but also a choice."

"About what?"

"It depends. Often it's about commitment, but it could mean a choice between opposing forces."

Oh yay.

Her hand drifted to the final card, sitting at the base of the cross, but she didn't touch it.

"That's the outcome, isn't it?" I guessed. "My future."

Part of me wanted to leap up from the table and flee the room before she could turn that card over. But I knew better.

I couldn't be sure that I'd chosen to go with the guys when they'd fled the city last Halloween *because* of Sabrina's reading, but if I hadn't been in the abandoned warehouse that night, Burke and his Keys of Solomon cohorts would have killed Ezra, and most likely Aaron and Kai too.

I couldn't risk not seeing this card. Bracing myself, I waited for her to turn it over.

She stole a glance at me, breathed deep, then flipped the card. It wasn't the Death card, nor was it the burning Tower from my very first reading. It was one I'd never seen before, its illustration revealing a tree in the shape of a cross, with a man hanging upside-down by one ankle. A halo shone around his head, and his expression was eerily peaceful despite his predicament.

"The Hanged Man."

My slight hope that it wasn't bad news snuffed out at her quiet murmur. "What does it mean? Give it to me straight, Sabrina."

"It means … sacrifice."

Dread rolled over me. "Are we talking about, like, the 'I need to give up booze for a month' sort of sacrifice, or … something else?"

Her gaze flitted away from mine. "There's no way to be sure."

"But you can make a diviner-educated guess, right?"

"I prefer not to stray outside the cards' guidance, as my own biases can influence my—"

"Sabrina." I waited until she looked back at me. "I know I haven't been the best about hearing my future, but I'm listening now. You know there's something going on—something besides all this." I waved at the pub.

Her throat bobbed as she swallowed.

I leaned forward. "This is life or death, Sabrina."

Biting her lower lip, she contemplated the spread, her forehead crinkled with anxiety. Finally, she straightened in her seat. "All right."

She laid her hands on the table on either side of the cards, her curled fingers and palms cupped toward them. She held perfectly still, breathing slowly, and for a second time, my awareness of the pub faded away.

Silence fell around us. Complete, impossible silence broken only by my drumming heartbeat and Sabrina's soft breaths. She exhaled in a long draft. Her eyelids lowered and her pupils disappeared, rolling back in her head.

The atmosphere grew heavy. All the hair on my body stood on end, and tingles rushed over my skin as an intangible weight settled over me. My perception of the pub, its paneled walls, and even the stool I sat on grew even more distant.

Sabrina didn't move, her back rigid and tendons standing out in her thin wrists.

As my alarmed gaze jumped from her to the cards, the Devil caught my eye. The ink lines of the illustration blurred. The creature's lips seemed to move with a sneering snarl. The chains he held rattled silently, and the naked man and woman he kept prisoner writhed.

The compass-like disc on the Wheel of Fortune card rotated sedately. The Lovers caressed each other. The woman of Strength pulled the lion's jaw wider, then faltered. Its jaws snapped shut.

The Hanged Man spun slowly on his dangling rope, turning until his hands, tucked neatly behind his back, were revealed. Leaves fell from the great tree's boughs as he rotated, but when his face came into view again, his eyes were closed.

No longer an expression of serene contemplation, he wore the lifeless visage of death.

My breath rushed through my throat, panic gathering in my chest as the pressure built. The illustrations seemed to expand, the Devil leaning forward out of his upside-down card, the branches of the Hanged Man's tree spreading onto the tabletop. The woman with her hand caught in the lion's jaws looked up at me, and her face had become my face.

Someone strode into our silent bubble of divination.

The pub burst into existence again and I pitched backward on my stool, almost toppling it. The room spun wildly before steadying.

"Deep breaths now, Sabrina. Slow. That's better."

Panting, I blinked to clear my confused vision. The new arrival was ... Darius?

He stood beside Sabrina's stool, one hand cupping the back of her head while he gently tugged her hands away from the cards. Her chest heaved as she sucked in air, her eyes squeezed shut and face contorted as though she were in pain.

When her breathing slowed to a more normal rate, Darius drew her off her stool. "Let's find a quiet room for you, shall we?"

She nodded shakily.

He glanced over his shoulder, his gray eyes somber. "Tori, will you please tidy up her cards? You can leave them in Clara's office."

"R-right." I watched numbly as he led her away, but before they got more than a few steps, I launched off my stool. "Wait!"

They paused. I stumbled over and grabbed Sabrina's hand. "That future you just—the things I saw on the—Sabrina, can I change it like last time? Will my choice change it?"

Holding Darius's arm for balance, she closed her eyes again. "No," she whispered. "The Wheel is turning. It's his choice now, and you can't change it."

"But—" My panic sharpened. "Sabrina, that can't—"

"Draw the last card, Tori. You'll see."

Darius guided her away. I stood there, hands trembling as I watched them cross the room and start up the stairs. The pub bustled with activity as teams prepared for the coming confrontation with the Court of the Red Queen, grimly cheerful in their determination to protect their city.

I rushed back to the bar. The five cards in the cross spread had returned to their original states, no more than mundane bits of cardboard and ink again. I stretched my hand toward the deck, waiting in two piles.

My fingers hovered over the next card. Steeling my heart, I plucked it off and tossed it down. A familiar illustration filled the card's face, a single word inscribed beneath it.

Death.

3

"**ARE YOU SURE** you don't want to wait until—"

"It's *fine*, Aaron. We'll be fine." I plucked the keys from his hand. "Quit worrying."

Standing beside the open driver's door of his SUV, the pyromage frowned at me and Ezra, then sighed. "Okay, fine. But be careful."

"I'm always careful," Ezra said in that somber tone that gave no clue as to whether he was teasing or not.

Aaron's frown deepened. He squinted between us, then turned on his heel and stalked toward the guild's front door to join the other officers for an early morning meeting.

Meanwhile, Ezra and I would complete the job Robin had given me.

Twenty minutes later, I pulled the SUV into the Capilano View Cemetery parking lot. When we'd shown up two weeks ago in search of the cult's lair, it'd been a ghost town—no pun intended. Today, however, a dozen cars waited for their drivers to return.

I parked at the farthest end and climbed out. The early February wind nipped at my cheeks as I checked that my combat belt was hidden under the hem of my jacket. Though I'd returned Justin's gun last week, I wasn't lacking in weapons.

Not only was my belt reloaded with alchemy bombs and a new paintball gun, borrowed from Lyndon, but I finally had an artifact back—after Friday night's meeting, Lim had delivered my brass knuckles, a force-amplifying spell imbued into the metal. Weldon, being significantly less reliable than the Arcana scholar, had yet to produce a replacement fall spell for me.

Ezra, unfortunately, had no weapon to carry—though considering his dual magics, he probably didn't need one.

I linked our arms as we walked onto one of the many paths that led through small fields of flat gravestones. A middle-aged couple meandered past us, their faces heavy with grief. Farther out, a family was gathered around another marker. An old man sat alone on a bench, a bouquet of white daisies in his hand and his weathered features holding a thousand memories as he gazed toward the distant trees.

I slid my hand down Ezra's arm and entwined our fingers. I'd never lost a loved one to death. There were no graves in the world that meant anything to me, but at just sixteen years old, Ezra had lost everyone he'd ever known.

"What happened to their bodies?" The question was out of my mouth before I could stop it.

Ezra glanced at me. "Whose bodies?"

"Your ... your parents. Do you know?"

"Unclaimed bodies are buried on private land managed by the MPD. I don't know where ... in Oregon, probably."

"When this is over, would you like to find out where they are?"

He considered my question as we roamed down the path, heading toward the forest at the northern end of the cemetery. "Maybe someday."

My fingers tightened around his. Against my will, the Death card slid into my mind's eye, followed by the Hanged Man, his face blank and peaceful in death. Sacrifice.

It's his choice now.

"Ezra ..." Words failed me.

"What is it?"

We stopped at the edge of the forest. The cemetery's other visitors were distant figures, and the rustle of branches in the cold wind was the only sound.

Searching his eyes, I opened my mouth—but again, I couldn't speak. I didn't know what to say. How could I demand he make no sacrifices? I might as well ask him to stop breathing. If his friends were in danger, he'd do anything to protect them.

He brushed his thumb over the corner of my mouth as though to rub away my frown. "What's wrong, Tori?"

"I ... I just ..." I sucked in a breath. "It's nothing. But I do have a question."

"What question?"

I headed up the path, searching for the spot where we'd hacked our way into the underbrush. "Did you know all that stuff Robin explained about demons powering up with heat?"

"I knew everything always goes cold when I tap Eterran's power, but I didn't know why." He shook his head in exasperation. "If I'd realized demons could turn fire into magic, I would've mentioned it a long time ago."

"Nice of Eterran to fill you in."

"He's never been free with his knowledge."

No kidding. Dick move, Eterran.

Ezra arched an eyebrow. "Now tell me what's really wrong, Tori."

Crap. I should've known I couldn't derail him that easily.

Luckily, we'd just located our two-week-old trail into the forest, and I pushed through the branches. Crunching steps and snapping twigs confirmed Ezra was right behind me, probably wondering what weird tangent my brain was on.

After our text-confessions of love and that white-hot kiss in the cemetery parking lot, Ezra and I hadn't had the time or privacy to really talk. Between our new arrangement with Robin and helping Darius prepare to take on—and take down—the Court, we'd been too busy.

And, as I'd told Sabrina, it was all just so … complicated.

I broke free from the trees, and as I entered the clearing, tension infused my muscles. The memories of our panicked flight hit me hard—Aaron barely able to walk, Kai limping badly, Ezra glowing with demonic magic.

The cenotaph was no more. Chunks of the shattered angel statue lay amidst the broken pillars, and the weathered chalice she'd held had fallen on its side near her dismembered hand as though she were reaching for it.

Unlike when we'd left, the underground stairway wasn't completely buried. Someone had uncovered the passageway's entrance—but we'd known to expect that. Darius hadn't neglected this crucial location. The morning after we'd uncovered it—and barely escaped with our lives—Darius, Girard, and Alistair had combed through the rubble inside, but Xanthe and Xever had removed everything important except the summoning circle. Not that they could've packed *that* up and moved it out, mind you.

The GM had stationed a surveillance team in the cemetery to watch for returning cultists, but no one had shown up. The cult had abandoned their lair.

Which was exactly why Ezra and I were here.

I pulled a flashlight off my belt. "Shall we?"

"Lead the way."

I started down the stairs, careful not to trip on the rubble. "Wouldn't it be great if we got to use a cult summoning circle to un-cult-ify you? The irony is delicious."

"Nazhivēr and I might have damaged it," Ezra said, referring to his battle with Xever's powerful demon. "If it survived, though, it would be …"

He trailed off as we reached the bottom. I shone my light across the cavernous storm reservoir.

"… almost too easy," he finished dryly.

I clenched my jaw. "Damn it."

My footsteps echoed loudly as I crossed to the circle I'd hoped we could hijack—but nope. The perfect summoning circle had been reduced to shattered rubble.

Darius had told me the circle was intact, which meant it'd been destroyed at some point between his visit to the underground lair and now. But our guild had been monitoring the site. How the hell had the Court snuck in here without our guys noticing?

The wooden altar had been demolished too, and the stone lectern where I'd found the cult grimoire had been smashed—rather angrily, I thought. How had Xanthe and Xever reacted when they'd realized I'd stolen the grimoire from its protective case? Something told me the cult leaders hadn't been happy about that.

I craned my neck back. Xanthe and Xever had even removed the scarlet crystals from the pillars and stripped away the sigil-emblazoned tapestries. Talk about an efficient cleanup. Had Xever put his injured demon to work after we'd escaped? I almost felt bad for the demon.

Almost.

"Do you think they've left Vancouver entirely?" I asked, kicking at a chunk of stone. There was nothing left that suggested a cult had operated here.

"They may have moved the High Court, but I doubt Xever is ready to leave yet. He's working on something."

"That stuff you were helping Robin with, right?"

Ezra nodded. "He's hell-bent on getting his hands on—"

Bzz-bzz-bzzzz.

The loud vibration of my phone filled the reservoir, and I dug frantically into my pocket, amazed there was any reception down here. I whipped out my phone, frowned at the unfamiliar number on the screen, then lifted it to my ear.

"Hello?"

"Tori?" a deep voice inquired.

"Who's this?"

"Blake."

I blinked. "Blake? Like, the Keys of Solomon terramage?"

"How many Blakes do you know?"

Relief flooded me. I hadn't heard a word from or about the terramage since we'd fled the Keys headquarters, leaving him bleeding on the floor. "I'm so glad you're alive."

A low, humorless laugh. "I told you I wouldn't die—though staying alive has proven more difficult than I'd expected."

"What do you mean?"

"That's actually why I called. We flushed out four Keys members corrupted by the cult—but we didn't get them all."

A rush of adrenaline hit me. "There's another one?"

"At least one more. After you left, I was almost killed three times before I could get out of Salt Lake City. I'm in hiding now, but it's too late."

"Too late?"

"Someone spread rumors through the guild that I've been suffering from PTSD since the Enright extermination, and after living alone on the site of the attack for eight years, I finally cracked. My guild membership has been suspended and there's a bounty to get me committed—for my own safety, they claim."

Ezra searched my face, probably reading the horror all over my features.

"Shit, Blake. If they catch you—"

"—I'll be dead before anyone realizes it's a setup. Yeah, I know. Don't worry, I'm well hidden."

"Is there anyone in your guild who can help you?"

He sighed. "I thought I knew who I could trust, but I'm not sure about anyone anymore. I wrote out everything and sent it to my GM, but I don't know if it'll reach him."

Not good. Pinning down the Court was like trying to hold water in your hands. There was no way to grab hold of it. It just slipped away.

"I can talk to my GM," I said. "I bet he can get through to your—"

"Too risky," Blake interrupted. "The Keys have no leads on the 'murderers' who killed Russel and the officers. You can't give them any reason to suspect your guild."

"We aren't *murderers*. We were—"

"It doesn't matter. If the cultist moles can convince the guild to turn on one of its own members, they can convince the Keys to turn on your guild too."

I swallowed hard.

"I'm calling to warn you and your guildmates to watch your backs. Stay away from the Keys—and stay away from that cult."

"Uh, well, it's not that simple. It turns out the top-level court thingy—what did you call it, Ezra?"

"The High Court," he supplied.

"Right. The High Court is here in Vancouver. I'm actually standing in their lair right now—their lair as of two weeks ago when we uncovered it, I should say."

Blake was silent for a moment. "Why the hell are you in their *lair*?"

"Former lair. They abandoned it after we broke in. Our guild's been watching it for two weeks but no sign of any cultists."

The terramage grunted. "The cult is trying to kill me because I know about them. They'll try to kill you too—and you're making it real damn easy for them."

"There's no one here, Blake."

"Have you forgotten about the mentalist?" he growled. "Even just walking around in the open is dangerous."

Grimacing, I glanced at Ezra. "We're leaving now anyway. The thing we came here for was a bust."

"Good. And once you're out, get your ass back to your guild."

I waved at Ezra to follow me and strode across the reservoir. "You're awfully bossy, you know."

"You'll thank me when you don't die. I just explained how the cult's been trying to kill me, remember?"

"Yeah, yeah." I started up the steps, phone in one hand and flashlight in the other. "So you're going to stay in hiding, right? You can just sit tight until my guild deals with the cult."

"Your guild?"

"Well, not *only* my guild." Grayish sunlight bloomed through the stairwell, and I flicked off my flashlight as I hastened toward the friendly glow. "We'll get help from other guilds too."

"Do you think that'll be enough?"

"Our GM is basically a genius." My head popped up out of the sunken, earthy stairwell, and I climbed the last few steps. "If anyone can do it, he—"

"*Tori!*"

A few steps below me, Ezra grabbed my legs. At the same time, something dropped past my face—and a rope snapped tight around my upper arms.

Someone behind me yanked me up out of the hole, tearing my legs from Ezra's grasp. I was flung down onto the rubble, bits of rocks digging into my back through my leather jacket—and a length of shining steel appeared an inch from my nose.

The stranger towering over me set the point of his long sword against my throat.

ᕴ

MY HAMMERING PULSE beat against the sword's cold steel edge. The constricting pressure of a rope cut into my elbows, pinning my arms to my sides, and its other end was in the swordsman's free hand. The stocky man with short blond hair standing near my shoulder was completely unfamiliar.

Well, shit. Blake had been right. My phone was no longer in my hand, and I had no clue if our call was still connected.

Ezra, halfway out of the sunken stairwell, stood unmoving, his gaze snapping between the blade at my throat and my captor.

"We finally meet, Enéas."

Without moving, I strained to see the speaker. A second man, tall and rail-thin, stood just beyond the cenotaph ruins, his arms folded over his narrow chest. He wasn't wearing the Court's oh-so-classy scarlet cloak of villainy, but he had the hood of his jacket pulled up, shadows covering most of his face.

"But you don't go by that name anymore, do you?" the man added.

"Who are you?" Ezra's voice was eerily calm—but frost was forming on the ground around him.

"The Magna Ducissa asked us to speak with you."

"Afraid to face me herself?"

The man smiled. "She's a busy woman."

"I'm sure she is."

"We're very pleased you survived, Enéas," the cultist said, sounding more sour than delighted. "If we'd known you escaped Enright, we would've extended a welcoming hand of support many years ago."

"Of course."

The man's thin lips twitched downward as he tried to parse Ezra's flat tone. "We wish to extend that helping hand now to a blessed child of the Goddess."

"Thank you. I accept."

Silence fell over the clearing, and despite the sword poised at my jugular, I almost laughed at the cultists' palpable confusion.

"Are—are you committed to returning to the Court's ways?" the lead cultist asked tentatively.

"Absolutely. You should've invited me sooner." Ezra ascended the last few steps, keeping his movements slow, then pivoted toward me and the blond swordsman. "Tori will come too. She's wanted to experience the Goddess's Light for herself ever since I told her about it."

Oh yeah. Sign me up.

Ezra raised his hand toward me as though indicating the awesomeness that was Tori Dawson and her burning desire to become a cultist. His expression was vaguely pleasant, and only because I knew him so well did I see the slight tightening of his jaw.

He snapped his fingers into a tight fist—and a burst of wind hit the swordsman. He and his blade flew backward, and I rolled in the opposite direction. Launching onto my feet, I sprang over the sunken stairwell. Ezra caught me in mid-leap and swept me behind him.

An instant later, the reedy cultist, the stocky swordsman, and a third mythic had surrounded us in a half-circle, fifteen feet away.

"This will be your only warning," the thin cultist intoned icily. "Return to the Court, or we will have no choice but to silence you."

Crimson light ignited over Ezra's fingers and snaked up his wrists. "Go ahead, then. Silence me."

"Perhaps you don't appreciate the ramifications of your actions. We will—"

Ezra raised his hand, fingers spread. Scarlet light blazed in his left eye and a swirl of magic erupted from his palm, solidifying into a hexagonal spell. Lips curling in a sneer, the cultist shoved his hood back to reveal a long face with flat cheekbones—and eyes sheened with red.

The man was a demon mage.

And I was standing in the wrong spot. No way did I want to be this close to a demon mage duel. I frantically wiggled my arms, trying to loosen the rope cutting off the circulation below my elbows.

The demon mage cultist bared his teeth. "You are a prodigy, Enéas. A child of the Goddess in true union with his *Servus*. You could become the first true apostle of the Goddess in living memory. Will you throw it away?"

Ezra's spell flared brighter, and when he spoke, a guttural accent had infected his voice.

"Ask your *Servus* what *he* thinks of your disgusting fairytale," he growled. "*Thāit ad hh'ainun, hrātir.*"

The glow in the cultist demon mage's eyes flashed brighter, and the man gritted his teeth.

The swordsman surged toward Ezra.

Ezra spun with unbelievable speed and unleashed his spell—spears of crimson light. But the swordsman had already changed direction and dove away, the attack missing him.

I scrambled backward. "Hoshi!"

She burst out of my belt pouch, her silvery glow washing over me.

"Get this rope off me!" I told her urgently, still retreating as the three cultists circled Ezra, none of them willing to get in range of his attacks—but that wouldn't last long.

She ducked behind me and I felt a hard tug on the ropes pinning my arms to my sides.

The demon mage cultist leered at Ezra, then raised his hand. A new spell snaked across Ezra's hand in answer. The demon mage vaulted toward Ezra, then swerved sideways as Ezra flung a blast of red power. It shot past the cultist, hit the ground, and exploded in a rain of dirt clods.

The rope around my arms dropped away.

Ezra spun on his heel and sprang at the demon mage cultist. The third man lunged in, and as the swordsman lifted his weapon, I launched into action.

"Come on, Hoshi!"

She zoomed ahead of me and flashed past the swordsman's face, causing him to pull up short. I jammed my brass knuckles on my fingers as the man pivoted toward me, his lethal blade angling for my chest.

I dove at his legs. As he stumbled back in surprise at my unexpected move, I thrust out my fist and shouted, "*Ori amplifico!*"

My knuckles hit his kneecap with a horrifying crunch. His leg flew backward from the blow, which caused him to pitch forward—on top of me.

The air puffed from my lungs as he flattened me into the grass. I whipped an elbow into a soft spot in his torso, then shoved up and sideways, throwing him off me. He rolled onto his side, clutching his leg, his face white and eyes bulging.

A few feet away, Hoshi clutched the pommel of his sword, the point dragging on the ground as she floated backward.

As I leaped up, a detonation of red power blasted me right off my feet again. A concussive wave of crimson magic swept out from Ezra, throwing his assailants back. The two cultists slammed down.

"*Ori celare caligine!*" the third one gasped.

Maroon-tinged smoke boiled out from him. It swept across the clearing, covering ten times the square footage of my smoke bombs. My vision blurred, and I rose into an uncertain crouch.

"Hoshi!"

Her glowing form appeared, and she flicked her tail. A powerful gust of wind blew across me, but the mist barely stirred.

Footsteps thudded loudly, and I tensed. Two shadows appeared, one with gleaming red eyes. The cultists. The sorcerer grabbed his newly gimped pal, while the demon mage swiveled toward me.

I didn't move, painfully aware that he could kill me before I could get my paintball gun out. Hoshi drifted closer, her fear dancing in my mind.

The demon mage sneered, then swept into the mist. His two minions rushed after him, one supporting the other.

I shot to my feet and whipped out my paintball gun, but they'd already disappeared. Shit.

"Ezra?" I yelled.

He rushed out of the mist, left eye glowing. "Where are they?"

I pointed in the direction they'd vanished. "That way."

He hesitated, then shook his head. "This spell is messing with my aero magic. I can't sense their movements."

"Then we find them the old-fashioned way," I declared, marching forward.

I got two steps before he grabbed my arm and pulled me back. "No ... we should let them go."

"What? Why?"

"Because I think they want us to follow them." His frown deepened. "Or ... maybe not, but they want *something*. They weren't even trying to kill me. The demon mage didn't use his magic."

I holstered my gun as my stomach sank with cold dread. "Then what was the point of ambushing us?"

"I don't know, but I don't want to walk into another trap."

The Court was good at setting traps. Even though our guild had watched this location for any sign of cult activity, it seemed the cult had been spying on *us* instead. And as much as I hated backing down, I had to agree with Ezra's assessment. Chasing them was stupid, especially when it was just me and Ezra against another demon mage.

But what had the cult wanted—and had they gotten it?

5

HOT WATER RUSHED DOWN my face and splashed over my shoulders. Head tilted back, I breathed the steamy air, trying to calm the tight, itchy anxiety in my chest.

Was there a point where fear and dread and urgency overloaded your system and you stopped feeling them? Could that happen? Numbness would be an improvement over this never-ending sense of doom.

Eyes closed against the spray, I reached out blindly and nudged the tap. The shower's temperature increased another degree, threatening to scorch my skin. The heat pounded down on me, something to feel besides the churning emotions.

Yesterday's attack in the cemetery wasn't the scariest thing I'd witnessed, or participated in, since falling into this secret world of mythics and magic, but it had confirmed our suspicion that there was at least one demon mage in Vancouver.

When Ezra had been the only demon mage I knew, his frightening power had been our special weapon. Now that destructive demonic magic was our enemies' weapon too. What if we succeeded in un-demon-maging Ezra? He'd get the world's biggest power demotion, going from "unstoppable paragon of destruction" to an average aeromage. And the cult would still be trying to kill him. He knew too many of their secrets.

My phone, sitting on the bathroom counter, chimed loudly. I ignored it, steaming myself like a lobster and hoping the heat would steady my nerves.

It chimed twice more, and when I still didn't reply to whoever wanted my attention, it began to ring. Swearing, I pushed the plastic curtain open, letting a rush of cold air into the steamy innards of the shower. I grabbed my phone, fumbled for the answer button with my wet thumb, then hit speaker.

"This better be good!" I barked at the unlucky caller.

"Am I interrupting something?" Ezra replied, the running water muffling his smooth voice.

My irritation vanished. "Just in the shower."

"Oh. Hmm."

I waited, allowing him all the time he wanted to think about me in the shower.

"Earth to Ezra," Aaron said sarcastically. "You were calling to tell Tori how she needs to get over here, remember?"

My phone wasn't the only one on speaker, it seemed. "Why do I need to get over there?"

"Robin is on her way." Ezra's tone gave no indication that my shower comment had derailed him. "You should come over too. Kai will be here any minute."

I snapped to attention. "Robin is going over there? Why?"

It took only an instant for Ezra to reply, but that moment in time seemed to stretch forever, the planet's orbit frozen as I waited for the words I hadn't dared to hope for so soon. Words I'd been afraid would never come.

"She figured it out."

———

I FLUNG OPEN Aaron's front door, rushed inside, and almost crashed into Robin's back.

She yipped in surprise and turned, her arms overflowing with long rolls of brown paper and a gray backpack hanging off her shoulder. Amalia was just ahead of her, halfway out of her leather boots.

Aw damn, I'd hoped to beat them here. I'd hurried as much as possible, but considering I'd been wet and naked when Ezra had summoned me, I supposed it had been a long shot.

"Hi Tori," Robin said, oddly breathless. "How are you?"

I arched my eyebrows. "If you've actually found a way to save Ezra, then I'm absolutely fantastic."

Ezra and Aaron were waiting for us in the living room, and standing between them was Kai, looking as cool and poised as always in dark jeans and a slim-fitting black sweater. He gave me a quiet smile when I rushed over to hug him.

Greetings were brief, then we moved to the dining table, where Robin laid out her armload of supplies.

"All right," she said, her voice higher than usual with nerves. "Amalia and I looked at every angle of the demon mage ritual. Like a regular demon contract, there's no way to break it. Once the demon spirit and human soul are bound, it can't be undone."

Standing beside Ezra, I waited silently. If that's all Robin had to say, she wouldn't be here.

"So we looked for ways to circumvent the contract instead of breaking it. After all, the biggest issue here is that Eterran is trapped inside Ezra's body. The contract between them is secondary to that."

Amalia put a hand on her hip. "From start to finish, contracting a demon requires three steps: summoning the demon, negotiating a contract, and binding the demon to the infernus."

Robin slid the cult grimoire out of her backpack and opened it to a marked page. "The demon mage ritual is four steps. Summoning is exactly the same—the demon is called into a summoning circle. Then negotiation."

"That's a bit different," Amalia noted dryly. "From what I've read, demon mages are damn near impossible to create in part due to ninety-nine percent of demons refusing to agree to it."

Tucking a damp curl behind my ear, I grimaced. "Yeah, well, what is the demon even getting out of the deal?"

"Lies," Ezra answered in a growl. "That is what they offered."

Robin frowned. "But you can detect lies. All demons can."

Aaron and Kai stiffened as Ezra's left eye burned crimson.

"Lies given as truth." Hatred chilled Eterran's quiet snarl. "A second man explained the contract. He did not lie, but every word he spoke was false. I knew nothing of humans and their ways. I did not think to make the summoner speak the same words."

"Wait." I peered at his crimson eye. "You know when you're being lied to?"

"Not in this body."

"Oh."

Robin glanced between us, then cleared her throat. "The contract for a demon mage is straightforward. Simply put, the demon agrees to bind itself to the human's soul. We're not really sure what that entails, but I'm assuming that bond gives the host enough control to keep the demon from immediately overpowering his mind."

We all looked questioningly at Ezra/Eterran, but he didn't speak.

"The third phase," Robin continued, "is the ritual that turns the host into the equivalent of a summoning circle. Then, for the final stage—"

"—the demon is summoned into the host," Ezra finished quietly.

A dark, haunted shadow lurked in his eyes, and I reached out, surreptitiously sliding my hand into his. His fingers closed tightly around mine.

"And that's the key," Robin said. "That's how we'll undo this."

I blinked dumbly. "How?"

"We're going to summon Eterran *out* of Ezra."

Silence.

Kai stepped closer to the table. "It's been a while since I studied Demonica basics, but from what I remember, summoners can call a demon of a particular type, but they can't summon an individual demon."

"Not from the demon world, no," Robin replied. "But making a demon mage requires summoning the already summoned demon a second time in order to insert him into the human host. We're going to do exactly that."

"There are complications," Amalia added. "The big one being blood."

I squinted at that ominous statement. "Blood?"

"The second summoning required Eterran's blood." Ezra frowned between the two women. "He doesn't have a body anymore. My blood isn't demon blood."

"No, your blood wouldn't work," Robin agreed. "But I think we can modify the spell to summon Eterran using blood from the same House. Are you familiar with demon Houses?"

"Yeah," Aaron answered. "Different demon types are called Houses and there are nine or ten of them."

"Twelve," she corrected as she lifted her backpack onto the table. "But yes. Their Houses are essentially lineages, so any blood from Eterran's House will be nearly identical."

A dozen demon Houses—and her demon was the *king* of one of them? That was what Ezra had said when we'd handed over the demonic amulet.

I pressed my hands to the table. "You want us to get *another* demon's blood? How are we supposed to do that? We don't even know what 'House' Eterran is from!"

"Dh'irath, the Second House," Robin revealed calmly. "The same house as Nazhivēr."

Nazhivēr? As in Xever's terrifying winged demon that Ezra had barely held off using demonic *and* aero magic?

With a happy little smile, as though she were presenting us with a basket of fresh-baked cookies, Robin slid a metal case out of her bag and flipped the lid open. Inside were five vials of dark liquid nested in a foam insert.

"This is Nazhivēr's blood."

I looked from the vials to Robin and back. "Where—and *how*—did you get his blood?"

"Well, um … technically speaking, I stole it." She shrugged. "Claude—or, rather, Xever was trading it to vampires in exchange for their saliva."

"Because vampire saliva affects demons," I murmured. "Is that why there are illustrations of vampires in the cult grimoire?"

"One of the reasons." Robin set the case aside and began unrolling one of the large papers. "Amalia and I put together a ritual that we think should work. We can't be sure … but this is the best we can do without any testing."

Aaron helped her flatten the three-foot-square paper. Drawn out on it in exhaustive detail was a summoning circle, the outer ring decorated with swirling lines and runes. Inside it were two more circles, their edges overlapping.

Ezra leaned over the drawing, and crimson sparked in his left eye again. He pointed to one of the inner circles. "This … what is this?"

"Zylas added that part," Robin answered. "He said it's for—"

Red light blazed off her chest. A streak of power leaped down to the floor, then stretched upward and solidified. Her demon appeared, his eyes glowing like magma and a mixture of fabric, leather, and light armor covering his lean, muscular body.

"It will bind the blood to its nearest brother." White teeth, pointed and predatory, flashed as the demon smirked. "You do not know this *vīsh, Dīnen et Dh'irath?*"

Ezra's—Eterran's upper lip curled. "I have never seen it before. Is it real *vīsh, Dīnen et Vh'alyir?*"

"You think that if you do not know a magic, it is not real?" His tail snapped sideways. "Smart. You will live long thinking that."

"I know more *vīsh* than most *Dīnen* ever see," Eterran snarled softly.

Zylas's smirk curved, a vicious tilt to it. "Because you are broken, so you needed greater power, *na?*"

Sticking out his right arm, he drew a line across his inner elbow with one fingertip. I couldn't guess what he was getting at with the gesture.

"You learned how to heal too late, Dh'irath," he mocked.

"You learned to fight like a coward, Vh'alyir," Eterran sneered back.

Call me crazy, but I was getting the impression that Eterran and Zylas didn't like each other.

Ezra blinked a few times, and the red glow faded from his left eye. I waited for Zylas to streak back into his infernus—but instead, he drifted behind Amalia, peering curiously around the dining room.

Robin began explaining the summoning ritual and the changes she and Amalia had made to it, but I was paying more attention to the demon in the room than anything she was saying. Judging by the way Aaron and Kai were tracking the creature's movements in their peripheral vision, they were equally distracted. Only Ezra seemed to be paying proper attention.

Zylas finished perusing the dining room, then drifted into the kitchen. He disappeared around the corner.

Pausing her explanation, Robin glanced over her shoulder and called, "Don't break anything, Zylas!"

"*Mailēshta*," came the grumbling reply.

Aaron frowned at her. "Uh, do you mind calling him back where we can see him?"

"He'll be fine. As I was saying, if the binding portion of the ritual works correctly, then …"

I forced myself to focus as Robin described the ritual in detail. The moment she stopped talking, Aaron zoomed toward the kitchen, muttering something about "checking on things," which probably meant, "checking on the demon wandering through my house unsupervised."

Kai followed warily, and Ezra trailed after him, more amused than worried. I dropped heavily into a chair as Amalia rolled up the papers.

Unconcerned about her demon's absence, Robin perched on the seat beside me, "Any luck with a location?"

"Not yet." I let my head fall back against the chair, staring at the ceiling. "I'll find something, though."

"We'll need a large circle. Much larger than standard so we can fit two circles inside it."

I squinted, picturing the temple ruins from Enright. We could always go back there to do it, but that was just asking for trouble.

"I'll find something," I repeated with more confidence than I felt. "How long will it take to set up the ritual and stuff once we have a location?"

"A couple of days, then the Arcana will need to charge for three more days."

So a week then, assuming I got my butt in gear and found a location in the next two days. A week, and we could save Ezra. A week, and this nightmare he'd lived for almost ten years would finally be over. He'd have the future he never thought he'd live to see.

I want you to be part of my future. My heart beat a little faster as I remembered him murmuring those words, his voice in my ear but hundreds of miles between us.

"Robin." I turned toward her. "Are you sure this will work?"

She looked at the grimoire on the table, open to the demon mage section. "As long as we can link the Second House blood to Eterran specifically, I believe it will work. The big question is … whether Ezra and Eterran will survive the separation."

That did absolutely nothing to ease my apprehension.

"Not to be insensitive or anything," Amalia interjected, "but they're going to die anyway. Better to try, right?"

Straightening in my chair, I shot the blond sorceress a cold look. "I never said I didn't want to try. Besides, it isn't my choice. It's Ezra's—and Eterran's—and they want to try."

"And what about after they're separated, assuming it works?" Amalia asked. "It'd be just great if we freed Eterran only for him to turn around and kill us all."

"You don't seem too worried about Zylas killing you."

She raised her eyebrows. "I worry about it every day."

That gave me pause.

Robin busily gathered her papers. "We don't need to worry about Eterran yet. We'll be summoning him into a circle, and he'll be trapped there until we free him."

"Trapping him in a circle isn't much better than leaving him stuck inside Ezra." It was better for Ezra, though. "I don't see him agreeing to a regular contract-infernus-type deal."

"We can cross that bridge when we get to it," she said reassuringly, returning the grimoire to her backpack. "There may be options you haven't considered."

"Options like what?"

She shrugged mysteriously. "We—"

⁻A muffled shout erupted from beneath our feet. I looked down at the floor in alarm. "Where are the guys?"

"Where's Zylas?" Robin yelped.

Another male voice exclaimed loudly from the basement, and I launched across the dining room. Robin and Amalia were right on my heels as I careened down the stairs and burst into the workout room.

Aaron, Kai, and Ezra stood amongst the exercise equipment—and Robin's demon was with them. Relief hit me—no one was fighting, bleeding, or dead—but it was swiftly followed by confusion.

For some reason, they were all standing around a barbell loaded with what looked like four one-hundred-pound plates—on *each side.*

"No way," Aaron declared. "It's impossible."

"But he just deadlifted six hundred pounds like it was nothing," Kai replied, his gaze flicking between the demon and the barbell.

"He's shorter than you." Aaron folded his arms. "It just isn't physically possible."

Ezra shook his head. "You have no idea what a demon can do."

Zylas's tail snapped back and forth, then he leaned down and grasped the bar. The hard, lean muscles in his arms and shoulders bunched. He heaved up, lifting the barbell. It bowed under the weights as the demon lifted it to his chest.

"Holy shit," Aaron muttered, inching away from the demon as though doubting whether he wanted to stand that close.

Puffing out a breath, the demon wrinkled his nose. "What is the point of this? Lifting heavy things?"

"Humans do it to make themselves stronger," Ezra explained dryly.

"This makes *hh'ainun* stronger?"

"Can you lift it over your head?" Aaron asked in a way that suggested he hoped the answer was no.

The demon braced his feet, then pushed the bar up over his head. It didn't look *easy* for him, but he wasn't struggling all that much either. My gaze ran along his arms, then down to his tense, defined abdominal muscles.

I glanced at Robin. Standing beside me, she was staring at the demon, mouth hanging open. Pink stained her cheeks.

As Zylas returned the weights to the floor, I nudged her with my elbow and whispered, "What did I tell you? Perfect abs."

She shot me a glare, her cheeks going even redder. "I dare you to say that to his face now that he can talk back."

I blinked and glanced at Zylas—only to find crimson eyes locked on mine. The demon bared his teeth from across the room. Er, maybe I shouldn't comment on his physique. Last time, I'd done it without thought, like he was a highly realistic marble statue—but statues didn't get angry when you ogled them.

"Okay." Aaron strode over to the weight rack and grabbed another big plate. "Let's find your limit, demon."

"Why?" Zylas adjusted a leather armor strap on his shoulder. "It is stupid."

"You can prove how much stronger you are than a human," Ezra told him.

"I already know *hh'ainun* are weak."

Robin cleared her throat. "We, uh, should probably get going."

"Just one more," Aaron cajoled, passing a plate to Kai to slide onto the bar's other end. "All males like to show off their strength. Whoever can lift the most wins."

"*Ch*," the demon scoffed. "There is no victory in this. It is only strength. *Hh'ainun* are stupid."

Robin cleared her throat again.

Aaron and Kai loaded up every weight they could fit onto the bar, then stepped back. Zylas peered at it, and I wondered if I was imagining uncertainty in his demonic face.

He grasped the bar, set his feet, and lifted. The weights rose off the floor—slowly. This time, the demon struggled. With a grunt of effort, he heaved it up to his chest, teeth bared.

He held it for a second—then one of the clips holding the weights in place gave out. The bar tilted and a plate slid off, crashing to the floor.

As Zylas pitched to one side, the three mages leaped forward—Aaron and Kai grabbing each end of the bar to stop more plates from falling, and Ezra bracing the center to take some of the weight off. The four of them lowered the bar to the floor.

As Kai counted the weights, totaling them up to see how much the demon had lifted, I glanced uncomfortably at Robin. She was watching her demon in a concerned sort of way, but when I shifted my gaze to Amalia, I found a pair of gray eyes tight with the exact same reaction as me:

The quiet, prickling fear of prey in the presence of its ultimate predator.

6

I PLANTED MY HANDS on my hips. "When I asked for a discreet location, this wasn't what I had in mind."

Beside me, Justin pushed the brim of his service cap up to peer at the two-story building across the street, its brick façade featuring lovely arched windows and old-world charm. A sign hanging by the wooden door read, "Police Museum," and below that, a temporary sign warned, "Closed for Renovations."

"Who'd expect mythic activity in a police museum?" he asked. "No one. Plus, the renovation won't be starting anytime soon. The whole roof needs replacing and they're having trouble getting funding for it."

"But ..." I eyed his dark blue uniform, then waved at the one-way road between us and the museum, a steady stream of traffic rushing past. "*You* can just walk right in. How are the rest of us supposed to get in and out of there without the whole street noticing?"

"The back door. Come on, I'll show you."

He led me to the nearby intersection, where we waited at the crosswalk for the traffic light to change, like proper law-abiding citizens. Crossing the street, we entered a narrow alley lined with dumpsters. Three buildings down, the back of the museum was almost unrecognizable, the pretty tan bricks covered by gray paint—to hide the graffiti, I assumed.

A large rectangular opening in the back of the building acted as a covered garage, and instead of an overhead door, it was blocked off with a chain-link fence. The only thing inside the dim space was another dumpster.

"Did you bring the stuff?" he muttered, glancing up and down the alley to ensure we were alone.

"Yep." I dug into my purse. "But bolt cutters didn't fit in my bag, so I borrowed the magic equivalent."

Retrieving what looked like a metal dog tag, I stuck its key-like end into the padlock on the gate and whispered, "*Ori clausum aperio.*"

Pale pink light shimmered over the artifact, and the padlock popped open. I slid it off, then fished a suitably worn-looking replacement out of my bag. Leaving it hooked on the fence, I pulled the gate open and walked in. Justin followed me.

The museum was a surprisingly cramped maze of halls and offices that had been converted into display rooms, but that wasn't what interested us. The basement was the place to be if you wanted to build an oversized summoning circle in secret.

The lower level featured a large, open concrete room interrupted by a few pillars, with all the museum's storage confined to the shelves along the back wall. The windows had been bricked over decades ago—this wasn't a great neighborhood—meaning the basement was completely private. Pending a thorough sweeping of the dusty floor, there was more than enough room for a summoning circle or two.

A spark of excitement joined the nervous foreboding that had taken up residence in my stomach. This was it. This was the place where we'd save Ezra.

"Will it work?" Justin asked, examining me in the glow from his phone's flashlight.

"I think so. If we dress like construction workers or something, nobody will think twice if they see us going in and out." I grinned. "Thanks, Justin."

"Sure. But if you get caught, don't mention me."

"Wouldn't dream of it. But are you sure you're okay with this? You shouldn't put your job at risk."

"What's my job compared to someone's life?"

"You don't even know Ezra."

He squeezed my shoulder. "But you do."

I smiled unsteadily, and we both hurriedly turned away from each other. As usual, us Dawson kids were no good with mushy feels.

We snooped around for a few more minutes, then started back up the stairs. As Justin poked his head into the shadowy garage area to check for witnesses, I glanced around the history displays. A police museum. I couldn't think of many locations more unlikely for an illegal demon summoning.

I used my borrowed padlock to secure the gate over the open garage, then Justin and I waltzed casually out of the alley and joined the lunch-hour bustle that had consumed the main street. Trying not to look too shifty walking next to a cop in uniform, I accompanied him to a coffee shop two blocks away where we bought a couple big chicken wraps to go. I'd monopolized his lunch break, so I couldn't send him back to work hungry.

Unwrapping our food, we walked and ate at the same time, heading toward his squad car, which he'd parked five blocks from the museum. Pedestrians hurried along the sidewalks, shoulders hunched against the chill wind, and traffic whizzed by in a steady flow. We halted at an intersection.

Justin swallowed a mouthful. "Tori, I was wondering …"

Tearing off a bite of my wrap, I leaned closer to hear him as half a dozen people gathered around us, waiting for the light to change. "Mm?"

"After you've helped Ezra and taken care of that cult …" He shifted his weight. "I was thinking … maybe I could swing by while you're at work one evening and get a drink?"

"Really? You want to?"

He nodded. "And, uh, if Aaron is around, that'd be cool."

My astonished gawking flashed into a beaming smile. I'd known Aaron could charm my brother given half a chance.

"Of course!" I threw my arm around him and squeezed, a cherry tomato spilling out of the wrap in my other hand. "I can't wait for you to meet everyone!"

The small crowd around us began to move, and I realized the light had changed. Still grinning, I stepped off the sidewalk. People streamed past us, marching toward the curb we'd just left.

"I *am* allowed to come into your guild, right?" Justin asked, uncertainty creeping into his tone. "That's not breaking the rules?"

"Rules, shmules." I dodged a power-walking businessman. "You're my brother!"

"That wasn't actually an answer, Tori."

"Yeah, well—"

A hand clamped over my mouth from behind.

As I was yanked off balance, adrenaline fired through my veins and I flung my head back. My skull met something equally hard and pain burst on impact. Dropping my wrap, I whipped my elbow out, hitting a soft torso and eliciting a grunt from my assailant. Then I was spinning, my arm cocked and hand clenched into a fist.

My gaze landed on the face of my attacker—the stocky blond cultist whose knee I'd shattered in the cemetery two days ago. His teeth-baring grin registered in my brain an instant before I saw the object in his hand.

The shiny length of steel.

Pointed at me. At my chest. Aimed for my heart.

My own momentum carried me straight toward it, and I had no time. No time at all. The mere second I needed to change my trajectory didn't exist.

The blade plunged into my chest.

I felt it. Felt the razor edges parting my skin, my muscles, my organs. Felt pressure and pain where I'd never felt anything before, in parts of my body that should never be touched by a foreign object.

My arm hovered in the air, halfway through the strike I hadn't completed. Motionless, I looked down at his hand curled around the dagger's hilt.

His fingers tightened, then he pulled the knife away. The blade slid out of my leather jacket, coated in shining red blood. Droplets spilled off the steel, falling in slow motion, sparkling as they floated down toward the pavement.

He drew the dagger back—and time snapped back to normal as he swung it toward me a second time.

Bang!

The sound exploded in my ears, and the cultist keeled over, shock splashed over his face and a bloody hole in his forehead.

People were screaming. Shouting.

"Tori!"

People were running. Fleeing.

"Call an ambulance!"

The ground was hard against my back. Was I lying down? When had I lain down?

"Prop up her feet! You, put pressure on the wound—hurry up! Tori, stay with me."

My vision was blurring. A face above me wavered in and out of focus, white as a ghost, hazel eyes just like mine shining with tears.

"Where's the goddamn ambulance?"

Hands were touching me, prodding me, pushing on my chest. A sound, growing louder. Sirens. Wailing, crying. I'd never realized how sad the sound of sirens was.

"Tori, stay with me."

"Tori."

"*Tori!*"

7

BEEP … BEEP … BEEP.

What an annoying sound.

Beep … beep … beep.

It wasn't an alarm. Not a cell phone. What else beeped like that? And why hadn't anyone shut it off already? So damn annoying. I was trying to sleep here. So tired. So exhausted.

Beep … beep … beep.

Just … shut … up!

"Relax, Tori." The cool female voice was accompanied by the scuff of shoes against a tile floor, drawing nearer. "I'm on it."

With a huge amount of effort, I cracked my eyes open. Light blasted my pupils, and my eyes were so dry they felt like sandpaper. Everything was so blurry that it took me a moment to make out the woman nearby.

She was in her late forties or early fifties with blond hair pulled up in a casual but elegant twist. She tapped on a monitor displaying a bunch of colorful numbers and lines, and the beeping went silent.

"Your blood pressure dropped again," she remarked, turning toward me. "How are you feeling?"

I blinked slowly. My face felt strange, and when I tried to wrinkle my nose, all sorts of weird sensations assaulted me. There was something stuck to my face?

The woman caught my hand as I reached for my nose. "Please don't pull out the nasal cannula."

"The what?" I croaked.

"The oxygen line in your nose." She pushed my arm down to my side, then produced a plastic cup of water with a bendy straw sticking out of it. She set the straw against my lips, and I greedily sucked down several mouthfuls of cool liquid.

Setting the cup aside, she perched on the edge of my bed. "Do you remember what happened?"

No images came to mind, but a horrendous rush of noise filled my ears—screaming and shouting and sirens and Justin calling my name over and over and over. Shuddering, I pushed the memory away and focused properly on the familiar face watching me: Elisabetta, the Crow and Hammer's best healer.

I blinked against the scratchy dryness in my eyes. "I was stabbed?"

"Yes. Would you like the short list of your injuries, or are you one of those patients who wants to hear every gory detail?"

"Gory details. How else am I gonna brag about it?"

"Just like your friends." She shook her head. "You were stabbed in the left side of the chest. The puncture caused a pneumothorax—a collapsed lung. The blade also nicked your heart, resulting in a condition called cardiac tamponade, which is where the sack around your heart fills with blood, squeezing your heart muscles. That caused you to go into cardiac arrest."

My abused heart lurched sickeningly.

"Fortunately, the paramedics had just arrived and were able to save you by performing a pericardiocentesis—they inserted a needle into your chest to drain the blood—"

"Actually, I changed my mind. I don't want the gory details."

Elisabetta smiled with faint humor that quickly faded. "It was close, Tori. Your friends sleeping in the waiting room right now don't even realize how close we came to losing you."

Waiting room? I glanced around and realized I wasn't in one of the converted rooms in Elisabetta's spacious home. This was an actual hospital room—beige walls full of weird sockets and panels and equipment, a sink and cupboard, and an ugly padded chair in the corner. Tubes ran from an IV stand with two bags on it, disappearing under my blanket in the vicinity of my left wrist.

"Am I gonna be okay?" I asked.

"You'll be absolutely fine—in a few days. We already removed your chest tube and healed the wound sites. Your X-rays look good, but damage to the heart is nothing to shrug off, even with healing Arcana to help." She stood. "Now, let's see how you're doing."

I submitted to a physical, too tired to do anything but answer her questions as she poked and prodded me. When she finished, she passed me the water cup for another drink.

"All right." She set the cup on the overbed table beside me. "I'll tell your friends you're awake."

"Can I see them?"

"Yes—if you can stay awake that long."

"Of course I can."

With a knowing smile, she headed for the door. It clacked shut, and I stared at it, determinedly ignoring the bone-deep fatigue weighing me down. I wanted to see them. The guys. My mages and my brother. They were here. I knew it. They were waiting for me, like we always waited when one of us got hurt.

They were here, and I'd stay awake so I could see them.

I kept repeating that to myself as the room faded and I slipped back into an exhausted sleep.

I SPENT TWO NIGHTS in the hospital, but no sooner was I discharged than Elisabetta shipped me straight to her house. She set me up in a healing room—significantly cozier than the hospital version, but the bed was the same—and only permitted brief visits from my friends. Probably smart since I was having trouble staying awake.

Still, I got to see Aaron and Kai, who fussed over me and tried not to show how freaked out they were over my near death. Justin, who'd seen the whole "almost dying" thing firsthand, didn't hold it together quite as well.

And Ezra. He hadn't said much, but he'd held my hand—his fingers ice-cold as he'd fought back his emotions.

The post-healing fatigue was intense, and time had gotten a little blurry. When I woke up to pale sunlight leaking through the drapes across the room's large window, I couldn't remember what day it was. My parched throat stung and I turned my head, searching for the ever-present cup of water.

Ezra was slumped in the chair beside my bed, his head resting against the wall and face slack as he dozed.

Forgetting about water, I stared at him. Just stared. Absorbing the sight. Letting it soothe me. The scruff on his jaw was thicker, approaching beard territory, and his long-sleeved shirt was wrinkled.

After a minute, I wiggled my arm out from under the blanket. My fingertips brushed his sleeve. He started, head jerking upright and eyes flying open. His attention snapped to me.

"Hey," I croaked. "Water?"

Sitting up, he grabbed the cup off the table and passed it over. I drained it, sighed in relief, and passed it back to him. He set the cup aside and turned back to me, his gaze roving worriedly across my face.

"Am I allowed to have visitors for more than five minutes now?" I asked. "What day is it?"

"Friday."

I wrinkled my nose. "Very funny."

His eyebrows shot up. "I'm serious. For real serious. It's Friday."

"But I was attacked on *Tuesday*."

He nodded. "You've been asleep. Healing always takes a lot out of a person."

"But … over three *days*?"

"You were stabbed in the chest." He brushed a scraggily curl off my face. "I thought we might lose you."

"*Pff.* One little stab wound can't keep me down."

He smiled, but there was no humor in it. "There was nothing little about that dagger, according to Justin."

"Where is he?"

"Work. Same with Aaron and Kai, but they'll be back tonight to check on you."

It took a bit of effort, but I sat up. "Any new developments?"

He studied me for a moment, somber and serious. "Aaron reported that Sin has been texting your brother."

I blinked. "Huh?"

"We're not sure when they exchanged numbers. They must've run into each other while visiting you."

I rolled my eyes. "Okay, but I meant *real* developments, not gossip."

His grin flashed before his expression turned thoughtful. "Preparations at the guild are ongoing. Everyone who can help has been making artifacts and collecting weapons and gear, and Aaron's been working the combat mythics hard."

"What about Darius? Have the other guilds decided what to do about the Court yet?"

"MagiPol finally launched their investigation, but the other combat guilds haven't done anything yet. With the temple in the cemetery destroyed, we have no hard evidence. Darius is trying to find the High Court so we have *something* to back up our claims."

"You mean not everyone believes him?"

"They think he's jumping to conclusions, either about the cult's existence or about how bad it is. No one wants to believe there are demon mages in the city." He shook his head. "He's doing everything he can. Once my little problem is taken care of, he won't have to tread so carefully."

His *little problem*. He said it so nonchalantly, as though he were getting a filling at the dentist.

"The museum basement is working well," he added. "We debated whether it was safe to use, but based on where you were attacked, Justin thinks the cultist staked out his cruiser instead of following you two to the museum. We haven't found any signs of cultists in the area, and Robin and Amalia have been working on the ritual circle at night."

A competing flux of dread and hope made my gut squirm. The Death tarot card danced in my mind's eye, only to be replaced by the Hanged Man dangling from one ankle with a lifeless expression of peace on his face.

Before my emotions could get away from me, I flung the blankets off. "All right. I'm taking a shower."

"You're supposed to rest."

"It's been *days*, Ezra." I slid my legs off the bed and pressed my bare feet to the cold tile floor. Aside from a few twinges in my torso, I felt nothing but overall stiffness and fatigue. "I need to be clean."

He huffed. "Then wait a moment while I start a bath for you. You can't fall down and crack your skull in a bath."

He disappeared into the attached bathroom, and the sound of water splashing into a tub trickled through the open door. After a minute, he came back out—just in time to rush over as I tottered across the room.

"I'm fine," I claimed, waving him off. "Just a bit weak in the knees, that's all."

He wrapped his arm around my waist anyway, so I allowed myself to lean into his sturdy warmth. He guided me into the bathroom, made sure I was steady, then stepped outside and closed the door. I used the toilet, washed my hands, then hobbled over to the tub to check the temperature. Too eager to wait for it to finish filling, I stripped off my medical gown and climbed in.

Sinking into the steaming water, I reclined against the slanted back of the tub. Wonderful. Amazing. The best feeling.

One I'd come so close to never experiencing again.

My fingers crept to my ribcage, and I found a tender spot where the dagger had pushed through my skin and into my organs. I prodded around a bit more, shocked as always by the miracle that was Arcana healing; you'd never know I'd had a hole punched through my chest. Remembering the feel of the blade, I hastily focused on pouring shampoo onto my palm and lathering it into my hair.

I slowly worked through a simple shampoo and soap process, but with each movement, I could feel exhaustion building in my limbs. I'd been healed before and bounced right back—but I hadn't been terribly injured those times. The guys, however, had suffered varying degrees of traumatic injuries, and I understood now why they'd needed days or sometimes a full week in a healer's care before returning to their usual routine.

Heaving out of the water, I stepped onto the soft bathmat, sloppily wrapped a towel around myself, and tried to decide whether my weak legs would make it all the way back to the bed.

"Ezra?" I called hesitantly.

He was through the door in an instant. "Should I get Elisabetta?"

"No, no." I forced a laugh. "I'm just pathetically tired."

"Pathetically?"

"Yeah, I mean, you'd think I could walk across a room—"

He slid his arm around my waist and tugged me closer. Pressing his hand to my cheek, he tilted my face up. "Tori, it's okay."

I blinked in confusion.

"You were attacked. You were hurt. You almost died. Don't pretend that didn't happen."

"I'm not—"

He leaned down, bringing our faces closer. "You don't have to be strong right now."

My mouth opened and closed, and that storm of emotions I'd been stuffing deep down since waking up post-stabbing stirred insistently. "N-no, I don't—"

"Do you remember what you told me when I hid my insomnia? You said, 'Don't try to be so strong all by yourself.'"

My breath caught in my throat—and my eyes stung.

He tucked me against his chest, and the warmth of his encircling arms spoke for him: *I'm here.*

The soft but unyielding resolution in his eyes spoke too. *I'll be strong.*

His steady heartbeat under my hand where it rested on his chest murmured, *I'll protect you.*

My mouth trembled. Tears spilled over, running down my cheeks.

He held me close, arms tight, one hand tangling in my wet hair. I clutched his shirt as emotions welled up inside me—fear and dread and weakness and vulnerability. So much vulnerability. I hated that feeling. Hated feeling like I was a victim. Hated feeling so defenseless.

That mythic had come at me from nowhere. I'd been happy. Laughing. Delighted that Justin wanted to visit my guild.

And then I'd been dying. The cult wanted me dead, and they'd almost succeeded. They'd keep trying until they accomplished their goal, and I would never know where the next attempt would come from.

I buried my face in Ezra's chest, shaking with sobs. I'd almost died. *Almost died.* So close to the end. To nothingness. To no longer being a person, only a memory in the hearts of those left behind.

I dragged my head up. Ezra gazed down at me as my hand slid up his chest, along his neck, and curled into his hair.

Before I could pull his head down, he was kissing me.

I clamped my mouth against his, kissing him back with equal ferocity. All my fear and helplessness fled as fire ignited in my blood. My arms were around his neck, both hands fisted in his hair. His arms held me against him, fierce but gentle.

Tilting my head, I opened my mouth for him and his tongue found mine. Fatigue forgotten, I pressed into him. My flimsy towel caught between us, the fluffy cotton rubbing against my bare skin as it slid down. His breath rushing out, he grabbed the back of the towel, the muscles in his arms bunching as he held it in place.

"Tori," he rasped. "You should be in bed."

"Only if you get in with me."

He stifled a groan. I arched into him, cold air finding my skin as one edge of my towel dropped, exposing my naked side.

Catching the towel's end, he swept it back around me—then scooped me off my feet. He strode out of the bathroom and into the bedroom. The sight of medical equipment tucked in the corner only slightly cooled my libido.

He set me on the bed, then flipped the blankets over me and my askew towel. Marching back into the bathroom, he returned with another towel and dropped it over my wet hair.

"Dry off," he told me. "Then get some sleep."

I pushed the towel up so I could see him. "I'm not tired."

"You looked ready to fall over a moment ago."

"Well, now I'm horizontal, so it's all good."

He choked on a laugh.

Pushing the towel off my head, I reached for him. He leaned down and our mouths met again. Soft, gentle, deep. A fire stoked by more than lust.

Slow, delicious heat unfurled in my center. My fingers curled around his wrist. Without breaking our kiss, I drew his hand downward. His warm fingers slid over my neck, trailing through droplets of cold water from the bath. Along my shoulder, tracing my collarbone.

I guided his hand farther down. Under the blanket. Pushing the towel aside.

He crushed his mouth against mine, breath rushing through his nose. I arched up into his palm—then his other hand was under the covers too. Sliding over my bare skin, tracing my curves. The bed dipped as he put his knee on the mattress.

I got my fingers back into his hair, holding his mouth to mine, not letting him pull away even for an instant. I would allow my own hands to wander later. Right now, I wanted him touching me. I wanted his hands on my body, exploring and teasing. Heat built in me, and the room spun as I sucked in air.

Uh, actually … the room was *really* spinning.

He pulled back, took one look at me, and muttered a curse under his breath. "I knew you should be sleeping."

I caught his wrists as he withdrew his hands. "Nuh-uh. I'm good. Just needed a breather."

"Nice try." He tugged his arms free, then pulled the blanket up to my chin. "I should've been on my guard against your seductress ways."

"Excuse me?"

"Luring me into your *hospital* bed." He shook his head, somber deadpan in full force. "Just think how I'd feel if you passed out while I was kissing you."

"To be frank, Ezra …" I arched an eyebrow. "I was luring you in for a lot more than mere kissing."

"Duplicitous," he intoned.

I laughed, and his grin flashed, its appearance stealing the air from my lungs. His smile was already sexy enough, but add in the faint flush in his cheeks and the way his gaze kept sliding down toward my blanket-covered chest as though he couldn't stop himself, and *hot damn*.

I was ready to drag him into the bed by force.

Puffing out a breath, I reminded myself that there was a slight chance I might actually pass out, and I didn't want to miss the moment when I finally got the aeromage out of his clothes and into my bed. I'd just have to be patient for a short while longer.

Considering Robin and Amalia had already begun preparing the ritual that would either save him or destroy him, I wouldn't have long to wait.

8

ROBIN PUSHED HER BANGS off her face. "It's ready."

The museum basement was transformed. The floor had been cleaned, the cracks and nicks smoothed out. Robin and Amalia had drawn the array using silver alchemic paint, and the hundreds of crisscrossing lines and runes were dizzying to look at. Two large circles sat inside the twenty-five-foot outer ring—one for Ezra to stand in, and one into which Eterran would be summoned.

I hadn't gotten to help at all. Elisabetta had only released me from her care yesterday, a week after Justin and I had checked out this spot.

"Ready?" I repeated, glancing between them, not quite daring to believe. "As in, we can start the ritual right now?"

"Uh, technically yes," Robin replied, "but I don't think we should attempt the ritual in broad daylight."

"We should wait for tonight," Aaron agreed, crossing his arms. "After midnight, at least. And I want Kai here too, just in case."

Just in case could mean anything, but I was afraid I knew exactly which worst-case scenario he was thinking of—the one where Ezra didn't make it out alive.

My stomach turned over.

A shrill ring erupted, and Aaron dug into his pocket. He pulled his phone out and lifted it to his face. "Hello? Oh, hey Girard." He listened for a moment. "Okay, yeah, I figured ice artifacts would be difficult to find … No, the teams I sent out haven't found any vampires. All the usual nest spots are empty. What about frost-bombs? Has Katherine had any luck making one?"

Still talking, he moved toward the far end of the room. I watched him go, trying not to worry about the guild preparations. Before we faced the cult, we needed to save Ezra—or kill him trying.

My stomach jumped again, and I pressed my hand against it. I'd never felt this nervous in my life—it was a sort of persistent, low-level panic that made me ill. I wanted the summoning ritual to be over with just as badly as I wanted to freeze time forever.

"How are you feeling?"

I blinked, bringing the room into focus. Robin was standing beside me, peering worriedly into my face.

"Your injuries … have they healed okay? Do you want Zylas to check them?"

That got my attention. "*Zylas?*"

"He's very good at healing. I could probably convince him to fix you up if you need it."

"Uh. That's very considerate, but I'm just tired." I shook my head, unable to imagine the savage demon volunteering to heal me. I'd trust Eterran with my health first. "How are you? According to the guys, you've been out here every night."

She squeezed her hands together. "It's the least I could do. Even without the amulet to trade, I would've helped Ezra. He saved Zylas's life."

"He did?"

"Yes." Her eyes clouded over. "I almost lost him."

The shadow of pain in her expression intrigued me. "Your demon means a lot to you, huh? What exactly is your relationship?"

She reeled backward as though I'd slapped her. "Wh-what? Our *relationship?*"

"Like … do you have a contract? Can you command him or what?"

She gulped a few times, her face beet red. "We have a contract, but I don't command him. We work together."

Work together. Despite my deal with Eterran for a mutual goal, the idea boggled my mind. "How did that come about?"

"We … we saved each other." She lightly touched the infernus hanging around her neck, then tilted her head questioningly. "Are you concerned?"

"About what?"

"That I don't command Zylas."

I shrugged. "I won't pretend he doesn't frighten me, but Eterran frightens me too, and he's not *that* bad … for a demon."

"You sound like Amalia. That's how she describes Zylas." With a glance around, she started across the room. "Speaking of Zylas, I should find him. He wandered off again."

I followed her toward the staircase, leaving Aaron to his phone call. "I didn't realize he was out."

She pushed the fire door open and started up the concrete steps. "He doesn't like spending hours and hours in the infernus."

"What's being inside an infernus like?"

"I'm not sure, but the gist of it seems to be 'boring.'" She opened the door to the main level. "Are you ready for tonight?"

As we ventured into the dusty halls of the small museum, I almost brushed off her question. But fear thrummed in my bones, and I needed to admit it.

"I'm terrified," I whispered. "I'm terrified to lose him. It feels like we're ushering him to his own execution."

Robin stopped beside me, sympathy softening her face. "You aren't ushering him. He decided this himself, didn't he?"

My throat tightened.

"There's a big difference between being forced to do something and choosing your own path." She gazed down the hall, her eyes losing focus. "Choosing … means something."

Her whispered words triggered a sudden memory: Zak leaning toward me, green eyes intent as he told me that I was as much a mythic as him. *Choice is more powerful than fate.*

Shivering, I shrugged off the memory—and realized Robin was still staring off into space. I waved a hand in front of her nose. "You all right there?"

She started. "Y-yes. Sorry. Just … just remembered something, that's all."

With a skeptical eyebrow arch, I glanced around. "So, do you wanna call for him, or what?"

"Hm? Oh, he already knows I'm looking for him. He's got some reason for not coming to find me. Let's check the second floor."

I was still frowning confusedly as she headed back to the stairwell. We hurried up to the second floor, and Robin led the way down a hall with small offices branching off it, each one converted into a display about some facet of the city's policing history.

We reached the end and turned into a wider corridor lined with glass cabinets. I peeked outside as we passed in front of a large arched window—and something dropped off the top of a cabinet.

Landing without a sound, Zylas shoved us both to the floor. I yelped as the demon's hand pressed between my shoulder blades, mashing me into the musty carpet.

"*Zh'ūltis,*" the demon growled. "Walking into the sight of hunters? I taught you to be smarter, *vayanin.*"

Spitting the taste of dust from my mouth, I craned my head. Zylas had merely rammed me into the floor, but he'd landed directly on Robin. She was sprawled on her stomach, the demon on top of her as he hunkered below the window.

"Zylas, get off me," she grumbled. "And what hunters?"

He raised his head enough to peer out the window. "They are watching."

"Someone is spying on us?" I started to sit up and the demon shoved me back down. "Who?"

"Humans. Three. They try to hide among the others, but they stay in one spot and watch, watch, watch. Hunting. Planning. They will ambush us."

Again, I raised my head, but more slowly this time. Zylas allowed it. With my nose practically resting on the sill, I peered into the street. People bustled about on the sidewalk, and it took me almost a minute to spot them: one man sitting at the bus stop, another leaning against a wall looking at his phone, and a third loitering near a boutique clothing store.

Shivers rippled over me. They had to be cultists. The Court must've noticed us using this building, and they were waiting for their chance to strike again.

Planning their ambush, as Zylas had said.

"What are we going to do?" I whispered. "Finding a new location and starting again now, when we're so close …"

Robin squirmed out from under her demon and crouched between us. "You haven't seen anyone watching us before this, have you?"

"No," Zylas answered. "They came today only."

She straightened her glasses. "The ritual is ready. It'll all be over tonight. We should stick to the plan, and if they're here when we return at midnight—"

"—I will hunt *them*," he finished, his husky voice layered with eager ruthlessness, his crimson eyes glowing.

If those cultists thought "*Servi*" existed to protect them, tonight they would get a very rude awakening as to what this particular demon thought of their ideology.

"NO, NO, NOOO!" I howled, waving my game controller as though that would somehow prevent my neon-green racecar from careening off the road and crashing into a building.

"Watch it!" Aaron laughed as he blocked my flailing controller with his elbow, hands glued to his own controller. "You're going to—shit!"

I cackled as his cherry-red car smashed nose-first into a light post. Ezra's and Kai's cars zoomed past his crumpled wreck.

"Thanks a lot, Tori," he grumbled.

"Go Ezra!" I cheered, steering my smashed car back onto the road, even though I had no chance in hell of catching up. "Show 'em who's boss!"

"He always wins anyway," Kai complained, his thumbs steady on his controller. "He doesn't need a cheerleader."

I turned, sticking my tongue out at the electramage, and Ezra made a *pfff* noise as I accidentally dug my elbow into his ribs. "Whoops! Sorry."

The sofa was more cramped than usual. We normally spread ourselves across all available furniture for game night, but somehow, we'd all ended up crammed on the sofa together. I was squashed between Ezra and Aaron, and I didn't mind one bit.

Aaron and I raced our steaming wrecks, half a lap behind Ezra and Kai as they battled for first place. Ezra won by a car length, and Aaron beat me easily. Oh well.

"Why do I always lose at my own games?" Aaron complained. "When you're undemonized, we'll see who wins all the time."

"Will he lose his enhanced reflexes?" Kai mused. "And his increased strength? Or are those permanent changes?"

"Who knows?" Ezra glanced at them, his expression grave. "The real question is whether I'll lose my demonic telepathy that allows me to hear all your thoughts."

The three of us stared at him uncertainly.

He cracked a grin. "Just kidding."

I blew out a breath, slightly panicked by the idea of Ezra having telepathy. I'd indulged in way too many naughty daydreams for that to be anything but an embarrassing nightmare.

He lifted his controller. "One more round?"

Aaron glanced at the clock beneath the television. "Let's call it a night. We only have a couple more hours."

"And Aaron and I have a job to do," Kai added, pushing to his feet.

"Yeah." Standing, Aaron stretched his arms over his head. "Let's go, Kai."

"Huh? A job?" I followed him and Kai toward the back door. "What job?"

Ezra followed us, stopping in the kitchen doorway, his expression the same blend of confusion and surprise I felt.

"Robin's demon spotted those guys scoping out the museum," Aaron explained. "We're going to sweep the entire neighborhood to ensure it's safe to go ahead with the ritual."

"Oh." I hesitated as the two mages pulled on their shoes. "Do you need any help?"

"Nope. You stay here with Ezra." Aaron grabbed his keys off the counter. "Make good use of the time while we're gone."

Good use? Huh?

Kai followed him out, saying over his shoulder, "We'll be back in an hour and a half."

I caught the door as it swung shut and hopped out onto the back step, cold from the concrete seeping through my socked feet. "Guys, is it really safe to—"

They stood a few feet away as though they'd known I'd rush out after them. The laughter of our game from a few minutes ago had faded, replaced by quiet worry and banked grief.

I drew up short, staring at them.

"We'll handle it, Tori," Kai murmured. "Go back to Ezra and don't worry about anything until we're home."

"But …"

"We have six years of great memories with Ezra." Aaron's voice was soft, gentle, sad. "You don't. Use this time for you two."

Pain slashed my chest. "Ezra isn't going to …"

He isn't going to die tonight.

But he might. And we all knew it.

"Get in there, Tori," Kai ordered kindly. "I'll text you when we're on our way back."

I nodded weakly, and they continued across the yard and through the gate. Vehicle doors opened and closed, then the engine started. As the SUV reversed out of the driveway, headlights flickering through the fence, I walked back inside.

Ezra was still leaning in the kitchen doorway, shadows draped across his face.

I trembled where I stood, terror and grief and hope and denial and simmering panic battling inside me—the emotions I'd been holding back all evening. I'd tried so hard to deny them, to keep this day positive, but now I couldn't dam the flood.

Ezra opened his arms in invitation.

I sprinted the length of the kitchen. He caught me, sweeping me against his chest, crushing me to him. I wrapped my arms around his shoulders, squeezing with all my strength.

A hundred embraces flashed through my mind, just like this one yet not like it at all. A hundred hugs filled with warmth, calm, safety, friendship, laughter, tears, and love.

The memory of our first hug, that awkward question I'd posed in Justin's apartment hallway, ballooned inside me. A week after my first shift at the Crow and Hammer, the night Aaron had been attacked while walking me home. Last May. Nine months ago.

Exactly nine months, I realized suddenly. Aaron had been attacked on May 19—a date I'd never forget—and today was February 19.

Was nine months all I'd get with Ezra? Three-quarters of a year? A summer, a fall, a cold winter of stress and worry … but no spring to thaw the ice and call back the sun?

A sob shook me, though I quickly stifled it.

Ezra's arms tightened, then relaxed. I tilted my head back, fighting the tears. Our eyes met, and there was sadness in his stare—but there was strength and steel too.

Taking my hand, he led me into the living room and guided me to the sofa before walking away. His footsteps padded up the stairs. The clack of a door opening, then closing. Returning footfalls.

He reappeared, carrying his acoustic guitar, and sat beside me. Settling the guitar on his lap, he plucked each string and adjusted the tuning pegs, then set his left hand against the frets.

With a sweep of his fingers, sound cascaded from the guitar. An unfamiliar melody emerged, the twanging notes soft and mournful. They danced a slow spiral, falling and falling, somehow growing even sadder until tears were streaking my face. The music slowed until he was plucking single notes, soft, fading, dying. I hugged myself, scarcely holding it together.

His left hand shifted across the frets, and his thumb brushed a new note. His fingers moved again, and the anguished melody began to rise instead of fall. It built, and somehow it was the sound of hope. It was the sound of a calling future, of a brighter day. The sound of renewal and rebirth.

The song swelled into a bright crescendo that rang with expectation before fading into silence.

He waited a long moment, then plucked out a simple scale. "I learned that song when I was a kid—I was twelve, I think. Whenever it all seemed like too much and I wanted to give up, I would play it over and over."

I twisted my hands together so hard it hurt.

"My whole life, I've been pushed by other people." He strummed a chord, then another. "Every big change I've experienced was because of someone else. My parents, the Court, Lexie, Eterran, then Aaron and Kai. And finally ... you."

"I ..." My voice warbled. "I didn't mean to—"

"It wasn't a bad kind of push, Tori," he murmured. "You helped me realize how passive I'd become ... how I'd stopped deciding anything. I'd stopped wanting anything, and I was just waiting for the end. I told myself I was just living in the moment, but I wasn't really *living* anymore."

He ran his hand along the neck of his guitar. "I really enjoy live music ... concerts and music festivals. Being a demon mage doesn't stop me from attending concerts. There's no reason I couldn't, but I never even told Aaron and Kai it was something I'd like to do. I just ... forgot it was okay to want things."

His eyes, soft and warm, rose to mine. "Then I met you."

My throat closed and I couldn't quite breathe.

"I don't want to die, but maybe I will. But I can do this because *I* decided. I'm not slipping into madness or waiting for Darius to put me down like a sick dog. This is my choice. This is what I want—a chance at a real life. I'm afraid, but it's a different fear than when it was all out of my control."

"Ezra," I choked.

Quiet sadness touched his smile. "I can't say I have no regrets, but no matter what happens, I'll never regret a single moment with you."

I pushed his guitar off his lap, grabbed his face in both hands, and kissed him. I kissed him so hard I was bruising my lips, and I didn't care. The pain joined the burning agony in my chest.

"You're going to survive," I gasped against his mouth. "You're going to be fine."

"Better than fine." He sank his hands into my hair. "I'm going to be myself for the first time in ten years."

I climbed onto his lap, our mouths locked together. Desperate. Urgent. His arms banded around me, one hand gripping my hair. I kissed him harder, deeper.

How could I lose him now? How could I lose this wonderful, terrible, agonizing, beautiful thing between us when it'd barely begun?

My fingers raked over his shoulders, then I reached down and grabbed the bottom of his shirt. I needed more. I needed everything. I needed all of him now, before it was too—

"Tori," he whispered.

I clutched his shirt, limbs quivering faintly.

"I want this to be just us. The two of us." He stroked the back of my neck. "I'm too tangled up with Eterran, and ..."

I raised my head.

His hand moved to my cheek, brushing away a streak of tears. "I want to be with you as myself, and until he's gone, I won't know who I really am. I haven't known since I became a demon mage."

"But ..." My voice was hoarse, almost soundless. "If we wait and you ... you don't ..."

"I'll just have to survive tonight. I want to discover myself … and I want to do it with you."

I nodded even as my heart tore itself apart. He wanted to love me as himself, not as a demon mage with another being interwoven through his mind and sharing his body. If that meant we would lose our last chance to share this kind of intimacy, I would respect his decision.

But he would survive. He would. He had to.

We lay together on the sofa, him stretched out on his back and me lying across him, our legs tangled. He stroked my neck and spine, and I touched his face, kissing him over and over. We held each other, waiting. Wanting the time to come. Wanting it to never arrive.

The back door clicked. Footsteps. A pause.

"That works better without clothes," Kai observed dryly.

"Mind your own business," I muttered, eyes closed and cheek resting on Ezra's chest. "How did it go?"

"Good. No sign of those cultists or anything else suspicious."

Ezra tensed under me, then sat up, lifting me with him. He drew me to my feet, and we faced Aaron and Kai. Terse determination had replaced their earlier grief.

The wait was over. It was time for battle now. I didn't know who or what we would fight, or if there was an enemy to fight aside from the magic that bound Ezra and Eterran together, but we would fight it with everything we had.

Ezra pushed his shoulders back, and with that steady, soothing calm that had amazed me from our first meeting, he looked across the three of us.

"I'm ready." He quirked an eyebrow. "Let's summon a demon."

9

BENEATH glaring fluorescent lights, Ezra stood in one of the two circles inside the twenty-five-foot outer ring that Robin and Amalia had drawn on the museum basement's floor. He was dressed in full combat gear, including his bad-guy-smasher gloves with their steel-reinforced knuckles and elbows.

Kai, Aaron, and I were arranged on his left, outside the silver array. We'd dressed in combat gear too, my belt around my hips, Sharpie in its sheath on Aaron's back, and Kai's vest loaded with small weapons. Had we dressed for battle because we felt stronger in these clothes? Or because it was a way of acknowledging the gravity of this night?

Robin stood opposite us. She hadn't dressed for a fight, wearing a gray sweater under her leather jacket, but I wasn't sure she owned real combat gear. Amalia was positioned across from Ezra, facing him, and she looked as "haphazard posh" as always in leggings, tall boots, and a leather jacket of her own.

I'd never paid much attention to Amalia. Next to Robin's mysteries, the apprentice sorceress had seemed kind of inconsequential—but I was revamping my impression of her big time.

Holding the ornate cult grimoire in her hands, Amalia chanted in Latin. The ancient words rose and fell with undeniable power, her voice smooth and confident, almost regal. It was as though she'd been born to read this spell—or as though she'd prepared since birth to read it. The thought that she might falter seemed ridiculous, and I had no doubt about her ability to perform the ritual flawlessly.

The final member of our strange group wasn't in the basement. Zylas was somewhere above us, prowling the museum rooftop as he watched for any sign of trouble. If any cultists showed up, he would warn us—and, depending on the intruders, eliminate them.

As Amalia's voice rolled through the room, Ezra waited alone in the circle, his left eye glowing faintly as both human and demon watched their fate unfold. Fighting to control my nauseating fear, I held on to Aaron's and Kai's hands. They gripped my fingers as tightly as I held theirs.

Amalia continued to chant, voice rising, then she paused. She gestured to Robin. The petite contractor knelt and opened the case at her feet. She withdrew a vial of demon blood—Nazhivēr's Second House blood, crucial to the summoning.

Walking into the empty circle, she uncorked it and tipped the vial, pouring the demon blood onto the central symbol. Instead of splashing across the floor, the thick liquid stuck to the rune, turning it dark scarlet.

She retreated to the circle's edge, and a heartbeat of silence ran through the basement.

"*Te tuo sanguine ligo, tu ut vocatus audias, Eterran of the Dh'irath House!*" Amalia declared.

A scarlet shimmer rippled out from the blood-coated rune. It spread across the silver array, turning the lines around Ezra's feet an eerie, iridescent ruby. He stiffened, the crimson gleam in his left eye brightening.

Amalia launched into the next phase of the ritual. Endless Latin flowed from her lips, then she pointed at the outer circle a foot in front of her boots.

"*Terra te hoc circulo semper tenebit!*"

The reddish glow imbuing the array whooshed upward in a shimmering wave, outlining a faint dome that arched over the outer ring. The gleaming dome faded, invisible, but according to Robin's explanation from a week ago, Eterran was now sealed inside the circle. Ezra would leave that silver ring as a human—or he wouldn't leave it at all.

My pulse drummed in my ears, a rapid beat counting down the minutes and seconds that remained.

Almost ten years had passed since Eterran had been summoned from his world and tricked into accepting a contract. Ten years since Ezra, deceived by the cult that ensnared his parents, had accepted his transformation into a demon mage.

Eight years since Ezra had run away from home, triggering the chain of events that had led to his parents' deaths and the destruction of Enright.

Six years since Aaron had encountered Ezra on the downtown streets and made a safe home for him.

Nine months since my first shift at the Crow and Hammer when I'd thrown a margarita across the three mages and Ezra had burst into laughter.

Three and a half months since I'd found out he was a demon mage.

Two months since our first kiss under the mistletoe.

One month since I'd realized I loved him.

And tonight, whether Ezra lived or died, none of our lives would ever be the same.

A silent buzz vibrated against my hip and I started, accidentally yanking my hands free from Aaron and Kai. Shit. Hadn't I turned my phone off?

I slid it out, the screen glowing with an incoming call from a number I didn't recognize. Amalia was still chanting, either too focused to have noticed my movement or ignoring me.

As I rejected the call, Kai glanced at my screen.

"That's Izzah's number," he whispered.

Izzah? I blinked at my phone, the screen dark. Why had Izzah called me? I hadn't heard from her in weeks.

The screen lit up, the phone buzzing. The same number appeared. She was calling again.

Amalia recited another Latin phrase. I hesitated, every nerve in my body prickling, then tapped the screen—answering the call. I brought the phone to my ear.

"Izzah?" I whispered as quietly as possible.

"Tori!" She was whispering too, but I could hear the urgency in her tone. "Where are you?"

"Where? I—"

"Is Ezra with you?"

The floor shifted under my feet. "Ezra?"

"I just overheard—two officers, they were talking about a classified bounty on Ezra. They're saying—"

Amalia's voice rose through another incantation. The air grew electric, scented with an unfamiliar tang of power.

"—Ezra is a *demon mage*."

The floor fell out from under me. The world fell. The universe was spinning out of control. Exploding. Imploding.

"A bounty," I choked out, scarcely making a sound. Aaron and Kai went rigid.

"Yes," Izzah whispered at top speed, "and the officers mentioned a team. I think they might be—"

Amalia stretched her hand out, pointing toward the blood-drenched rune as Latin flowed from her lips. The swirl of power through the two circles shifted back and forth, rippling across the interconnecting lines.

Izzah was still talking. "—already started, and you need to warn him before—"

"I have to go." I yanked my phone away and ended the call. My hand shook, the device almost slipping from my fingers. I shoved it into my pocket.

Aaron's and Kai's expectant stares were scorching the top of my head, but I couldn't look away from Ezra as he waited in the circle. Power sizzled in my nose and throat as Amalia's voice swirled through the room.

We couldn't stop now. We were so close.

Zylas was on the roof, keeping watch. No warning yet. We had time. Just enough time to unmake a demon mage. Just enough time to save Ezra not only from Eterran and madness, but from the justice of the mythic world that had just been unleashed.

I grabbed Aaron's and Kai's wrists, holding on to hope as I held back my terror. Every molecule in my body vibrated with urgency. Faster. Hurry. *Quickly!*

But Amalia didn't chant any faster. A single error would ruin the ritual. She continued at the same steady pace, power rising, the eerie glow of crimson magic in the circle deepening until it was more black than red.

Drawing herself up, Amalia lifted her hand toward Ezra. "*Tenebrarum auctoritatem da mihi, da super hunc imperium sine fine! Eterran of Dh'irath, bearer of the power of Ahlēa, wielder of the king's command, by your blood and your oath, I summon—*"

In a flash of glinting armor and reddish-brown skin, Zylas appeared behind her. His hand clamped over her mouth, halting her final words.

His eyes glowed like pits of magma. "They are inside."

My thundering heart plunged toward my feet.

"Who's inside?" Kai demanded.

"Odin's Eye."

The answer rasped from my dry throat. Odin's Eye was here. A team responding to a top-secret bounty on a demon mage.

"We have to get out of here!" Aaron barked urgently.

As one, Aaron, Kai, and I turned toward the lone exit. The open doorway led into a dark landing, and beyond it was the stairwell.

Zylas grabbed Robin's arm, shoved the petite contractor toward Amalia, then stepped in front of the two women and sank into a defensive stance. His fingers curled, claws unsheathing, crimson eyes fixed on that dark doorway.

"Aaron Sinclair," a deep male voice called, echoing out of the stairwell. "Kai Yamada. Tori Dawson. You've been charged with harboring a demon mage, a capital offense under MPD law. Surrender now, or we will attack with lethal force."

My lungs locked.

"Ezra Rowe. You've been identified as a demon mage and the MPD Emergency Judiciary Council has ordered your immediate execution." A short pause. "If you have any integrity or humanity left, you will surrender as well."

Tremors ran through my limbs. Ezra's secret was out. The world knew he was a demon mage.

I slowly slid one hand up my thigh to my hip. As my fingers curled around a cool glass sphere, I flicked a glance at Aaron and Kai. Aaron gave the slightest nod.

I yanked the alchemy bomb off my belt and flung it. As it arched through the air, Zylas launched toward the summoning array. His fist swung down, knuckles smashing into the concrete floor at the circle's edge. The concrete cracked under the blow, splitting the lines and runes.

My alchemy bomb smashed on the floor—and with shouted battle cries, the Odin's Eye mythics charged through the doorway.

I caught only a glimpse of familiar and unfamiliar mythics in dark gear before the billowing smoke obscured them. Its peppery tang filled my mouth as the room went white with mist.

Aaron and Kai leaped ahead of me, drawing weapons, and chaos exploded everywhere. Fire burst outward as Aaron's sword swept into a charging mythic, and their blades met with a ringing clang. Kai flung his throwing knives, and electricity leaped into the fog. A pained shout revealed that his attack had landed.

I yanked out my paintball gun, scouring the darting shadows for a target.

Something hit me in the back and I landed painfully on my knees. I swung my gun toward the bulky Odin's Eye mythic attacking me from behind, but he caught it and twisted it out of my hand. His fist flashed out—one, two, three strikes—and pain struck me in the jaw, the sternum, and the gut.

I went down. He flipped me onto my face, put a knee in my back, and wrenched my arm behind me. Through locked lungs, I felt a zip tie pull against my wrist. He yanked my other arm over to bind my wrists together.

That fast, I was done. Beginner's luck, a couple months of training, and a gutsy attitude were no match for professionals. I was nothing more than an amateur against the practiced bounty hunters of Odin's Eye.

Flashes of white electricity and orange firelight blazed nearby, but Aaron and Kai were too busy fighting off the Odin's Eye team to help me. My cheek ground into the floor as I squirmed violently, but the far stronger mythic forced my wrists together and looped the zip tie around them.

Hoshi burst from my belt pouch.

I didn't see what she did, but the mythic reared back with a shout. I pulled my feet in and kicked as hard as I could. My boots met his stomach, protected by an armored vest, but the strike was enough to throw him off balance.

Rolling away, I slipped my hand from the zip tie he hadn't had a chance to tighten and snatched my paintball gun off the floor. As Hoshi shot up toward the ceiling, I pulled the trigger.

The yellow ball exploded against his left cheekbone, and he pitched backward with a pained grunt—but he didn't collapse into unconsciousness. Sleep potions were common, and some pros dosed themselves with the antidote before heading out on jobs.

As I scrambled in my belt pouch for my brass knuckles, Hoshi dove at the mythic's head, buying me time. She whipped him with her tail—and he caught it. Yanking her down, he smashed his huge, gloved fist into her small body. The blow hurled her into the floor.

I shoved my brass knuckles onto my fingers and lunged at him with a scream. "*Ori amplifico!*"

My punch connected with his chest, and the air boomed. He flew backward and hit a shelf. Cardboard boxes tumbled down on his head.

I whirled around, but I couldn't see the sylph through the smoke screen. "Hoshi? *Hoshi?*"

She didn't appear. Had she shifted into the fae demesne?

A concussive burst of air swept through the room. The smoke ballooned outward, carried on an expanding ring of wind. In the center of the clear space was Ezra, unarmed except for his gloves. He was completely surrounded by mythics.

Faster than any human, he lunged into his opponents and unleashed rapid blows on his attackers, each strike punctuated with a blast of wind that threw his victim backward—but the mythics behind him closed in, weapons gleaming.

"Mario!" someone bellowed over the cacophony. "Get your demon over here!"

Crimson light flared through the room, and the shadow of a demon appeared in the fog—recognizable by its terrifying height, messy mane of hair, and lion-like tail. The demon advanced toward the corner where the Odin's Eye mythics had pushed Ezra.

I stood alone in the chaos, unnoticed by the other combatants, and in that moment, I understood the hopelessness. I couldn't tell how large the Odin's Eye team was, but we were outnumbered by at least three to one. I'd heard over and over that Odin's Eye was a tough guild. Aaron and Kai had talked about the skill of their combat members. They were the second most proficient bounty hunting guild in the city.

And they were supposed to be our allies. Rivals, yes, but allies. Now, all that skill and experience was our enemy. Our only hope was for Ezra to unleash his demonic magic, but that would mean killing our former allies and condemning himself as a violent demon mage.

The haze swirled wildly, flowing in and around the combatants—and a dark shape with glowing red eyes shot out of the misty shadows. As Ezra fended off his attackers, Zylas rushed in.

He dove for the floor, sliding into the legs of the nearest mythic. The man was still falling as the demon launched up into the next mythic. Swinging off the larger man like a fulcrum, Zylas slammed both feet into a third mythic—then wrenched the second one off the floor and threw him into another man.

My jaw hung open. I'd witnessed how much weight the demon could lift but seeing him hurl a larger man across a ten-foot distance was still a shock.

The horde of Odin's Eye mythics surrounding Ezra broke apart as Zylas smashed through them, inconceivably agile and unstoppable. Ezra flung two mythics away from him with powerful gusts.

"Ezra!" Aaron roared over the raucous noise. "Whirlwind!"

The aeromage thrust his hand into the air and a gale erupted through the room. The wind howled, spinning around us and whisking the smoke from my alchemy bomb into a spiral. I leaped out of the buffeting gale and into the safe eye of the storm with Aaron and Kai. Where was Zylas? I couldn't see him, Robin, or Amalia.

"Counter!" an Odin's Eye man bellowed. "Jerome—"

Orange-white flames raced up Aaron's arms and across his shoulders. His sword was blazing. Fire rippled off his hair, and I couldn't tell where man ended and flame began.

He extended his sword, then snapped it in a tight circular motion.

Ezra's whirlwind exploded with fire.

I reeled away from the roaring inferno as it whooshed around and around the room—and I realized Ezra had made it over to us. He stood a few feet away on Aaron's left, and on his right, Kai held two short knives.

Power crackled over the electramage's arms, and with the terrifying tornado of flames surrounding us, he calmly pointed his blades at the ceiling.

Outside the ring of fire, every strip of fluorescent lighting shattered and electricity leaped for the floor. Shouts and cries erupted from the Odin's Eye mythics as lightning rained down on them.

Fire, wind, and lightning undiminished, the three mages backed toward the exit. I moved with them, the elements raging around us but nothing reaching us except the heat pouring off Aaron. I retreated into the stairwell. Kai darted in after me, then Ezra, and finally Aaron. With a twist of his sword, he sent a wave of boiling fire shooting through the doorway back into the basement room.

"What about Robin and—" I began in a panicked shout.

As Aaron's fireball swept out the door, Zylas skidded across the threshold just beneath it. He had Amalia over one shoulder and Robin under his other arm. He spun in a neat pivot and tossed Amalia and Robin toward us. Ezra and Aaron caught them as Zylas leaped right back into the hazy basement room.

A man's howl of pain rang out as the demon found his next victim.

"Go!" Aaron shouted.

I didn't stop to ask where Zylas was going all by himself. I sprinted up the stairs, Robin and Amalia on my heels. Up, up, up, then I flew through the door at the top—and right into the first of three mythics waiting in the hall, reinforcements for the team below.

My fist flew and my brass knuckles smashed the guy's nose. As he lurched back, a small hand grabbed my shoulder. Robin?

"*Ori eruptum impello!*"

With her incantation, an expanding silvery dome hurled the mythics into the wall so hard they smashed through it.

"Go left!" Ezra ordered sharply.

I spun left and streaked down the hall—away from the exit. Pounding footsteps told me the others were following, but there was nowhere to go. The corridor ended in an arched window.

As my steps slowed, Ezra charged past me. He thrust both hands out and a blast of wind shattered the window like a battering ram, blowing out all the glass. He leaped over the sill and disappeared outside.

Adrenaline burning in my veins, I ran to the window and sprang through it.

Six feet down, Ezra caught me. He pushed me aside and lunged forward to catch Robin as she leaped out next. He tossed her toward me as Amalia plunged down. As I steadied Robin, objects tumbled from her arms—the case of demon blood and her gray backpack, a corner of the grimoire sticking out the top.

"You—you grabbed it—" I gasped, scarcely able to believe she'd managed it amidst the smoke and battle.

As Aaron and Kai landed on the pavement beneath the window, I crouched and shoved the metal case into the backpack. Robin gripped her infernus, her eyes going out of focus.

The pendant lit with crimson light—and a red streak of power shot out of the lower wall of the building. It sucked into the infernus, then burst out again. Zylas reformed from the light, the red glow of his power washing over the alleyway.

The instant he was solid, he swept Robin off her feet and onto his shoulder. He snatched Amalia with his other hand, throwing her over his other shoulder.

"*Run*," he snarled at us—then bolted across the alley.

With one leap, he was over the chain-link fence bordering the opposite property. Two more leaps, one off the roof of a rusting van, and he was on top of a building. He disappeared on the other side.

Gone. I blinked stupidly, clutching a strap of the backpack.

A shout sounded from inside the building. Ezra seized my arm, and the four of us sprinted away. Unable to follow Zylas's escape route, we raced down the alley to an intersecting back street and wheeled around the corner.

Light flared behind us. The Odin's Eye mythics were giving chase.

We came out on East Hastings Street. Ezra sped across the four lanes, causing two cars to blare their horns, their tires squealing. The flash of their headlights disappeared as we ran into another dim alley.

My lungs burned. Clutching the precious backpack, filled with the irreplaceable materials Robin had saved from the basement, I kept running, Ezra beside me and Aaron and Kai right behind.

Run. Just run. Alley after alley. Across another street. Into the shadows again. Headlights suddenly blinded me as a black SUV screeched to a halt beside us.

"Get in!" Kai barked.

I glanced back at him, shocked by the order, and saw the cell phone in his hand, screen glowing. Gasping for air, I wrenched the back door open, dove inside, and slid across the seat to make room for Ezra and Aaron. They dove in after me while Kai sprinted around the SUV's hood and jumped into the passenger seat.

We were still closing the doors as the engine roared and the vehicle tore away. I craned my neck, looking back. As the SUV took a turn on two wheels, men in black combat gear barreled out of the alley. They'd been right behind us.

I slumped in my seat, lungs heaving, and looked toward the driver. The rearview mirror reflected Makiko's pale face as she clutched the steering wheel.

"Kai, what happened?" she asked tersely.

He didn't answer. None of us spoke a word.

10

NUMB INSIDE AND OUT, I held an icepack to my jaw as I watched Makiko clicking on her laptop. On the sofa beside me, Ezra was hunched forward, elbows on his knees and chin resting on his fists.

Aaron and Kai were a dozen paces away at the small condo's kitchen island. Kai had his shirt off, and Aaron was stitching a gash in the electramage's bicep, first aid supplies scattered over the counter. Kai stared at the ceiling, jaw tight.

The apartment belonged to Makiko, but she didn't live here. It was one of half a dozen secret properties her family owned in Vancouver—places to retreat during emergencies. This one was located in Coal Harbour, high in a tower with a view of the inlet, the dark water tinged with yellow as the morning sun peeked above the horizon.

Aaron knotted off the stitches and selected a jar of white cream from the large first aid kit. He liberally dabbed the ointment over the bloody line in Kai's arm.

"Here it is," Makiko murmured.

Ezra raised his head, and I lowered my ice pack as she pointed a remote at the wall-mounted TV. The screen came on. A few clicks on her laptop, and the MPD's white website filled the television so we could all see it.

The webpage layout was familiar—a bounty posting—but large red text at the top declared, "LEVEL 2 CLASSIFIED."

I skimmed the text, the chill in my blood deepening with each line. Ezra's personal details were clearly laid out, from his age to his guild to his home address. The dates for the MPD investigation—February 13-14—were followed by a description of the "Emergency Judiciary Council Hearing under Code 12-03-006," with their ruling of the death sentence.

"'Investigation results,'" I read aloud. "'A witness from the Keys of Solomon guild reported on February 12 at 18:08 that mythic Ezra Rowe assaulted and wounded a combat team in the Capilano View Cemetery. The witness further alleged that the suspect demonstrated magic consistent with illegal demon magery. Witness testimony has corroborated submitted evidence.'"

As I finished reading, Makiko guided her cursor to a file attached to the case, labeled "C19-1382-Evidence-01", and double-clicked it. A window popped open and a video filled it. The shaky phone camera blurred in and out of focus as it was pointed through winter-bare shrubs at a patch of green grass.

Three men circled a fourth, who had a weird red smear obscuring his outstretched arm. It sort of looked like a glitch in the recording or a light reflection.

Scarlet flashed, and the screen went completely red, then white. A female voice gasped.

"*Demon magic!*" she exclaimed in a horrified whisper. "*He's using—oh my god!*"

The video cleared, revealing craters in the ground and dirt sifting down to earth. In the bottom corner, a woman with wild red hair—me—tackled a guy in the legs while a pale streak flickered nearby. Hoshi, I was guessing.

"*He's going to kill them!*" the camerawoman gasped. "*Oh god, he—no!*"

The screen went crimson again, and explosive noise screeched across the speakers.

Makiko paused the video, and silence fell over the room. The frame frozen on the screen showed a weird streaky smear of white and red. Magic didn't photograph—or record—well, but the camera had picked up enough.

Aaron rubbed a hand over his face and into his hair. "You were set up."

"By a Keys of Solomon member?" I ground out. "Why is a Keys member even here? Were those other cultists affiliated with the Keys too?"

Ezra's jaw was clenched. "I don't know about them, but the woman recording the video—I'd know her voice anywhere."

Our heads swiveled toward him as he stared at the screen, crimson flaring in his left eye.

"Xanthe. She set me up, recorded the video, and reported me to the MPD."

The "Magna Ducissa" of the Court of the Red Queen, Xanthe was a mentalist with the power to control anyone in her line of sight and force them to commit any act she desired.

"*Xanthe* is a Keys of Solomon member?" I rasped, fighting the emotions clogging my chest. "She was—the whole time we were—they—"

I stammered into silence as the urge to scream ballooned in my chest, compressing my lungs. I wanted to rage and shriek and cry at the unfairness, at the hopelessness. We'd tried to identify cult moles in the Keys guild. We'd wondered who was left. We'd puzzled over how the Court could've infiltrated such a powerful, anti-demon guild.

And all along, one of the cult's dangerous leaders was inside the guild, using her terrifying psychic ability to sway its members.

"Don't jump to conclusions," Aaron muttered. "This doesn't mean she's actually a member of—wait. *Shit.* How did I not realize it?"

"Realize what?" I demanded.

"Remember the video footage Blake showed us of the cultist who hanged himself in the Keys' lockup cell eight years ago? A dark-haired woman visited him before he committed suicide."

My limbs went cold. Xanthe again. It had to be her. She must've used her power to make that man kill himself—which meant she'd infiltrated the Keys eight or more years ago.

"*Why?*" I burst out. "Why set us up? Why reveal Ezra to the MPD? Wouldn't it be safer for the cult to just kill us all?"

Kai shook his head. "That was probably their plan until Darius started telling everyone there was a demon cult in Vancouver. Killing Ezra can't undo that, so the Court has given MagiPol and the other guilds a demon mage to hunt instead."

"And they've discredited Darius in the process." Makiko clicked out of the paused video. "Now everyone will think Darius has no idea what's going on in his own guild, or that he's throwing around accusations to hide his own secrets."

That urge to scream—or cry—was getting stronger and stronger, and I had to gulp several times. "Can't you do something? A second GM confirming his story about the cult could make a big difference."

"I have no proof," she said quietly. "And if I reveal I was traveling with you, it'll cast more doubt on our stories. Besides …" Her lips thinned. "The family comes first. I can't jeopardize that."

Aaron's hands formed tight fists. "So, Ezra has a death-sentence bounty on his head, and Tori, Kai, and I have been charged with harboring a demon mage, and"—he gestured at the screen with the bounty information—"the Crow and Hammer's guild license has been suspended pending an investigation. Now what?"

"If I'm not a demon mage," Ezra said, "then the Keys of Solomon's evidence is no more than baseless allegations. We can turn the spotlight back on them and the cult."

"But they have a video of you using demon magic," I pointed out despairingly.

"They have a video of a woman claiming I'm using demon magic. Magic doesn't record properly. The video only shows splotches of red light." He looked between us. "There's no way to convince MagiPol that I'm not a demon mage unless I'm not a demon mage. It's the first and most important step to saving you three and the guild from these charges."

"Then we have to finish the ritual as quickly as possible." I bit my lip. "We can't go back to the museum basement."

"No," he agreed. "We need a new location. We'll have to build the circle array again, let it charge, then perform the ritual."

Aaron paced across the living room. "The array creation could be done in half the time if we can get Robin and Amalia to work on it nonstop instead of only at night, but the charge time won't change."

"So a week or a little less," Ezra concluded. "That's how long we have to avoid capture."

"Every combat guild in the city will be hunting you." Makiko closed her laptop. "The bounty on Ezra is three hundred thousand dollars. That'll bring in other guilds."

"And there's Xanthe to worry about," I added grimly.

Makiko pursed her lips. "I can think of a few obscure locations where you could hide for a week and prepare the ritual. It's just a matter of getting you there without drawing any attention."

"We'll need Robin and Amalia too," I said. "We aren't sorcerers. Even if we knew how to set up the array, it wouldn't work for us. How will we contact them?"

Ezra, Kai, Aaron, and I had destroyed our phones before arriving at the condo. Technology could be tracked.

Makiko set her laptop aside, walked into the condo's second bedroom, and returned a moment later with a flip phone. She handed it to me.

I dialed Robin's number—good thing I had it memorized by now—and listened to it ring. It clicked to voicemail. I ended the call and redialed. It rang over and over, then went to voicemail again.

Flipping the phone shut, I glanced across the guys. "Do you think … did they get away safely?"

"Even carrying two people, Zylas is faster than a human," Ezra said. "There's no way they didn't escape the Odin's Eye mythics."

I wrapped both hands around the cell. "I'll try again in a few minutes."

Makiko tugged her black sweater straight. "Then I'll pick a location and begin preparations for smuggling you out of the city, and—"

A phone rang loudly, and I eagerly opened my hands—but the flip phone's tiny screen was dark.

Makiko pulled a sleek black phone from her pocket and lifted it to her ear. "Yes?"

The tinny sound of another voice leaked from the phone.

"How long ago?" she asked brusquely. "I see … Report back to them that I'll present myself within the hour."

She ended the call and tucked her phone in her pocket. Her dark gaze turned to Kai. "I've been summoned to the MPD precinct for questioning about the charges against you."

My fingers dug into the cushions, but I was the only one who seemed shocked. "But what about getting us to a safe location?"

"I'm Kai's GM. If I don't present myself, it'll look suspicious." She offered a faint smile. "I've dealt with the MPD before. I'll tell them I have no knowledge of a demon mage and promise to deliver Kai into custody as soon as I can locate him. It'll buy us some time."

As she collected her jacket, I fought the urge to protest. I didn't want her to leave. Makiko wasn't my favorite person by any stretch, but she was cool-headed, competent, and the acting GM of a powerful guild that could shield and hide us.

She set the TV to the security channel, which displayed the video feeds of all the cameras positioned throughout the condo building, then picked up her jacket. "Get some rest. I'll be back before noon."

I waved half-heartedly as she headed for the door. Kai followed her, and they murmured together for a moment before she slipped out. He bolted the door behind her, armed the security system, and turned to face us.

The silence was back, heavier than before.

There was nothing we could do except wait. The Court of the Red Queen had outmaneuvered us again, but they didn't know we were planning to transform Ezra from a demon mage into a regular aeromage. If we succeeded, we'd turn this all back on them.

We could make it happen. Somehow, we had to.

II

MURMURING VOICES drew me out of a restless sleep. Groggily, I lifted my head off the pillow I'd jammed against the sofa armrest. A heavy weight pinned my legs—Ezra had slumped sideways in his sleep and had his head pillowed on my thigh.

At the kitchen island, Aaron was prodding Kai's upper arm. The skin around the sutures was red and inflamed, and Kai flinched with each press of Aaron's fingers.

"I don't know, man," he muttered as he examined his friend's wound. "It doesn't look good. Might be infected. You need proper medical attention."

"If Makiko were willing to risk calling a MiraCo healer, she would've done it." Kai lowered his arm. "Wrap it up and I'll take a vitality potion."

Nodding unhappily, Aaron pulled a thick white pad and a roll of gauze wrap from the first aid kit. As he positioned the pad on Kai's wound, my gaze swung toward the floor-to-ceiling windows, where daylight leaked around the blackout shades.

"Makiko isn't back?" I asked.

Ezra stirred sleepily and raised his head. He blinked at me, then at the other two.

"Not yet," Kai answered as Aaron wound gauze around his bicep. "She should be back any time now."

"What time is it?"

"Twelve-thirty."

She'd expected to be back before noon. Nervous energy buzzed in my chest, and I slid the burner phone from my pocket. No messages from Makiko explaining the delay. Did she know this phone's number?

I dialed Robin. It rang and rang, then went to voicemail. I called again. And again.

No answer.

Slowly, I lowered the phone. "Something happened to Robin. Something's wrong."

Kai and Aaron didn't reply, their silence confirming my worries. The chances that she was sleeping or missing my calls were diminishing by the hour, but there was nothing else I could do except keep calling.

Staring at the phone, I considered all the numbers I could call. Darius. Clara. Sin. I could reach out to almost anyone from the Crow and Hammer, but contacting them would incriminate them.

The only person I could possibly contact was Justin. He was human and outside the MPD system—but he was also my family. Someone could be watching him.

The MPD had classified the case against Ezra, ensuring it wouldn't leak back to him or his guild, but Odin's Eye had been brought in on it—and possibly other guilds too. There was no way to know, but I suspected the men Zylas had noticed scoping out the museum hadn't been cultists. They'd probably been Odin's Eye scouts.

We were on our own. Not even Darius could swoop in to save us this time. He needed to protect the Crow and Hammer.

Our only chance was to separate Ezra and Eterran, and for that, we needed two people who weren't here—and whom we couldn't reach.

I pressed the call button again and listened to Robin's phone ring and ring.

I TRIED TO SLEEP again but my restless brain would only doze for a few minutes at a time. Aaron, snoring softly, had replaced Ezra on the sofa beside me, and Kai had retreated into the bedroom to sleep. Ezra sat on a kitchen chair, which he'd placed in front of the TV. He watched the security feed, the rise and fall of his chest the only sign that he wasn't a highly realistic mannequin.

My mind whirled, questions and worries and fears and dread leaving me dizzy and antsy. Another hour crept by, and I gave up on sleeping. Pushing off the sofa, I stretched my arms over my head, then tugged the flip phone from my pocket and called Robin again. No answer.

Ezra's head turned as I walked over to his chair, and I stopped dead at the twin crimson eyes glowing in his face.

Fear uncoiled in my gut. "Uh … Eterran?"

"Ezra is sleeping." A guttural accent tinged his words. "I am keeping watch."

"Don't you need sleep too?"

"Not the way a human does. Demons will rest, but sleep is dangerous."

Pondering that, I walked to the kitchen table where our gear was stacked. Unearthing my combat belt, I opened the back pouch. Empty. Hoshi hadn't returned. Whenever we'd been separated before, she would find her way back to me within a couple of hours.

That Odin's Eye mythic had smashed her with his fist. Was she okay? Had he injured her? Had she escaped that basement or was she still there, too hurt to find me?

Chewing the inside of my cheek, I grabbed a kitchen chair and carried it over to Ezra—or Eterran, rather.

I set it beside him and sank down. "We haven't talked about what you'll do once you're no longer trapped inside Ezra."

"I do not know yet. Only when I am myself again will I know."

"What do you mean?"

"I have been trapped inside a human for ten years." His jaw tightened, then relaxed. "If I am still demon enough, I will find a way to return to my world. If I am not …"

Trailing off, he resumed his observation of the security footage. I caught my lower lip between my teeth.

"Eterran …" I leaned closer, lowering my voice. "How much are you influencing Ezra these days?"

"Another question I cannot answer, *payilas*. Our minds are bound. Our thoughts mix in strange ways."

"You mean … you can't tell who's who anymore?"

"Nothing so simple. I know my mind, and he knows his."

I swept a lock of hair off my face. "Then what? I don't get it. Are you the one who's determined to survive, or is Ezra really fighting for it too?"

"He has always fought, but against me instead of for himself." He exhaled harshly through his nose. "I have despised him for that more than anything else. His weakness, his foolish guilt. But there was always strength in him. If he had been *kanyin* instead of human, I could have taught him how to become a fearsome fighter."

"If he'd been what?"

"A juvenile male demon. A young warrior." His lips curved up. "Like the *Dīnen et Vh'alyir*. Zylas is past his *kanyin* years, but he has much to learn yet."

My mouth quirked in a frown, but before I could ask any more questions, the crimson glow faded from his eyes. Ezra squinted blearily, then covered a wide yawn with one hand.

"Were you talking to Eterran?" he asked, rubbing his face.

"Yeah. He said if you'd been a demon boy instead of a human, he could've made you into a proper warrior."

Ezra stared at me.

I shrugged. "That's what he said."

Shaking his head, Ezra pushed to his feet. As he arched his back in a stretch, I got up from my chair and slid my arms around his waist. He engulfed me in a hug, and I leaned into him, resting my cheek on his shoulder.

"Makiko still isn't back," I whispered. "I can't reach Robin. Kai's wound needs a healer. We can't ask anyone for help. What are we going to do?"

He brushed his thumb across my cheek, wiping away a tear. "We'll figure it out."

The bedroom door swung open and Kai appeared, his hair rumpled. Joining us, he held his hand out. "Tori, the phone please. We can't wait any longer without knowing what happened to Makiko."

Plucking it from my pocket, I handed it over. "Are you going to call her?"

"No. If they have her phone, they'll be waiting for us to contact her." He flipped it open. "I'm going to try some other numbers and see what I can learn."

Already punching buttons on the phone, he headed into the spare bedroom, swinging the door half shut behind him.

Ezra leaned down and pressed a soft kiss to my tense mouth. "Let's make something to eat."

In the kitchen, we investigated the fridge, freezer, and cupboards. There were no perishables to speak of, so I got out a frozen pack of ground beef, tomato sauce, and noodles. Our spaghetti wouldn't include any cheese—a crime, if you asked me—but it'd be hot and filling.

Aaron woke up while we were clanking pots around, and the three of us quietly discussed our options as I mashed the frozen beef in a hot pan until it broke apart. Not my best work.

Kai rejoined us as I was dishing out pasta onto white plates.

"She arrived at the precinct this morning," he said without preamble, setting the phone on the table and dropping heavily into a chair. "Since then, she hasn't returned home or shown up at the MiraCo office. Her head of security is going to contact the precinct for information on her whereabouts. I'm supposed to call him back in an hour to see what he found out."

The guys polished off huge portions of spaghetti, and I forced down most of my plate despite a complete lack of appetite. While Ezra and I tidied up, Aaron checked Kai's arm again. The angry red inflammation around the wound had worsened. We dosed him with another vitality potion from the first aid kit, hoping to boost his immune system, then I made him lie across the sofa and relax as much as he could.

At exactly one hour, he asked for the phone. I heaved off the chair in front of the TV and crossed to the table. As my fingers closed around the device, a buzzing vibration shook it.

"Ah!" I yelped. Afraid it might stop ringing before I could get it over to Kai, I flipped it open and hit the speaker button. "Hello?"

"Kaisuke Yamada?" an unfamiliar male voice inquired.

Kai's jaw tightened, and I knew why—he was supposed to call Makiko's security guy back, not the other way around. As Kai sat up, I rushed the phone over and held it in front of him so he wouldn't have to jostle his injured arm.

"Kaisuke here. To whom am I speaking?"

"Yamada-*dono*," the man replied in a muted Japanese accent. "I'm a member of the Miura household and work with Miura Futoshi-*dono*."

"Has Miura-*dono* returned to the country?" Kai asked. "Makiko didn't mention it."

"He is still on health leave. However, he has been informed that his daughter was taken into MPD custody. The agents claim to have evidence that she is protecting the demon mage in Vancouver, as well as shielding you from justice."

Aaron sucked in a breath.

"If a guild master is arrested for a capital crime," the nameless man continued, his words terse and rapid, "the MPD can investigate any and all facets of their guild, with or without cause for suspicion. They've begun an examination of MiraCo's business dealings."

"I see," Kai murmured.

"If the MPD proceeds with this investigation, they'll uncover … *transactions* that are intrinsically tied to the Yamada family. Exposing MiraCo's discreet dealings will expose the

Yamada family as well, and the family cannot allow that to happen."

"Do you mean—"

The man on the phone cleared his throat quietly. "Miura-*dono* can't ask you himself, but he begs you to save his daughter."

A pulse of silence.

"Save Makiko?" I blurted. "From what?"

"The family is going to have her killed," Kai replied flatly. "They'll make it look like an accident or a health-related death, but even if it triggers an investigation, the MPD can't legally continue to examine MiraCo."

My knees weakened. Ezra stepped behind me, his steadying hands on my waist.

"The decision has been made," the caller said. "There is no time left. Yamada-*dono*, if there is anything you can do, the Miura family would be greatly in your debt."

Kai stared at the phone, his eyes eerily dark against his pallid skin.

"I …" His throat moved as he swallowed. "I can surrender myself in exchange for Makiko's release."

"*What?*" I shouted.

"Kai—" Aaron began angrily.

He held up a hand. "Mute the phone, please."

I pressed the button.

"I'm injured," he said before we could resume shouting. "Without Makiko, there's no safe way to get me to a healer. And if I don't do this, Makiko will be killed."

"But if you do, you'll be killed in her place!" I yelled, panic constricting my throat.

"I'm not a GM. Holding me doesn't give the MPD any special privileges to investigate my guild. My family won't have any reason to kill me, and once Makiko is out of MPD custody, she can protect me."

Aaron stepped to his friend's side. "But we need you."

Kai closed his eyes. "No, you don't, Aaron. You can protect Ezra and Tori without me." Eyes opening, he smirked. "At least for a little while."

Aaron swore.

Slipping past me, Ezra tugged the phone from my hand and held it out to Kai. "Do what you need to do. We'll manage the rest."

Kai took the phone, pressed a couple buttons, and lifted it to his ear. "Tell them I'm on my way to the precinct." He listened for a moment, then ended the call.

Aaron swore again, his hands balled into fists.

Kai passed the phone back to me. "Wait for darkness, then leave. This place isn't safe."

"Where will we go?" I whispered. The city outside these flimsy walls had never been more terrifying. "What about the safe place Makiko was talking about?"

"She can't help us anymore. Once they release her, the MPD will dog her every move. You need to find Robin and Amalia. Without them, it doesn't matter where you hide."

Denial spun in my head, insisting this couldn't happen. We needed to be together. That's how it worked. We accomplished things together, and we struggled and failed when we were apart. It would take all of us to survive this. Kai belonged with us.

Only moments later, he was pulling on his jacket, his wounded arm held stiffly. And only moments after that, he embraced Aaron, then Ezra.

My brain was still howling its refusal to accept this when he wrapped his good arm around me. I clamped myself against him.

"Kai," I choked.

"Take care of Ezra," he murmured. "Get that demon out of him, and I'll be back before you know it."

"You don't owe Makiko anything. You don't have to do this for her."

He squeezed me gently, then stepped back. "I owe her a lot more than I ever realized. I can't let her die because of me."

I knew that. Kai wasn't the type of person who'd let someone die when he could stop it—even if it meant sacrificing himself to save her.

Sabrina's tarot card flashed in my mind, the Hanged Man spinning on his rope.

As I blinked the vision away, Kai stepped out into the hall. Our eyes met one final time before he swung the door shut, and the soft click of the latch was like an ominous strike of thunder in my chest.

12

OUR FOURSOME was down to three, and every step I took away from Makiko's secret condo made me wish even more that Kai was still with us.

Aaron walked ahead of me, a black beanie covering his copper hair and Sharpie hanging down the center of his back; its silver pommel peeked above the collar of his coat, and the bottom of the sheath stuck out from beneath the hem. Ezra trailed behind me, wearing a ball cap pulled low to shadow his pale eye and scarred cheek, watching everything from beneath its brim. I strode along the sidewalk between them with my hood pulled up. Robin's gray backpack hung off my shoulders, stuffed with the cult grimoire, our customized summoning ritual, and the case with Nazhivēr's blood.

My combat belt was around my waist, hidden under my jacket, but the back pouch remained empty. Hoshi hadn't returned.

We didn't know yet where we'd build a new summoning ritual, or even where we'd hide out tonight, but like Kai had said, none of that mattered without Robin. Though we had the ritual and instructions, we weren't Arcana mythics. Only sorcerers could build working sorcery arrays.

So our destination? Robin's apartment.

It was a risk. Odin's Eye knew about her involvement, and they were probably hunting for her too. However, unlike me and Aaron, Robin hadn't listed her real address in the MPD database. She might be hiding at home, and that gave us a chance to beat the bounty hunters to her.

At least, that's what I told myself as we left the high-end Coal Harbour neighborhood and entered Gastown, the always-bustling tourist area where I'd once attempted to land a waitressing job. Old-fashioned streetlamps glowed cheerily as we followed the redbrick sidewalk past quaint historical buildings.

As we stopped at an intersection, waiting for the light to change, I noticed a café with an empty sidewalk patio, the yellow umbrellas folded up. Inside, a waitress carried a tray of food past a brightly lit window.

That café was the last restaurant I'd applied to, where the manager had revealed that no one in downtown Vancouver would hire me.

As I'd been standing outside the door in despair, a paper with three mythic job postings had blown into my face—and one of the postings had been for the only guild in the city that would've considered hiring a human out of the blue, on a day when Clara had been so desperate for help that she'd overlooked my paperwork in favor of a trial shift.

That was some next-level luck. Maybe some would call it fate. Like with Sabrina's tarot cards, there was magic at work in this mundane world that I didn't comprehend. That maybe no one comprehended.

But *choice* was more powerful than fate.

I'd chosen to read a piece of garbage, discovering the job listings. *I'd* chosen to venture into a bad neighborhood. *I'd* chosen to accept a trial shift.

And I'd stuck around. Every time things got messy, got ugly, got scary, I'd chosen to stick it out.

Now here I was, nine months later. The hot mess of a girl who'd thrown a margarita across three customers in a fit of temper had grown so much, changed so much, shaped by happiness and love as much as by fear and anguish.

I clasped Ezra's and Aaron's hands. Ignoring their questioning looks, I waited for the crosswalk light to change, then marched across the road.

Gastown's quaint buildings disappeared, replaced by utilitarian structures that grew increasingly dilapidated as we ventured into the disreputable Eastside. We wound through an alley and halted where it met a cracked sidewalk. Several blocks north of us was the Crow and Hammer, and a block south was Robin's apartment building.

"Do we split up to scout the neighborhood?" Aaron muttered. "Or stick together?"

I tightened my grip on their hands. "Together."

Aaron nodded and set out again. I finally released them so we could assume a more casual formation, trying to blend in with the sparse foot traffic—except the number of pedestrians was increasing. And they were all heading in the same direction as us.

Ahead, unusual light leaked past the three- and four-story buildings: red and yellow flashes, with a steady orange glow that tinged the dark sky.

The breeze shifted, and the potent tang of smoke hit my nose.

Ezra, Aaron, and I exchanged alarmed looks, then sped up. Not quite jogging, we raced to the intersection, sprinted across, and wheeled around the corner.

A huge red firetruck with lights flashing blocked our way forward. A large crowd of people and two news vans filled the street behind a temporary barrier. Beyond it, five more firetrucks were haphazardly parked on the road, and a group of firemen strode out of the building's smoky front entrance while others aimed heavy-duty hoses, thick streams of water raining down.

An apartment building was engulfed in fire. Black smoke billowed upward, disguised by the dark night, and angry flames leaped from the shattered windows.

"Oh my god," I whispered, my hands pressed to my mouth.

A gaping hole marred the building's face, as though a wrecking ball had demolished a third-floor unit. The ragged maw belched fire and smoke, and it didn't take an expert to guess that's where the inferno had started.

A fireman shouted a warning, and the watching crowd gasped as a balcony railing plunged three stories and crashed to the pavement. A moment later, the entire balcony broke away. It smashed into the ground, debris flying everywhere.

"Is that ... Robin's apartment?" I asked numbly.

Ezra nodded, his lips pressed into a thin line. My hands shook as I slid the flip phone from my pocket and dialed Robin's number. Instead of ringing, it went straight to voicemail.

"What if she's in there?" I turned to Aaron. "Could you …?"

He shook his head. "I can protect myself from burns, but I'm not immune to smoke inhalation."

Ezra stretched onto his tiptoes to peer over the spectators. "There are ambulances on the other side. Let's circle around and see if Robin and Amalia are getting treated."

Aaron and I followed as he backtracked up the street and cut into the alley. Several barricades prevented civilians from approaching the burning building's rear, but no firemen or police guarded them, so we jumped over and continued on. The worst of the flames were consuming the opposite side of the structure, and as we walked closer, I could hear the fire alarm blaring through a wide-open emergency exit.

Our steps slowed, and I glanced around anxiously for any sign of Robin, Amalia, or Zylas. Had they escaped out the back? Was Zylas the one who'd exploded the wall of their unit? What on earth had happened?

Drawing level with the rear door, I peered up the steps and into the hallway. Orange light flickered, but I couldn't see any flames as the black smoke twisted and coiled, thick and impassable.

I squinted. I could almost see something in the dark haze … something solid. Something *moving*.

With crunching steps, Ezra and Aaron joined me, and all three of us stared into the boiling blackness. The shape grew clearer—big, solid, steady. Whatever it was, the smoke didn't bother it. My pulse drummed in my throat.

A demon walked out of the smoke and fixed its crimson eyes on us.

I gaped in disbelief. A demon? But why? What was it doing in there? I'd seen this type before—it was the huge, stocky type with spines on its back, same as Burke's demon, but it couldn't be the same demon. That one had escaped this world when I'd killed Burke.

The air around Ezra chilled warningly.

"Well, well." A gravelly voice drifted down the alley. "Look what we have here."

A man with a full-on biker beard and an infernus hanging in plain sight on his chest walked toward us—and three others followed him, all big, burly, and clad in leather. I spotted a second infernus.

"We've been waiting for someone to show up," another male voice remarked, satisfaction oozing from every word.

My head snapped in the opposite direction. Four more men—two with those distinct silver pendants around their necks—strolled toward us from the alley's other end. We were trapped between them.

"Grand Grimoire," Aaron growled under his breath, naming the city's notorious Demonica guild.

"We were hoping to catch little Robin Page and her little demon," the first man sneered, "but this is even better. We get to take down the demon mage instead. Once in a lifetime opportunity, boys."

The mythics laughed.

Aaron shifted closer to me. "Don't try to fight the demons," he whispered. "The contractors are our targets."

"I've got to ask, though," the beefy contractor added. "How did you become a demon mage, Rowe? I didn't think there were any summoners left who could do it."

Ezra's arm brushed mine. "The champions will protect the contractors. We'll handle them. You—"

"Well, kid?" the mythic demanded. "Have anything to say?"

"Got it," I whispered, my hand drifting toward the holster on my hip.

The contractor's sneer returned. "Well, in that case—"

Aaron plunged his hand under the back of his jacket. Sharpie's hilt appeared as he yanked the sword free, the razor-edged point tearing through his jacket collar.

Crimson light flared over the three contractor's pendants, and the fourth contractor's demon lunged for us.

Aaron and Ezra charged up the alley, and I ran after them, paintball gun clutched in both hands. With the demon on our heels, we raced for the waiting mythics.

The two champions sprinted to intercept us, one of them brandishing a machete with water coalescing around the blade. Without breaking stride, Aaron flicked his sword.

The champion, still ten feet away, burst into flame.

Screaming, the man dropped his weapon and threw himself onto the ground, trying to smother the flames.

If the situation hadn't been so desperate, I would've stopped to gape at Aaron. I'd seen him throw fireballs, create moving inferno walls, and engulf *himself* in flames, but I'd never seen him light another human being on fire like that. I shouldn't have been surprised. He was highly skilled at discorporate ignition. He could light anything on fire.

He'd merely *chosen* not to turn people into flesh torches—until now.

As the burning man collapsed, Ezra blasted the other champion off his feet with wind. I aimed my gun past the aeromage's shoulder and fired a shot at the nearest contractor. The yellow ball flashed across thirty feet and splattered all over the man's chest.

He grinned. "We know your M.O., witch!"

Cold rushed through me. The Odin's Eye mythic I'd shot had been immune to my sleeping potion too. They knew to dose themselves with an antidote before battle.

Baring my teeth, I unloaded the clip, firing all the shots into his face. He roared in agony, reeling back and clutching his eyes.

Ezra yanked me off my feet—just as an inhumanly long, muscular arm swung at me from behind, so close I felt the wind of its passing.

One demon—belonging to the contractor I'd blinded—wasn't moving, but the other three had caught up to us. Aaron slashed with his sword, tearing the nearest demon's stomach open, but it didn't even flinch. Its fist smashed into his chest, knocking him clear off his feet.

Ezra clapped his hands together, then swept his arms out. A hurricane-force gale erupted from him, shoving the heavy demons back several steps. Grabbing my hand, he bolted away. Aaron was back on his feet, and sword in hand, he followed on our heels—but the thundering steps of the demons were right behind us, and the contractors whooped gleefully as we fled.

My legs pumped, thighs burning. If we faltered, we'd be dead. Three demons were too many, and Aaron's fire wouldn't stop them.

"This way!" I yelled, wheeling left into a narrow gap between buildings.

Aaron and Ezra careened after me, the latter ducking a demon's snatching hand. I seized a smoke bomb and chucked it over my shoulder. It shattered behind us.

"The fire escape!" Aaron called.

A rusting fire escape clung to a brick wall twenty yards away, the ladder retracted with only a few rungs hanging below the second-floor platform. We sprinted toward it, and Ezra grabbed my waist. As he threw me upward, orange fire burst off Aaron's sword.

I caught the bottom rung of the ladder and heaved myself up with an extra push from Ezra. Aaron sent an inferno blasting into the haze of my smoke bomb—and a demon charged out of it, skin blackened from the fire. The damage wasn't slowing it down, nor was the fact that its contractor was out of view.

"Aaron!" Ezra shouted.

The pyromage turned and ran at Ezra, who cupped his hand to form a foothold. He launched Aaron upward, and I scrambled higher on the ladder as Aaron caught it with one hand, his sword in the other. He pulled himself up.

Ezra leaped, grabbing the bottom rung. He started to draw himself up—

The demon grabbed his ankle. It yanked, and Ezra clamped his arms around the ladder rung, holding on for dear life.

Aaron thrust his hand out. The demon's head burst into flame—but it didn't release Ezra. It didn't react at all and kept dragging down on Ezra's foot. The fire escape creaked, metal groaning.

Laughter rang out. Shadowy shapes appeared in the fog— the rest of the Grand Grimoire team.

With no better idea, I plucked my brass knuckles out of their pouch, shoved them on my hand, and jumped off the ladder, plunging past Aaron and Ezra.

"*Ori amplifico!*" I screamed as I dropped.

My fist slammed down on the demon's broad shoulder, the momentum of my fall powering the strike. The amplified force smashed the demon into the ground.

I landed on top of the beast and launched up again so fast my head spun.

"Get her!" someone shouted.

"Tori!" Ezra yelled.

He'd pulled himself up the ladder, and with one elbow hooked over a rung, he leaned down, arm outstretched.

I leaped, reaching for his hand. He caught my wrist, and pain burned through my shoulder as he hauled me off my feet. With impossible strength, he swung me up, and Aaron caught me around the waist, pulling me against the ladder beside him.

A flash of gold light whipped past our heads and hit the wall in a burst of sparkles. The Grand Grimoire champions were attacking us.

We scrambled up the ladder and jumped onto the second-level platform. As another blast of magic ricocheted off the metal railing, Aaron smashed a window with the pommel of his sword. Knocking the glass out, he dove through.

I swung over the sill into a dingy bedroom, and Ezra vaulted inside after me. Together, we charged into an equally derelict living room that reeked of cigarette smoke. No one seemed to be home.

As Aaron unbolted the front door, metal clanged from the direction of the bedroom. The Grand Grimoire mythics were on the fire escape.

Aaron pushed me out of the apartment. We sprinted down the hall and through a metal door into a stairwell. Back down to ground level, along another hall, across an empty foyer, and out the main entrance.

We burst out onto the same street as Robin's apartment, two buildings down. Lights from the firetrucks flashed, and nearby, two ambulances sat with their back doors open, the paramedics talking to a handful of forlorn-looking evacuees.

I looked around wildly for the best direction to run. With any other guild, I would've run into the nearest group of humans, but I didn't trust the Grand Grimoire to hold back.

The three of us hesitated, unsure what to do.

"Tori!"

Waving frantically, a woman ran toward us from the far side of an ambulance, her face shining with perspiration and pale blond hair tied back in a short, messy ponytail.

"*Sabrina?*" I shrieked.

She flew into me, crushing my chest with a hug. "I'm so glad I found you! I wasn't sure where—the fire was the only clear sign—if I'd missed you—"

I pried her off and held her shoulders so I could gawk at her face. "What are you *doing* here?"

"This way, quickly!" She tugged on my arm to get me moving.

"What—" Aaron began.

"There's no time!" She hauled me into motion. "Come on!"

Aaron and Ezra ran after us as she led me farther up the street. Skidding to a stop, she plucked a key chain with a single key out of her pocket and held it out.

When I just stared, she shook it urgently. "Take it! Escape!"

"Esc—" Breaking off, I realized we'd stopped beside an old white car with rust around the bottom of the doors. "But—"

She stuffed the key into my hand. "They're coming. Look!"

I looked over my shoulder. A group of burly men was silhouetted against the flashing lights, clustered in the middle of the street. One of them pointed in our direction, and the whole group broke into a run.

Heading straight for us.

"Get in the car!" Aaron barked, plucking the keys from my hand. He raced around the front bumper and yanked open the driver's door.

Ezra opened a back door and dove in. "Tori!"

Tears spilled down Sabrina's cheeks. She pushed me toward Ezra's open door. "Go, Tori. Please—please be safe!"

The engine rumbled to life. Ezra grabbed my arm, pulling me backward.

"Sabrina," I babbled frantically, "what about y—"

"I'll be fine. Go!" Turning, she dashed into a nearby alley.

As she vanished in the darkness, Ezra hauled me into the car. I sprawled across his lap, and with the door still hanging open, Aaron hit the gas. The tires squealed and the car shot forward.

Ezra caught the flapping door and slammed it shut. With my legs across his lap, I pushed myself up, peering out the back window.

The Grand Grimoire team stood in the center of the road, watching us escape. There was no sign of Sabrina.

13

I SLUMPED in an uncomfortable swivel chair, staring listlessly as Aaron paced the length of the office, over and over. Ezra stood at the window, peering through a gap in the cheap plastic blinds.

We'd gone to ground in a rundown industrial neighborhood in the Eastside. Our car was parked in a back lot, and we'd broken into a small, shabby office building belonging to an HVAC company—a struggling one, by the look of things.

"Did Robin and Amalia go home after the Odin's Eye ambush last night?" Aaron muttered as he swept past. "I know their address isn't registered, but still not smart."

"Robin isn't a combat mythic." Ezra tugged on the blinds, closing the gap he'd been looking through. "But Zylas is a hunter. He knows the danger. If they went back, it's because they had to."

"Who attacked their apartment? Was it that Grand Grimoire team?" I thought of how swiftly Zylas had plowed through combat mythics in the museum basement. Would those Grand Grimoire mythics have even slowed him down? "Was Zylas the one who blew out the wall?"

"He'd only use magic as a last resort." Ezra folded his arms. "Same reason I can't use Eterran's magic to defend us."

Claiming the charges against Ezra were bogus would be difficult to pull off already; if anyone saw him using demon magic, we'd have no chance of convincing MagiPol not to execute him. And Robin had the same problem. She couldn't afford any witnesses blabbing about her illegal contract with Zylas.

"Does it matter who attacked them?" Aaron growled, pacing back across the room. "We can't contact her and we can't search for her—not while every guild in the city is hunting us."

My hands clenched. "We *have* to search for them. Without them, we can't do the ritual."

Aaron came to a halt and pressed both hands to his face. He pushed his fingers up into his hair, and when he finally turned to me, his expression was as bleak as I'd ever seen it.

"We'll be caught before we have any chance of finding her ... and we don't even know if she's alive."

Silence fell as we let that terrifying possibility sink in.

"Can we hire an Arcana mythic to set up the ritual for us instead?" Ezra asked.

"If Kai were with us, maybe." Aaron paced another circle. "We could look for a rogue Arcaner, but—shit, guys. I've never hired a rogue before. We're just as likely to walk into a sting as find a rogue guild."

I pressed my hands tightly together. I could think of one mythic who knew his way around the rogue underground, but I had no way to contact him—and no desire to put Ezra's life in his hands a second time.

"All mythic attention in the city is on us," Aaron continued, "and even rogues will have heard about a demon mage bounty. Approaching anyone would be a huge risk."

"Then what?" I asked. "How do we set up the ritual?"

"I think …" He blew out a breath. "I think we need to get out of the city."

I was shaking my head before he even finished. "We can't do that."

"We run for it," he repeated. "We fall back on the plan we made with Darius six years ago in case Ezra was ever discovered. Everything's already arranged. We flee north to Alaska, and once we're far enough away, we can find a mythic who'll do the ritual."

I stood up, shoving the office chair. It rolled into the wall with a thump. "But what about Kai? He's in MPD custody right now! Are we just going to abandon him? What about the Crow and Hammer? The guild could be disbanded. One week to prepare the ritual is already pushing it. If we disappear for two or three weeks, we'll never be able to convince the MPD that Ezra is innocent!"

"I know, Tori." Aaron's gaze was quietly distressed. "I just don't see any other option."

Turning away from him, I shoved the chair into the wall again. Despair warred with a dozen other emotions—frantic fear, seething fury, suffocating guilt. Everything hinged on the ritual, and without Robin or Amalia, we were screwed. Why had they disappeared? Why weren't they helping us? We'd made a deal! I'd given them the damn amulet!

I shoved the chair a third time. The impact jarring up my arms didn't distract me from the churning fear and anger. The bang of it hitting the wall didn't drown out the voice in my head telling me we were doomed.

It wasn't fair! We'd been so close! We'd been *minutes* away from separating Ezra and Eterran. Now every possible worst-case scenario was playing out before our eyes and there was nothing I could do to fix it. *Nothing!*

As a shout of despairing fury wrenched from my throat, I grabbed the chair and swung it into a filing cabinet with all my strength. It struck with a ringing clang, but it didn't help, and I reached for the chair again.

Ezra stepped in front of me, blocking my reach, and wrapped me in his arms.

For a second, I considered shoving him away. I didn't want comfort. I wanted to rage and scream and curse at the whole damn world.

His arms tightened, sturdy and unyielding. "Breathe, Tori."

I realized my chest was heaving with fast, furious inhalations. Jaw tight, I buried my face in his shoulder and focused on slowing my lungs. Gradually, the agonizing tension in my muscles released and the raging storm of emotions quieted.

Ezra rested his cheek on my head. "Kai is in MPD lockup, not a dungeon. He may not be comfortable, but he's safe. And Darius knows how to handle the MPD. He'll protect the Crow and Hammer."

Eyes squeezed shut, I didn't answer. Kai wasn't being tortured, but I had no reason to trust the MPD. And neither did

Darius, who could only play loophole chess with them for so long before he ran out of moves.

Nothing was guaranteed. No one was safe.

Including us.

I gripped fistfuls of Ezra's shirt. The worst thing for Kai, for Darius, for the Crow and Hammer, and for us would be getting caught. Ezra would be killed. Kai, Aaron, and I would be convicted of capital crimes for protecting him. The Crow and Hammer would be disbanded.

The best way to help everyone was to get out of the city before we lost our chance.

"All right," I whispered. "When do we leave?"

"We'll wait for morning," Aaron answered, and I started, surprised to find him leaning against the desk right behind me. "The Grand Grimoire guys saw our car. All the bounty hunters will be watching for a white sedan, so we'll try to blend in with the morning commuters."

I nodded, my cheek pressed to Ezra's chest. Untangling my fist from his shirt, I grasped Aaron's warm hand and entwined our fingers, connecting the three of us together.

As long as we were together, I could hold back the dark despair.

CURLED AGAINST Ezra's side, the floor cold and hard under my butt, I wearily listened to the low rumble of his voice as he and Aaron debated the best route out of the city. The three of us were tucked in a corner of the office, leaning against the wall and waiting for the first tinge of dawn to touch the horizon.

I let their voices wash over me, my eyes closed. I was exhausted, but also wired with anxiety. My thoughts spun and spun, and it was so hard to quiet my mind enough to catch a little sleep. The unpleasantly hard floor didn't help, but there was nowhere remotely comfortable in this barren office to sleep.

"… wasn't expecting Sabrina to show up." Aaron's voice filtered through my jittery drowsiness. "I never suspected she might not be a diviner."

I cracked my eyes open, frowning. "What are you talking about? Why wouldn't she be a diviner? She predicted where we'd be with her tarot cards."

"Have you ever seen a tarot reading include something as specific as a location?" Aaron asked dryly. "Tarot cards are all about your present state, big decisions, directions your life is taking, that sort of thing."

My frown deepened. "Her readings haven't been super specific, but everything she's predicted for my future has come true."

"Everything?"

"Yeah."

He rubbed his stubbly jaw. "I'd say that's further confirmation that something's fishy, then. Diviners are usually vague about the direction your future is headed because tarot cards aren't reliable that way."

Ezra nodded. "I was surprised when she predicted you'd save my life back in November."

I massaged my temples. "How can you believe in her predictions but not believe she's a diviner?"

"I never said I didn't think she could predict the future. Whatever she can do, knowing where to show up to help us is next-level predictive power. I get why she would hide it."

My gaze flicked up to Ezra. How many other guild members hid their secrets within the ragtag group of misfits known as the Crow and Hammer?

"You know what'd be nice?" I muttered. "A future prediction about us winning the lottery and spending a month in Hawaii."

"Aaron doesn't need to win the lottery," Ezra pointed out.

Aaron leaned his head back against the wall. "If you're craving a tropical vacation, I can just tell my parents I'm interested in checking out the IEA's Polynesian branch. They'll fly us there for as long as we want."

I was too tired to remember what IEA stood for. Some huge Elementaria guild. "Yeah, just don't mention that Ezra is a demon mage."

Aaron grunted.

"What do your parents think of your promotion?" I asked after a moment. "Did you tell them?"

"Nope." His smile was surprisingly relaxed. "I don't need to hear what they think. I'm happy about it."

I grinned, finding happiness in that even with everything else going on.

Now we just needed to fix this whole mess so he could go back to enjoying his promotion instead of fleeing for his life as a wanted rogue.

I climbed off the floor and stretched again, my muscles painfully stiff from a night sitting on the floor. More out of habit than hope, I called Robin's number—straight to voicemail—then pocketed the phone and picked up my combat belt, which I'd left on the desk. My fingers brushed the empty pouch at the back. Still no Hoshi.

We gathered up our things. I shouldered the precious backpack with the ritual, demon blood, and cult grimoire, and Aaron strapped Sharpie against his back under his jacket. Ezra donned his steel-reinforced gloves, then pulled his leather coat on over them.

This was as ready as we'd get.

My stomach grumbled miserably as we slipped out of the dark office. We'd eaten—sort of. The HVAC company's staff room had included a vending machine of drinks and snacks. We'd smashed the glass and dined on chips, chocolate bars, and bags of trail mix, washed down with bottles of water. Not exactly nutritious, but better than nothing.

Once we were out of the city, Aaron could access one of his secret bank accounts. With cash in hand, we could buy real food, but that wouldn't be happening for hours yet.

We approached the back door, and Aaron cracked it open to peer outside. A line of large work vans with company logos on their sides filled the lot, and our old white sedan was tucked between two of them. I wondered where Sabrina had gotten it. As far as I knew, she didn't own a car.

Dawn was a mere suggestion of light in the eastern sky, and the still air was fresh and crisp. Seeing nothing moving in the lot, Aaron opened the door all the way.

Ezra clamped his hand on Aaron's shoulder, halting him. The aeromage stood unmoving for a moment, then slammed the door shut.

"There are people out there."

14

MY HEART SKIPPED A BEAT. "There are people out there? As in, like, people who work in this area?"

"They're grouped in an alley." He turned to Aaron. "How long will it take to get in the car and drive out of the parking lot?"

Aaron considered it. "Too long. I don't want to be trapped in a vehicle when they attack."

"They're probably watching all the exits. We need to make a new one."

Aaron nodded. "The buildings to the west are a maze. We can run that way and lose them in the alleys."

In agreement, the two mages marched back down the hall, and I rushed after them. We'd been cornered again. Which guild was preparing to ambush us this time? The same Odin's Eye mythics? More Grand Grimoire contractors?

The guys chose a west-facing window. Ezra drew himself up, then waved a hand. His blast of wind blew out the glass, and as it smashed on the ground outside, we leaped over the sill.

Distant calls rang out as our feet hit the pavement—and then we were running. Aaron shot ahead, leading us into the nearest alley. This industrial area was full of interconnecting alleys and back roads for accessing all the rear businesses and commercial lots. If we could lose our pursuers anywhere, it was here.

I ran hard, Ezra right behind me. My gasping breaths were too loud for me to hear if anyone was coming up behind us, but I didn't dare hope we'd left them behind already. Warehouses flashed by on either side. Thirty yards ahead, the alley split in a T-intersection.

As we sprinted toward that first turn, the air grew sickeningly damp—then a wave of water crashed over my ankles, sweeping my feet out from under me.

I slammed down on my ass and skidded on the wet pavement. Defying all laws of fluid dynamics, the water reversed direction and flowed over my legs, encasing them.

With a crackle, the water froze into solid ice.

The guys were down too, but fire blazed off Aaron, melting the ice on his legs, and Ezra wrenched free with his inhuman strength. They leaped up. I didn't have their extra special abilities, and my legs stayed frozen to the ground. Yanking out my paintball gun, I smashed its metal butt against the ice.

The ground trembled, then shattered into zigzagging fissures. As Aaron and Ezra staggered for balance, the crumbling pavement broke the ice holding me down. I scrambled onto my knees as the earth rocked.

Wind erupted, howling down the alley and blasting into the off-balance mages. Aaron dropped to one knee, but Ezra caught himself and whipped his arm out, his buffeting wind countering the assaulting gale.

Orange light blazed—but not from Aaron. Forty feet away, a man glowed with flames. A pyromage. And arranged around him, illuminated by his fire, were five others.

Universally tall, well-built, fit as professional athletes, and decked out in identical gear. I would've laughed at their dorky matching uniforms, except the black garments, each emblazoned with a logo over the heart, didn't make them look silly. Their unifying attire made them all the more terrifying.

They could only be the Pandora Knights, the city's most accomplished bounty hunting guild, populated entirely by mages. Highly skilled, notoriously aggressive, powerful mages.

My frightened stare swept across them. Hydromage, kryomage, terramage, aeromage, pyromage.

The unknown mage on the far left pointed a thin-bladed rapier. Electricity crackled down the steel, then leaped toward us. Aaron thrust Sharpie out, catching the bolt. It sizzled over the blade, then leaped down into the pavement, unable to bypass the insulated hilt.

The Pandora Knights team didn't waste any time on conversation, banter, or threats. Three darted forward and two fell back, one mage in the middle, their movements fluid and practiced. An attack formation.

Aaron held his sword out, placed his hand against the blade, and slid his palm down the steel in a sharp movement.

Fire exploded over the six mages.

The attack would've incapacitated any other team, but not this one. Ice burst from the kryomage, water flooded the hydromage, wind swept over the aeromage. The pyromage extended his hands toward the electramage and terramage, extinguishing the flames on them in a heartbeat—while completely ignoring the fire crawling harmlessly over his own limbs.

"Run," Aaron rasped. "I'll distract them."

I shot to my feet, clutching my useless paintball gun. "But—"

"I'll be right behind you!" He raised his sword, concentration tightening his face. "I need you two out of the way!"

Right. We were flammable. Whirling, I shoved my gun in its holster and grabbed Ezra's arm.

"Aaron—" he began sharply.

"This one is my fight," Aaron shot over his shoulder. "You know what yours is, Ezra!"

Confusion sparked amidst my urgency. Ezra hesitated, his face twisting, then pivoted on his heel and sprinted away. I ran beside him, clutching his hand. Firelight flared behind us. A rush of pounding footsteps, a crackle of electricity—then roaring flames exploded outward, filling the alley.

We reached an intersection and I spun around, staring back at the fire. Waiting for Aaron's silhouette to appear. Waiting for him to dash out of the blaze and run to join us.

Ezra's hand crushed mine.

The fire was withering—and electricity flashed. The earth quaked, pavement cracking with a sound like a gunshot. Wind whooshed across the alley, bending the flames, revealing the silhouettes within the dying inferno.

Six men surrounding a seventh.

"*Aaron!*" I screamed.

Fire surged, hiding the battle. I lunged, ready to race back—and Ezra caught me around the middle. He pulled me against his chest, his harsh, rasping breath filling my ears.

Frost covered the ground around us. My frightened gasp sent a puff of white into the wintry air.

I twisted to look at him—and saw his glowing left eye, his features contorted with agonized rage. His arms were so tight around me I could scarcely breathe.

"Ezra—" I gasped.

"I'm all right. I'm—" He broke off, jaw clenched, teeth bared. "He's buying us time. We can't waste it."

Buying us time? But no, he was coming too. He'd be right behind us. He—

He'd said that so I wouldn't argue.

Another burst of fire leaped skyward, and in the dancing flames, I glimpsed the eerie shape of the Hanged Man.

Ezra dropped me back onto my feet, grasped my hand, and ran into a connecting alley. The mage battle disappeared behind us, and every step I ran drove a splinter of steel deeper into my heart.

They wouldn't kill Aaron. He was the famous Sinclair heir. No Pandora Knights mage would blacklist themselves by killing him.

They wouldn't kill him. He'd be okay. He'd be okay. *He'd be okay.*

Ezra pulled me down alley after alley. My lungs screamed and my legs burned. As I started to stumble, my stamina spent, he slowed his steps. Just ahead, the alley opened into a parking lot. For a second, I thought it was the same one where we'd parked our white sedan, but this one was empty except for two flatbed trailers at the far end.

Ezra scanned the lot, then pulled me into a jog, aiming for the street on the opposite side. Ten paces away from the shelter of the alley, he drew up short, pulling me to a stop beside him.

Four men strode into view, blocking the parking lot's exit.

Black uniforms, guild logos on their chests, weapons in hand. More Pandora Knights mages.

Fifty feet away, they spread into a defensive formation, waiting for us to attack—and that was our only option. We couldn't run back the way we'd come or we'd risk fleeing right into the larger group of mages who'd no doubt defeated Aaron and were chasing us down.

For the first time, I considered giving up. I imagined putting my hands in the air and letting them come. Running, fighting, escaping—it was so hard. The fear and panic and pain. I couldn't take it.

But if I gave up, Ezra would die. Which meant I had to keep fighting.

Arctic cold rolled off him, and the ground turned white with frost. He was going to fight. He was going to unleash his demonic magic to save us—but he'd also be condemning us. We couldn't run but couldn't fight. What the hell were we *supposed to do?*

As despair gripped me, I started shivering—but not because of the cold emanating from Ezra. Something else hung in the air …

A shivering essence of threat.

Dawn had reversed itself. The sky was black as midnight. Shadows crawled along the ground. The Pandora Knights faded to indistinct silhouettes.

In the eerie silence, a sound reached my ears, so out of place it took me a moment to identify it: the slow clop of hooves on pavement.

The measured beat of a walking horse grew louder. Drawing closer.

From out of the swirling darkness, a ghostly equine shimmered slowly into view. Its steel-colored coat darkened to black on its legs, with an inky mane and flowing tail. Muscles rippled over its body, its powerful neck arched. Acid-green eyes glowed, pupilless and otherworldly, and its nostrils flared as it tossed its head.

A rider sat astride its back, clad all in black, his long coat flared across the horse's haunches, a deep hood drawn up. No saddle, no halter, no reins. He guided the powerful creature with a gloved hand on its neck.

Death had come, mounted on his nightmare steed.

The stallion stopped midway between the mages and where Ezra and I stood in silent shock. It lifted a foreleg and slammed it down with a loud clang. Again, the horse struck the pavement, tail swishing and snapping, ears flat against its head. A throaty, aggressive snort rushed from its nose, puffing white in the chill air.

The rider's shadowed hood turned toward the group of mages.

Black flames rippled and danced around the horse's legs, and shapes appeared, stepping out of the darkness. Shaggy obsidian fur. Ridged muzzles and bared teeth. Burning scarlet eyes. Two ebony wolves prowled around the stallion, their snarls rumbling through the silence.

The black rider waited.

Twenty-five feet away from the unearthly specters, the Pandora Knights mythics didn't move. Not even the best-trained mages from the top bounty guild in the city were brave enough to challenge this enemy. Not when the shadows coiled so menacingly. Not when the wolves snarled so hungrily. Not when the ethereal stallion smashed that powerful hoof into the ground again, shattering the asphalt.

With another toss of its head, the horse turned and broke into a quick trot—heading straight for us. I recoiled into Ezra as the towering beast drew level with us, its shoulder higher than the top of my head. The rider twisted toward me, and I looked up into a familiar face.

He extended his gloved hand.

Once before, he'd offered me his hand just like this. Under a gazebo in a night-swathed park, he'd told me to walk away … or to come with him and never return.

I hesitated only for a moment, then grabbed his hand.

Zak hauled me up, and I scrambled onto the horse behind him. Ezra swung onto its back behind me, settling into place more smoothly than I'd expected.

As I clutched Zak's jacket, the beast leaped forward, hooves hammering against the pavement. With the vargs racing beside us, we thundered across the parking lot—then the horse's pounding hooves deadened into silence as white mist engulfed us and we slipped out of human reality.

15

THE STALLION'S HOOVES beat the ground in a quick trot, the sound alternating between the dull thump of wood and the sharp crack of gravel. The horse was following a triple set of train tracks, heading east toward the sunrise. The gray water of the harbor rippled on our left, and on our right was a dirt bank with businesses and commercial buildings on its other side.

We'd left our pursuers behind—but we'd also left Aaron. There was no guild in the city less likely to seriously wound him, not when every member of the Pandora Knights knew who Aaron Sinclair was. An Elementaria guild would never risk the wrath of one the richest and most powerful mage families in North America.

But abandoning him had still torn my heart from my chest.

A guild catching Ezra was the worst-case scenario, I reminded myself, fighting my despair. Ezra using his demonic magic in front of witnesses was the second-worst scenario. Both would doom us.

The line of buildings on our right ended, replaced by a hundred yards of trees. The horse continued onward for half that distance, then swerved toward the twelve-foot bank.

I grabbed Zak around the waist as his fae steed surged up the steep incline like it was a gentle knoll. The horse cut into a thick stand of spruce trees, their heavy boughs blocking out the weak morning light, before coming to a halt.

Zak swung his leg over the stallion's neck and dropped to the ground. Turning, he reached up for me, and I let him pull me down. Ezra slid off the beast last.

Pushing his hood back, Zak swept his piercing green eyes across me.

Human eyes, I noted. His irises weren't iridescent with Lallakai's power.

Zak opened his mouth—and the stallion swung its head toward me, ears pinned. The druid grabbed a double handful of its mane and hauled back an instant before those big blocky teeth could bite down on my shoulder.

"Enough, Tilliag," he snapped, putting his shoulder into the horse's chest and pushing it back a step. "Get over it."

Tossing its head, it snorted angrily.

"Uh," I muttered. "Get over what?"

"Nothing. His grudges are his problem."

My confusion deepened as I looked from the druid to the fae stallion. Why would the creature have a grudge against me? What had I ever done to upset a horse?

Wait ... that steel-gray coat with a bluish tinge was familiar. Back during the battle to save Llyrlethiad the sea fae, the enemy witch had tried to escape on a fae horse—and, channeling Llyr's power, I'd blasted the horse's legs out from under it in mid-gallop.

"Is that the same fae horse that the Red Rum witch was riding?" I asked, narrowed eyes returning to Zak.

"Tilliag was injured, and I helped him."

"You disappeared for, like, two days after that fight. You said you were busy."

"Treating Tilliag's injuries was one of the things I was busy with." He rubbed the stallion's forehead. It swished its tail, then lowered its head and nosed at the sparse winter grass.

"If you want to go, the street is that way." He canted his head to the south. "Or we could … talk."

Biting the inside of my cheek, I glanced at Ezra. It'd been a month since Zak had betrayed me, Ezra, and our entire guild so he could kill Varvara and recover his grimoire. Ezra had nearly died that night, and the memory was painfully fresh.

Ezra considered me, memories haunting his eyes too, then nodded.

Turning back to the druid, I assessed him, not sure what to make of his appearance. His hair was shaggy again, overdue for a trim, and a short beard darkened his jaw. Faint circles smudged the undersides of his eyes.

I had a hundred questions, but the most important first: "How did you find us?"

"Everyone in the city is talking about the demon mage from the Crow and Hammer." He brushed his hair off his forehead. "The Pandora Knights are the best bounty hunters in the city. I tailed them until they found you."

"Why?"

"To help you."

I pressed my lips together. "Where's Lallakai?"

"She's not here."

"I can see that much. Where, specifically, is 'not here'?"

"I don't know." He ran a gloved hand over Tilliag's shoulder. "We … had a falling out."

My eyes widened.

He glanced at my expression, tightened his jaw, then faced the horse. "I wanted to … deal with some things. She wanted me to disappear into the wilderness where bounty hunters could never find me." He tugged his fingers through the stallion's tangled mane. "When I wouldn't do what she wanted, she … left."

"So you replaced her with Tilliag?"

The stallion's head came up, ears pinned angrily, a poisonous green eye fixed on me.

Er … "no," I was guessing.

"Tilliag owes me." Zak leaned against the stallion's side and looked between me and Ezra. "What happened?"

I drew in a deep breath. With Ezra flanking me in supportive silence, I pushed my shoulders back. "Zak, I appreciate that you got us away from the Pandora Knights, but you've made it abundantly clear that you don't do charity. Helping us—there's nothing in it for you."

He gazed at me for a long moment, and I couldn't decipher the intensity in his sharp eyes.

"You asked me if it was worth it." He exhaled roughly. "It wasn't, and I'm sorry for taking advantage of your trust, for lying to you, and for putting the lives of people you care about in danger."

It was the first time I'd ever heard Zak apologize—and it wasn't nearly enough. "You betrayed me. Being nice now doesn't change that."

"I know."

"Do you? This isn't a fae exchange. You can't just throw helpfulness dollars at me until I sell you my forgiveness."

"I know."

"Even if you save us, I'll probably go right on hating your guts."

His mouth thinned unhappily. "I can get you both out of the city—out of the country, if you need it. I know how to keep you under the radar, and I can help you start again with a new identity."

Zak was a rogue who'd lived on the wrong side of the law his whole life. He knew how to evade the MPD, how to slip through the clutches of bounty hunters, and how to escape our seemingly inevitable fates. If anyone could get us out of this, it was the Ghost.

But that wasn't the future I wanted.

I pinned him with a stare. "If you're going to help us, Zak, then you better commit. No half measures, no bailing when it gets tough, no saving your own skin first."

He frowned. "I'm here to help you, not sacrifice myself— but yes, I'll do whatever I can."

"Not good enough."

I started in surprise. Ezra had been so quiet that I hadn't expected him to speak at all.

His mismatched eyes were cold as ice. "You don't need to sacrifice yourself, but how much are you willing to risk? Time, money, inconvenience, injury? What about *everything*? Will you risk that? Because that's what Tori risked for you."

Zak's expression darkened. "I've already risked—and lost— plenty."

"For your own ambitions." Ezra folded his arms. "We've seen what your 'help' looks like. It stops the moment you decide the potential gains aren't worth it anymore."

"What do you think I plan to gain from this?"

"From what I can see, nothing—which is why I'm wondering if that's what your help will be worth. When the next guild comes down on us, will you bail? Will you throw me to the hunters to save yourself?"

"If the situation were different, I'd put you down myself."

"Oh my god, Zak!" I snapped. "If that's how you feel, then—"

"He's unstable. You may not trust me, but I'm not one wrong word from flying off the handle and killing you or your allies."

My hands clenched into fists. "Ezra wouldn't—"

"He killed three of my vargs." Zak's jaw flexed. "They'd been with me for ten years."

A moment of silence.

"I'm sorry," Ezra said quietly. "You created the circumstances that caused it, but I'm sorry it happened and that I was part of their deaths."

Zak made a dismissive gesture, brushing the topic away. "I won't die on anyone's altar, especially not yours. But"—he turned to me—"I'm offering my help, whatever you think it's worth. If that's not good enough, then we're done here."

Tension vibrated between the three of us.

"I don't want your help running away," I told the druid. "What I need won't be as easy as smuggling us out of the country, but if you're still willing, then I have one question for you."

"What's that?"

I smiled—a grim, humorless smile. "Have you ever summoned a demon before?"

ZAK, as it turned out, had not summoned a demon before. But he was about to learn how.

I greedily stuffed a burger in my mouth as I watched the druid. He stood at a plastic folding table pushed against a water-streaked concrete wall, its surface spread with everything from Robin's backpack—the case of demon blood, the cult grimoire, and her notes and diagrams. He pored over them, shoulders stiff with concentration.

Me, I just kept eating my burger, too exhausted to worry about anything for a few minutes.

For Ezra, Aaron, Kai, and me, finding a safe, private location for conducting illegal activities had seemed like an insurmountable challenge. For Zak, it was just a day in the life of a career criminal. In a matter of hours, he'd found a location, moved us into it, and stocked it with everything we needed, including food, water, and cots to sleep on.

The faintest spark of hope burned in my chest. We had a location for the ritual. One obstacle down.

But we still needed an Arcana mythic to prepare and perform it, and I didn't know yet if Zak could do it. And we didn't know if the ritual would even work. And if it did, we didn't know if Ezra would survive it. And if he did, we didn't know if we could convince the MPD to let him live.

And even if we somehow, impossibly, accomplished all that, we still had to survive—and destroy—an insidious cult that had its invisible tentacles snaking all throughout Vancouver.

Crumpling his burger wrapper into a ball, Ezra stuffed it into the paper bag. "I'm going to scout around a bit."

I nodded. "I'll keep an eye on Zak." As he began to stand, I caught his wrist and tugged him back toward me. "Wait. Actually ... maybe you shouldn't."

The painfully fresh memory of Aaron being overwhelmed by Pandora Knights bounty hunters made my dinner churn in my stomach. Ezra had demonic magic, but he couldn't use it. He didn't even have a switch.

He smiled faintly. "I'll be fine."

Probably, but considering the way things had gone so far ...

Still holding his hand, I rose to my feet and crossed the concrete floor, our footsteps echoing through the large room. A warehouse, really. Zak had rented the storage facility for us— or rather, he'd used a fake identity to pay a man to rent the facility under another fake name.

"Zak," I said as we joined him at the table. "Do you have a weapon Ezra can borrow? He's got nothing."

The druid looked up, his gaze skimming across Ezra. "I only have knives."

"That's fine," Ezra replied. "A larger blade would be closer to my usual switch, if you can spare it."

Zak flipped open a buckle that ran around his upper thigh. It came free and he held the leather belt out, a sheathed blade hanging from it.

Taking the weapon, Ezra pulled the handle. A twelve-inch blade, wickedly serrated, slid from the sheath. I wasn't sure if the serrated edge had a purpose—did it double as a utility knife?—but it certainly added to the terror factor.

With raised eyebrows, Ezra sheathed it and buckled the belt around his thigh.

"Thanks," he murmured, then touched my elbow. "I'll be back soon."

I nodded. His fingers ran down my arm and across my hand as he turned away. He headed toward the door, but I kept my attention on Zak, whose eyes had followed the trail of Ezra's touch.

He returned my silent stare as the aeromage's footsteps grew distant and the door clacked shut.

Zak faced the table and resumed studying the myriad of papers. He'd shed his long coat, and his black t-shirt was clean but wrinkled. A tangle of artifacts hung around his neck, the colorful crystals resting on his chest.

My gaze ran down his sculpted left arm, free of Lallakai's feather markings, to the tattoos on his inner forearm. Four of the five circles contained fae runes, and I craned my neck to peek at his right arm, curious to see how many more he'd replaced since his battle with Varvara.

My breath caught. I snatched his right wrist and pulled his arm up. White scars, edged in pink, raked through his druid tattoos.

"Why didn't you get that healed properly?" I demanded.

He tugged his wrist free. "I was busy."

"What's more important than permanent damage to your arm?"

"The entire city knows who I am now. There's no healer, rogue or otherwise, who wouldn't see my tattoos, realize I'm the Ghost, and betray me in an instant."

I clenched my jaw. "What about a fae healer? They have healing magic, don't they? Could they fix your arm?"

"Probably, but I can't leave the city to find one." He set a diagram down. "Without Lallakai, I'm stuck here. Powerful fae rarely enter cities. They hate all the pollution and concrete and human filth. If I still had my farm ... but I don't, so I can't venture anywhere I might run into a fae I can't fight."

"But you can fight most fae, can't you?"

"I used up or lost almost all my fae magic. What I have left isn't very powerful." He slid his hand into his pocket and pulled out a square of purple. "Except this, but it isn't particularly useful."

The Carapace of Valdurna. It'd saved Ezra's life a month ago, almost killing him in the process. Couldn't say I was pleased to see it.

Zak's fingers curled around the fabric, his scars pulling taut. "Lallakai will return once she decides I've had enough time to stew about how helpless I am without her."

"Shit, Zak. That's ... not a healthy relationship, you know?"

He let out a surprised laugh. "Healthy? It's survival. I knew Lallakai was a darkfae from day one, and I took my chances with her anyway."

"She's actually a darkfae?"

"More or less. There are worse fae." He tucked the Carapace back in his pocket and slid another of Robin's drawings closer. "You've been busy over the last few weeks."

"Doing my best to save Ezra, yeah." I pointed at the papers. "So? Can you do it?"

"My area of expertise is alchemy, and the sorcery I've learned is nothing like this. Parts of it are written in ... in demonic, I think? And even if I can construct the array, I'm not sure it'll work. Summoners have their own demon contracts. Is that because the arrays require demon blood, or is there some other connection?" He rubbed his short beard. "In other words, your guess is as good as mine."

Well, my slightly decreased anxiety levels were through the roof again. Yay. "So what, then?"

"I'll try it, and if it fails … we'll figure out what to do next." He flipped the cult grimoire open to a page written entirely in Latin. "Do you have a plan for what to do with the demon, assuming the ritual works?"

I leaned a hip on the table. "Not really, but Eterran is reasonable for a demon."

Zak's eyebrows rose. "If he seems reasonable, it's because he's in a vulnerable position. Once that's no longer the case, you can't know what he'll be like."

"Robin said he'll be stuck in the circle, so we can figure that out when it's time."

"Mm," he agreed vaguely. "Before I forget …"

My forehead crinkled as he reached for his coat, lying on the corner of the table. He fished around inside its many inner pockets, then withdrew a silver orb the size of a small melon.

I gasped. "Hoshi!"

Before he could even offer the fae to me, I'd snatched her from his hand. I cradled her against my chest, stroking her warm, ridged shape. "Where did you find her? *When* did you find her? Is she okay? Is she hurt? Hoshi? Hoshi, can you hear me? Is she—"

"She's dormant," he said, cutting through my babble with a frown. "One of my vargs found her near that museum where you were first attacked. I'd planned a whole lecture for you on abandoning her, but it doesn't look like you need it."

I hugged her tightly. "She disappeared. I can't see into the fae world so I couldn't find her. When will she wake up?"

"I'm not sure. I think this is how sylphs heal from injuries. She needs time to recuperate her strength. Just keep her safe until then."

"That might be difficult when I can't even keep myself safe. Good thing you're going to make this ritual work, right?"

He grunted in a way that didn't suggest confidence.

Cradling orb-Hoshi in the crook of my arm, I patted his shoulder. "You can do it. You're the best alchemist on the west coast, remember?"

He snorted. "You didn't actually believe that, did you?"

I had, but then I'd met a few more west-coast alchemists—like Kelvin Compton, the transmutation genius, and his possibly even more brilliant apprentice, who'd mutated werewolves into furry super soldiers.

"I'm a powerful druid, a good alchemist, and a mediocre sorcerer," Zak added. "I have no idea what kind of demon summoner I'll be."

I looked down at the grimoire. "We're about to find out, aren't we?"

16

EIGHT HOURS of preparation.

That's how long Zak spent studying the cult tome, Robin's diagrams, and a small leather book I recognized as his personal grimoire. He drew out a quarter-scale version of the three-circle array, getting a lesson from Eterran on how the demonic runes were supposed to work in the process. Once he had the array down, Zak practiced the incantations, his low voice echoing through the small warehouse while Ezra and I went over every inch of the concrete floor, filling and sanding all cracks and imperfections.

Twenty hours to draw the full-sized array.

Zak painted every precise line, curve, and angle of the three-circle array. Ezra and I did what we could to help—adjusting the metal rulers and angle tools as he directed us, passing him the alchemic marker he was using to draw it, holding up his cheat sheet of incantations whenever he needed to read one—which was every ten minutes.

Seventy-two hours for the array to charge.

Before it could be used, the collection of arcane lines and runes had to passively absorb the earthly energies all around us. Zak caught up on the sleep he'd missed, then split his time between practicing the intensive incantations required for the actual summoning and checking that none of the guilds searching for Ezra were getting too close to our hideout.

Sitting on a cot with my back against the wall, I wrapped my arms around my legs. Beside me, cocooned in a nest I'd made with my jacket, Hoshi was still an orb, cool to the touch and unresponsive to my voice.

I stared at the silver lines drawn across the floor. So much time and effort. So much risk and suffering. So much riding on this ritual.

We didn't even know if it would work.

If it failed, we'd have to find a rogue Demonica expert to figure out why. That meant more time spent hiding here. More time that Aaron and Kai would spend in lockup—assuming they were both relatively safe in MagiPol's care and nothing worse had happened to them—and more time in which the guild could be disbanded, if it hadn't already. We had no way of knowing what was going on outside this warehouse.

Quiet footfalls broke into my thoughts. Ezra crossed to the cot and handed me a granola bar from our stash of food. Water droplets shone on his leather coat, and Zak's long dagger was strapped to his thigh; he'd been on the warehouse roof, surveying the rundown commercial streets around our hideout.

"Zak still out?" I murmured, turning the granola bar over in my hands. My appetite had disappeared sometime this morning.

"He should be back soon." Unzipping his jacket, Ezra shrugged it off his shoulders. I watched the leather slide down his arms, dragging over bands of muscle, his bronze skin marked with faint scars.

As he tossed his jacket onto the end of the cot, probably intending to sit beside me, I pressed a hand against his stomach. He paused, blinking down at me. I nudged the hem of his shirt up, revealing the white scars that raked his torso from hip to sternum.

I splayed my hand across them, the unyielding ridges rough under my palm. "You've survived so much."

His surprise softened. He ran his thumb along my jaw.

"You'll survive this too," I whispered, pressing my fingers into his warm skin. "Won't you?"

He combed his fingers into my tangled hair. Neither of us had showered properly in a week, but Zak had procured some basic hygiene supplies. I'd washed my hair, but the lack of hair product was showing.

"I don't know," he murmured. "I can't guess what will happen, but whatever it is, I promise I'll fight to survive however I can."

Tears stung my eyes. "I'm so afraid I'm going to lose you."

"I'm afraid too." He tucked a lock of my hair behind my ear. "I'm afraid it won't work. I'm afraid it will. I'm afraid it'll kill me. I'm afraid my body might survive but my mind won't."

I swallowed against the sob building up in my chest.

"I'm afraid because I don't know who I am if I'm not a demon mage. What if I don't like myself? What if you don't like me?"

"Why would I suddenly not like you?" I huffed.

His fingers trailed down the side of my neck. "Maybe I'm actually a jerk."

My hand drifted across his abs, my thumb following the waistline of his jeans. "You could never be a jerk."

He was quiet for a moment. "People like me because I'm easygoing. I don't get upset about anything ... but that's because I *can't*."

I looked up at him, my lips quirking in a faint frown.

"If I'm not suppressing myself all the time and worrying about Eterran, I'll be different. Maybe ..." He smiled ruefully. "It's a stupid thing to dwell on right now, but what if I'm different and you, Aaron, and Kai don't like me as much anymore?"

"Oh, Ezra." I pulled on his waist and he sank to his knees in front of the cot, putting us at eye level. "Of course you'll change a little bit, but everyone changes. We change throughout our entire lives. Are you exactly the same now as when you first met Aaron and Kai?"

"No. I was ... a lot more defensive back then."

"And they still liked you, right?" I combed his hair back from his face. "It's okay to change."

His warm hands were on my hips, and he slid me forward on the cot until our bodies pressed together, his waist between my thighs. "There are a few things that I won't allow to change."

"Like what?" I whispered.

He slid his hand up my spine. "Like how I feel about you."

Leaning in, he pressed his lips to mine. Our mouths moved with a quiet passion that swiftly escalated into urgent heat. I pressed against him, fingers digging into his shoulders, and his arms clamped around me, squeezing so tightly I could scarcely breathe. I kissed him harder. Held him closer.

I wrapped my legs around his waist, clinging to his warmth and strength. He was alive, and I desperately, frantically needed him to stay that way.

I crushed our mouths together, needing him more than I could express. More than I even understood. Nine months since I'd first laid eyes on him, and I had changed in irreversible ways. He had helped me change.

If I lost him now …

The clatter of a door interrupted us, and I jerked up with a frightened gasp. Zak stepped into the warehouse, raindrops chasing him inside. As he closed the door and bolted it, Ezra rose to his feet.

Zak assessed the demon mage with one swift, piercing look. "It's time to begin."

ZAK'S RASPY VOICE filled the empty concrete room. His chanting was slow, measured, each word delivered with care. Lacking Amalia's confidence, he took his time with each phrase, the cult grimoire braced in his hands. Whenever he paused to check his place, my nerves wound tighter.

For a second time, Ezra stood in one of the two circles within the larger ring, and where Robin had stood with the case of Nazhivēr's blood, I waited with a glass vial clutched in my hand.

Dizziness spun in my head, and I reminded myself to breathe.

Zak continued the incantation, the hollow echo of his voice emphasizing the barren emptiness of the room. Aaron and Kai should have been here. They'd saved Ezra, protected him, loved him like a brother. They deserved to be here, but it was just me.

Zak's voice rose, then went silent. He canted his head, a silent command. If he said anything that wasn't part of the ritual—or made a mistake chanting the endless Latin verses— it'd be ruined and we'd have to wait another three days for the array to charge.

Gripping the vial of blood as though it were a live grenade, I skittered across the outer line, drawn in shining silver. In the center of the empty second circle, I crouched and positioned the vial over the rune. At Zak's nod, I dribbled the thick blood over the marking. Like before, the liquid clung to the silver line.

I rose to my feet and faced Ezra across the circle. His left eye glowed brightly, and I could see both the mage and the demon in him. Ezra's fear, his determination, and his quiet, steely readiness for whatever would happen. Eterran's far more savage resolve, his burning drive for freedom, and his violent need to survive.

Zak waited until I'd returned to my spot outside the circle, then resumed. "*Te tuo sanguine ligo, tu ut vocatus audias, Eterran of the Dh'irath House.*"

The center rune I'd covered in blood glimmered with scarlet light that swept across the array until the entire thing glowed. Ezra stood rigid as Zak continued the incantation.

He pointed at the ring that marked the outer circle. "*Terra te hoc circulo semper tenebit.*"

The faint radiance swept through the lines, then arched upward. A semi-transparent dome whooshed over the circle, then faded. The barrier was up. Only one part of the ritual remained.

Speaking even more carefully, Zak began the final chant. Once again, I experienced the eerie sensation of staticky energy building in the air, heavy and flavored with unfamiliar power. The shimmer of magic flowed between the two circles until it gathered in the empty one, that central rune rippling with blood-red light.

Zak paused. His shoulders moved as he drew in a deep breath, then he slowly raised his hand toward Ezra, the grimoire braced on his other palm.

"*Tenebrarum auctoritatem da mihi, da super hunc imperium sine fine.*" He fixed intense green eyes on the demon mage. "*Eterran of Dh'irath, bearer of the power of Ahlēa, wielder of the king's command, by your blood and your oath, I summon you!*"

The glowing rune in the empty circle blazed, and answering light erupted over Ezra.

He arched, limbs going rigid—and threw his head back in a roar of agony.

"Ezra!" I screamed.

Glowing veins snaked over his limbs. Red power boiled over his body and surged outward. Phantom horns sprouted from his head and wings took form in the rippling power, rising off his back. The power expanded, dragged out of him.

Ezra was screaming and I was screaming. I lunged toward the circle—and Zak caught me, hauling me back from the silver line before I could cross it. I thrashed against his hold, crazed, anguished, incoherent.

The power erupting from Ezra shuddered into a discernible shape. Into shoulders far broader than Ezra's, built to support those huge wings. Into a head half a foot above Ezra's, sporting four long horns.

For a horrifying instant, Eterran's phantom form overlaid Ezra's human body.

Then Eterran's shape dissolved into a bright streak of crimson that arced across the circle and slammed into that glowing rune. The power ballooned upward, reforming the phantom demon—crouched on the floor, his fist braced on the concrete, wings half furled.

His body solidified and the glow on his limbs extinguished. The radiant lines of the spell array flared one last time, then dimmed to burnt black.

Ezra collapsed to the floor.

My scream rang out again. My elbow whipped back, hitting Zak in the ribs so hard he staggered, then I flew toward Ezra, hands reaching for him.

I slammed into an invisible force and ricocheted off, pain bursting through my limbs from the impact. The outer ring marked the floor just in front of me. Gasping, I lunged forward again. My hands slapped against nothing. I pushed into the invisible wall, then felt across it.

The barrier—the invisible dome that was supposed to keep demons inside the circle.

Zak appeared beside me. His hands connected with the unseen obstacle, just like mine. I smashed my fist into it, and the air rippled faintly. We couldn't pass through the barrier.

Ezra couldn't get out, and we couldn't get in.

17

"EZRA!" I screamed.

His shoulders shifted, and he slowly drew an arm under himself. He pushed up onto his hands and knees, motions jerky, limbs trembling.

He raised his head. Blood trickled down his left cheek. The white scar down his face, eight years old, had reopened. His shirt, damp with fresh blood, stuck to his right side, where the old gashes from that same attack raked up his torso. His old injuries, healed by demon magic, had torn with Eterran's exit from his body.

Shoulders heaving, Ezra looked across the circle at the demon.

Eterran was crouched where he had appeared. His left knuckles were propped on the floor, a leather bracer around his wrist, but his right elbow ended in a scarred stump, white lines running up his reddish-brown skin toward his shoulder. The old injury did nothing to reduce the demon's aura of power. His near-decade-long imprisonment inside Ezra hadn't withered the thick, heavy muscles that banded his torso.

He raised his head, crimson eyes fixing on his former host. Dark blood leaked down the left side of his face—Ezra's reopened wound was mirrored on the demon. His countenance wasn't as human as Zylas's, but his sharp features were recognizable. Long black hair hung over one shoulder, tied with a leather string, and from the waist down, he wore lightweight demonic body armor.

Those powerful muscles rippled as the demon braced himself, then stood.

With the movement, dim streaks of crimson flashed inside the circle—and Ezra crumpled to the floor with a hoarse cry. Eterran dropped back to his knees.

Faint ribbons of power rippled between them. They ran from mage to demon, twisting and writhing.

"What is that?" I gasped, near soundless with panic.

"Are they still bound?" Zak pressed his hands to the invisible barrier. "I think … the contract is linking them together? Eterran is still tied to Ezra's soul."

I remembered what Robin had said. *Once the demon spirit and human soul are bound, it can't be undone.*

So she'd created this ritual to circumvent their contract, not break it. We'd all thought separating them would be enough.

With painful effort, Ezra pushed up onto his knees, panting for air.

"Get him out of the circle, Zak!" I shouted, hysteria edging my voice. "Hurry!"

"They're still bound."

"But—"

Eterran gathered himself again. When he stood, the strings of power—of essence, of soul—that tied him to Ezra rippled, and Ezra shuddered, his breath rasping more violently. Eterran's broad torso was streaked with wounds that mirrored his former host's scars, and blood trickled down the demon's reddish-brown skin.

"Stand, Ezra."

I recoiled slightly. Eterran had spoken through Ezra more than once, but hearing his real voice sent terror cascading through me. Deeper than baritone, growling, bestial. Inhuman.

Ezra stared at the demon.

"We are dying," Eterran snarled quietly. "I feel it. You feel it. We cannot exist like this. The bond cannot be broken while we both live."

Ezra's jaw tightened.

Crimson flared in the demon's eyes. "Stand."

As terror-laced confusion ricocheted through my head, Zak's voice filled my ears, words he'd spoken when I'd first told him I wanted to save Ezra. *Any form of demon contract is for life. They only ever end with a death.*

They only ever end with a death.

With a death.

"No," I gasped.

With a deep inhalation, Ezra climbed to his feet and straightened his spine. Wiping the blood off his chin, he faced the demon. Eterran's wings unfurled, filling his half of the circle.

"We finally learned how to be allies," Ezra said, quiet and hoarse. "Don't you want to try to find another way?"

"There is no time. We are dying."

"I don't want it to end like this."

The demon's upper lip curled. "*Want*. A weak word for a weak male. Have you learned nothing?"

Ezra sucked in a sharp breath.

"If you want your life, take it from me," Eterran snarled softly, "before I take mine from you."

For a second, Ezra didn't move—then he reached for the sheath on his thigh and drew the long knife Zak had lent him. In answer, Eterran curled his fingers, claws unsheathing. The faint streaks of power between them rippled.

The demon launched across the circle.

"*No!*"

My shout was still ringing through the room as Ezra thrust his knife out. With a boom, a gust of wind shoved the huge demon back before his claws could reach the aeromage's fragile human skin.

The demon staggered, tail snapping. The crimson ribbons running from demon to mage shuddered, and they panted harshly.

"It feels …" Ezra gasped unsteadily. "It feels like it's pulling my heart out."

Eterran bared his teeth, revealing predatory canines. Crimson flashed up his arm and six-inch talons formed on his fingers, magically extending his claws into deadly weapons.

The demon lunged again. Wind burst from Ezra, and the demon's talons raked across the dense barrier of air. As the wind blew outward, Ezra slashed with the knife.

Eterran twisted aside, and his tail slammed into Ezra's legs. He fell. Eterran pounced, stabbing downward with his glowing talons, and Ezra rolled, kicking out. Another boom of wind.

The threads of magic linking them writhed, and Eterran's talons flickered, half dissolving before they solidified.

Gulping air, Ezra rolled onto his hands and knees, the knife in his fist clattering against the floor. He shoved up, stumbling for balance as the soul link fluctuated wildly.

Eterran raised his arm, palm pointed at Ezra. Crimson spiraled out from his wrist—and the link between them blazed. Pained gasps rushed from both of them as Eterran's attempted spell broke apart.

"Eterran," Ezra panted. "We can't do this. We can't—"

"*Nailēris!*" the demon roared, the deep boom of his voice shocking me. "Do you only want life if it is easy? If it tears your soul to fight me, then tear your soul. While your heart is still beating, do not tell me you can't fight."

He raised his arm again. The demonic spell flared around his wrist, and the threads of their link burned again. This time, Eterran didn't flinch. The spell solidified, the distorted runes igniting with power.

Shuddering with pain, Ezra cast his arm out in an arc, the dagger flashing.

A howling gale hit Eterran as his spell unleashed. The crimson power exploded, throwing demon and mage backward. They crashed into opposite ends of the barrier, the invisible dome shimmering on impact.

I hammered my fists against it. "Zak, do something! Break the circle! *Help him!*"

For a second, he didn't move. Then he stooped, grabbed the dropped grimoire, and started flipping through it. Searching for the ritual—for the key to breaking the circle.

Wings stretched wide, Eterran clambered up. The soul link frizzled. Its glow had grown fainter, and I didn't think that was a good thing.

"Stand," he growled.

Ezra braced his elbows on the floor, shoulders heaving with each rapid breath.

"You are weak. You *want* life, but you do not need it."

Ezra's head came up, his teeth bared. He shoved to his feet, one hand pressed to his bloody side, the movement making the threads of power dance sickeningly. "I survived being a demon mage for ten years. I'm not going to die now."

"Then *fight*." The demon's eyes burned. "Hold back nothing. Rip your soul out to kill me, so you can die with pride."

Air whistled through Ezra's clenched teeth. Eterran's crimson talons reformed—and they charged each other.

They met in the circle's center. Flashing crimson. Howling wind. Eterran drove into Ezra, slashing with his talons. A buffeting gust. A thrust of the knife. Talons grazed Ezra's side. Ezra raked the knife across Eterran's ribs, but the wound did nothing to slow the demon.

The soul link flashed and writhed, and demon and mage staggered and stumbled even as they fought. Battling through the link. Battling through the pain.

Battling desperately for survival.

Snarling, the demon smashed his forearm into Ezra so hard he slammed into the barrier directly in front of me. He slid down to the floor, legs sprawled in front of him.

"Ezra!" I shoved against the invisible wall, trembling from head to toe.

He pulled his legs in and pushed himself up, back pressed to the dome. Across the circle, Eterran raised his arm and magic flared out from his hand. A seething orb of demonic power blasted from his palm.

Ezra dove for the ground and the magic exploded against the barrier right in front of my face. Lunging up, Ezra charged. His knife slashed the air, and a gust shoved Eterran back a step.

Demon and mage clashed again. They were slowing. Weakening. Their lives draining away as the soul link leeched the strength out of them. In a minute or two, maybe less, neither would be able to continue.

And they knew it.

Gasping, Ezra threw a burst of wind at the demon—but it was weak. Way too weak. Instead of being driven back, Eterran snapped his wings out, repelling the gust.

With a roar, he launched at Ezra, his talons flashing for the mage's chest.

Ezra should've ducked. Blocked. Countered.

Instead, he clutched his blade and lunged to meet the demon. They slammed together, and my scream rang out—a cry of anguished terror.

Blood splattered the floor.

In the center of the circle, demon and mage didn't move. Ezra held Eterran's wrist. He'd forced the demon's arm down, deflecting those lethal talons away from his heart—but not far enough.

The six-inch talons were buried in his stomach, right on top of his old scars.

In Ezra's other hand, he held the hilt of his knife, the full length of its blade rammed between Eterran's ribs, a few inches too low to strike his heart.

Their chests heaved for breath. Blood spread over Ezra's shirt. A line of thicker, darker blood ran from the knife in Eterran's chest.

The aeromage's gasping inhalations slowed. His stare locked on Eterran's and his hand, clutching his weapon's hilt, tightened.

Time seemed to distort, one second dragging into the next. Mage or demon. One of them had to act—was about to act—would deliver the killing blow. Whoever moved first would survive.

Ezra sucked in a deep breath, gathering the dregs of his strength. Steeling himself.

A final instant, a heartbeat, a reckoning.

Then he twisted the knife.

A spiral of air blades tore through the demon's chest. Wind burst from Eterran's back, carrying a mist of dark blood, and the demon lurched away, his talons tearing from Ezra's stomach.

A gory hole in the center of Eterran's chest wept blood down his front. His limbs quivered faintly, and the demon sank to his knees. As the glow in his eyes dimmed from crimson to dark scarlet, he slumped onto his side.

Ezra dropped onto his hands and knees. Ripples of transparent power shivered between him and the demon as they stared at each other—then Ezra leaned forward. Reached out.

He grasped the demon's hand, holding it tight. Eterran's eyes darkened from scarlet to black as blood pooled beneath him. Bitterness flickered across the demon's features, then softened into weary peace.

"*Vh'renith vē thāit.*" The unfamiliar words rasped from his throat. "Never forget."

His eyelids slid closed over ebony eyes, and the shudder of his body stilled. As quiet fell across the room, the faint radiance of the soul link dissolved into nothing.

"Victory," Ezra whispered, "or death. I'll remember."

18

I KNELT ON THE FLOOR with both hands wrapped around Ezra's. Crouched opposite me, Zak dribbled a gray potion into the puncture wounds in Ezra's stomach. The druid had elevated Ezra's legs, thrown his jacket over the mage's lower body to keep him warm, and fed him three potions—but Zak was neither a true healer nor a surgeon.

All he could do was try to keep Ezra alive as long as possible.

My limbs rigid, I watched Ezra's chest rise and fall with short, rapid breaths. He was conscious, but his stare was frighteningly blank and I wasn't sure if he knew I was beside him.

I clutched his hand tighter. "Hold on, Ezra."

Bang.

I jerked around. The small back door to the warehouse bounced off the wall, and a man swept through the threshold. Tall, fit, salt-and-pepper hair, piercing gray eyes. Darius gave the room a brief, assessing look, then strode toward us. On his heels, two mythics hurried inside, both carrying large fluorescent-orange cases.

Elisabetta and Miles, our guild's healers.

Leaping up, I backed away to make space, and Elisabetta knelt in my spot. Miles, a well-built man with a shaved head who looked like he should be crushing rogues on a combat team, crouched beside her and unzipped his case to reveal bundles of medical supplies and Arcana paraphernalia.

"Five puncture wounds to the abdomen," Elisabetta observed brusquely as she took hold of Ezra's wrist, feeling for his pulse. "His lips are cyanotic. No radial pulse. Miles, prep an IV while I get him on oxygen. You, keep pressure on the wound."

The second order was fired at Zak, and he pressed both hands to the punctures in Ezra's stomach while Miles dug into his case. Elisabetta opened hers and pulled out a zippered bag. In it was a lunchbox-sized device with a mini oxygen canister. She strapped the plastic mask to Ezra's face and turned a knob on the device.

"How's that IV coming, Miles?" she asked as she clipped a small electronic gadget to Ezra's finger. "His O_2 sats are"—she peered at the gadget—"eighty-nine percent."

"Almost there," Miles murmured as he prodded Ezra's forearm, then inserted a needle. "Get a vasoconstriction potion on those punctures."

"I already did that," Zak said. "It'll last another five minutes at most. I also fed him a blood replenisher, blood-loss stabilizer, and high-potency vitality draft."

Elisabetta looked surprised for less than half a second. "I need to suture these wounds before we begin the healing. Can you assist me so Miles can prep the array?"

"Yes."

She and Zak gloved up. As Zak wiped a yellowish-orange liquid from Elisabetta's supplies over Ezra's stomach, she flipped open a case to reveal rows of shiny surgical tools. I scrunched my eyes shut, fighting a wave of nausea.

A hand settled on my shoulder. Opening my eyes, I found Darius standing beside me. How long had he been there?

He nodded toward the other end of the summoning circle, and I followed his gaze to Eterran's body, untouched since his death, a pool of dark blood surrounding him.

"You succeeded," he murmured.

While Zak had disabled the barrier sealing Ezra inside the ritual circle, I'd called Darius. Our brief conversation had included no details except our location and "Ezra is dying, bring healers now!"

"We did," I whispered. "Ezra won."

But he might still die.

"Darius …" My throat constricted. "Kai and Aaron …?"

"Safe. They're in the MPD lockup."

Faint relief sparked through me. "Robin and Amalia?"

Darius's mouth thinned and he gave his head a small shake. I wanted to ask what that shake meant, except I knew it would be bad news and I couldn't handle that right now.

We didn't speak again as Elisabetta leaned over Ezra. Miles had moved to a clear patch of concrete where he began drawing out a large Arcana array with rapid strokes of an alchemic marker. His low chanting filled the room, occasionally joined by Elisabetta's quiet orders for Zak.

Miles and Elisabetta finished at the same time. Zak helped the healers shift Ezra onto the array, then retreated as they knelt on either side of the mage. While Elisabetta checked his IV bag and finger gadget, Miles began another chant. Faint light shimmered across the array.

Peeling off his bloodstained surgical gloves, Zak crossed toward us, stopping a few steps away. He and the GM eyed each other—Zak with wariness and Darius with cool appraisal.

After a long moment, the druid jerked his chin toward the demon body. "That should be dealt with immediately."

Darius nodded. "I noticed the yard out back is dirt. I have shovels in my vehicle."

"Shovels?" I muttered, most of my attention on Ezra and the healers. "Do you always tote shovels around?"

"Yes. I never know when I might need to bury a body."

My gaze snapped to the GM. With anyone else, I would've assumed they were joking, but with Darius …

Zak gave me a rag and a bottle of "cleaner potion" from his supplies, then he and Darius headed outside together. My heart beat in a sickening rhythm of fear as I moved to the farthest edge of the summoning array from Eterran and began wiping away the evidence of our demonic ritual.

Miles continued to chant, the minutes dragging by. Every time his voice stopped, I'd whip toward the healers, but they would merely add something to their array—a new rune, an earthy ingredient, a talisman—before resuming.

An hour passed, then another. I scrubbed my way across the floor until only the markings around Eterran remained. With my back throbbing after too long bent over, I inched toward the healers, peering down at their work.

White lines and runes marked Ezra's bronze skin, similar to the ones that spanned the floor beneath him. The punctures in his stomach had closed, the angry lines smudged with dried blood, the stitches removed.

I exhaled shakily.

The door clattered. Darius and Zak walked in, their faces shining with perspiration. Zak carried a large black tarp and a coil of rope.

My chest ached strangely as the two men spread the tarp out and dragged the heavy demon onto it. The ache intensified as they tucked Eterran's wings in—those huge wings that had unfurled with surprising elegance. What had the demon looked like in flight? Had he been graceful, agile?

I bit down on the inside of my cheek as Zak drew the tarp over the demon's still face. I'd seen so many of his expressions through Ezra's features, but so little from the demon himself. He'd waited so long, fought so hard, to return to his own body.

Had it been for nothing? His suffering, his struggles, his determination?

The memory of the demon and mage in their final moments of battle shivered through me—each one's weapon buried in the other's body, their wounds not a true reflection but mirrored in an unnerving way.

Darius and Zak tied the tarp around the demon's body, and when they hauled it across the floor, I followed with numb steps.

In the dirt lot behind the warehouse, its perimeter stacked with abandoned junk and scrap metal, Darius and Zak had dug an oversized grave. They dragged the body into the hole, then picked up their shovels.

"Zak." I held out my hands. "Let me."

His gaze flicked across my face, then he handed me the shovel. Darius waited as I dug the blade into the dirt heap beside the grave and threw the first shovelful into the hole. The soil landed on the tarp with a terrible sound.

When I stuck my shovel into the pile a second time, Darius joined me. Zak waited off to the side while Darius and I buried the demon in his unmarked grave.

With every turn of my shovel, I wondered what I was feeling. How could I experience sorrow and relief at the same time? How could I be glad the demon was dead, but also mourn him? He'd been an ally and enemy both. An adversary but also a comrade. He'd been a victim, deceived and abused by the Court, just like Ezra.

Demon and human. Warrior and child. They'd hated each other, tormented each other, relied on each other. They'd survived together for ten years, but only one of them would continue on. Eterran, who'd been so driven to live, had died.

My throat closed. I shoveled the last of the dirt onto the grave, my arms shaking.

Zak's hand closed around the shovel's handle. He pulled it away, then held out a black object. Staring in confusion, I cautiously pulled it from his hand and turned it over. A leather bracer with a protective metal plate, upon which was etched a strange symbol.

It was the bracer that had been around Eterran's wrist.

"When did you ..." I whispered, unable to finish the sentence.

"It's for Ezra." Zak's low voice blended with the night. "When someone has that much influence over your life ... protector and oppressor ... then suddenly they're gone—" He broke off, mouth thinning. "Ezra may not want it, but I think he will."

My fingers tightened around the bracer.

He joined Darius in spreading the dirt out to disguise the loose earth that warned of something buried beneath. I swallowed against the scratchy ache in my throat. I needed to go back inside. To check on Ezra. To finish cleaning the floor so that when we left this place, there'd be no evidence of what had happened here.

But I continued to stand there, staring at the disturbed soil. There were no graves in the world that meant anything to me.

Until now.

I **WAS SITTING** on the floor again, this time beside the cot. Ezra was stretched across it, a thermal blanket laid over him, and I rejoiced over each slow breath he took.

The warehouse was quiet. As soon as the healing was completed and Ezra was comfortable, Darius had whisked Elisabetta and Miles away—returning them to the guild before anyone, namely the MPD, noticed they'd left. Lucky for all of us, our GM's lumina magic made stealth operations simple.

Zak had slipped away to scout the area and ensure no one had noticed anything unusual, while I kept my butt parked beside Ezra. I wasn't leaving him, period.

He'd survived—the ritual, the battle afterward, and his injuries. Joyful relief shivered in my gut, but a layer of utter emotional exhaustion muted the feeling. I was spent. Waiting in a numb stupor, I lost all sense of time.

It wasn't until Ezra's fingers tightened around mine that I stirred back to full awareness. I lifted my head.

A warm, weary brown eye gazed at me. The left side of his face was bandaged, exacerbating his usual asymmetry. Elisabetta and Miles had focused on healing Ezra's worst wounds, leaving the damage to his old scars to be healed later.

I pushed onto my knees. "Ezra?"

He squeezed my fingers. "Am I in one piece?"

"All limbs and digits presently accounted for." I pressed my hand to his cheek. "How do you feel?"

"Like I took the worst beating of my life." His forehead scrunched, then smoothed. His eye slid closed, and his expression went alarmingly tranquil. "Hmm ..."

"Ezra?" I squeaked.

"I can't even remember the last time ..." As he trailed off, his eye opened and he gingerly turned his head to stare across the room where the ritual circle had been. "He's gone."

"Yes. He ... he's dead. We buried him." I hesitated. "Do you think he ...?"

Ezra said nothing, his gaze distant. Was he reliving the final moments of his desperate battle with Eterran, analyzing each moment?

Eventually, he refocused on me. "You're okay?"

"I'm fine—though if not for that barrier, I would've been in there with you. I thought the damn thing was supposed to keep demons in, not people out."

"Hmm. That's true of a regular summoning circle, but it sort of makes sense for a demon mage ritual to trap the human too." A shadow passed over his face. "In case the human host tries to change their mind."

Had that ever happened? During his time at the cult, had he seen a prospective demon mage try to flee in mid-ritual?

"I'm glad it kept you safe," he added.

I scrutinized him as though I'd never seen him before. "So, you're alone in your own head now. How does that feel?"

"It feels ... empty."

"I think that's normal. You'll get used to it." I tilted my head. "And you're no longer doomed to die. How does *that* feel?"

He reached up, his arm quivering with the effort, and cupped my cheek. "It feels like I can breathe properly for the first time in a very long time."

Tears welled in my eyes.

"Tori …" His thumb caressed my cheek. "I want to kiss you without a demon in my head."

He was still finishing his sentence as I pushed up off the floor. I slid onto the cot beside him, pressed gently against his side, and brought my mouth to his.

We kissed, and my heart swelled in my chest until it threatened to burst from my ribs. My lungs struggled for air through the hot bubble of relief lodged inside me—the respite from the terror and grief and anguish of the past hours, days, weeks, and months.

We'd saved him—his life and his soul. We'd done the impossible. We'd unmade a demon mage.

With reluctance, I drew back from Ezra's mouth. "You need to rest and recover your strength. We still have to deal with MagiPol and the Court."

"That," Ezra murmured with a faint smile, "is Darius's arena. He'll already have a plan. He always knows what to do when it comes to the MPD."

Very true. Darius was our expert tactician for anything and everything involving MagiPol and their laws.

I combed Ezra's hair away from his face. "You should still rest, though."

He obediently closed his eyes, a low sigh sliding from his lungs. His breathing slowed again, and I wrapped my hands around his, watching as he drifted into a weary, healing-induced sleep.

Even injured and exhausted, his sleep was more peaceful than I'd ever seen it.

19

EZRA PULLED ON a black t-shirt and tugged it down his torso, careful of the bandages taped over his damaged scars. The five punctures from Eterran's talons didn't need to be covered—they'd healed to pink lines—and after ten hours of sleep, the aeromage was looking half alive instead of half dead.

"I cleaned your shoes," I told him. "You can't even tell they were drenched in blood."

"If not, you'd be going barefoot," Zak added helpfully, his black backpack—containing what I suspected was everything he owned, from which he'd just donated a shirt—hanging from his shoulder.

"I can face any trial or tribulation as long as I have shoes." Ezra sat on the cot, and I nudged his shoes over to him with my foot. "Are we forgetting anything?"

I glanced around the warehouse. I'd scrubbed all the ritual lines and blood from the floor. The cots we were leaving behind, and Zak had packed the remaining food into his bag. Robin's gray backpack hung from my shoulders, stuffed with the cult grimoire, the ritual notes, the case of demon blood, Ezra's combat gloves, Eterran's wrist bracer, my heavy-duty belt, and orb-Hoshi, still dormant and tucked in the belt's back pouch.

"We're good," I said.

Zak drew the hood of his coat up, though without Lallakai's magic, the shadows didn't completely hide his face. "Then let's go."

I grabbed Ezra's hand and led the way to the doors. He was moving stiffly but without a limp. The bandages on the left side of his face, covering his eye, looked starkly white against his bronze skin.

Opening the door, I walked outside. The warehouse was one of many near-identical structures on an industrial back road, with a storage lot full of steel pipes opposite it. With no trees in sight, the only greenery was the occasional weed poking through a crack in the asphalt, but the dreary concrete maze was brightened by the afternoon sun shining down from a clear blue sky.

Less unexpected than the break in Vancouver's perpetual winter overcast was the vehicle parked in front of the warehouse.

Stepping out of his gunmetal gray SUV, Darius pushed his sunglasses up on top of his head and surveyed us with intent gray eyes. Like his last visit to our hideout, he was smartly dressed, his short salt-and-pepper beard groomed, and the corner of his mouth curled up in a half smile. Did *anything* faze this man?

Zak walked through the door behind me. He paused long enough to stare down the GM—no happy feelings of burgeoning comradery there—then turned sharply. As he walked away from us, hooves clacked against the pavement. Tilliag shimmered into view, acid eyes burning in its dark face.

The steel-colored stallion tossed its head, nostrils flared and ears pinned, and barely slowed its sharp trot as it drew level with the druid. Zak caught a handful of its mane and swept onto the horse's back.

"I'll be waiting, Tori," he called over his shoulder.

With another aggressive head toss, Tilliag launched from a trot into a gallop, and as they sped away, both horse and rider faded into the ethereal fae demesne.

I sighed. Zak and his dramatic exits. He could never arrive *or* leave like a normal person.

"What's he waiting for?" Darius asked.

"He wants me to call him when we're done with MagiPol." I shrugged. "Not that he admitted he's worried."

"Hmm." His gaze turned to the aeromage beside me. "Welcome back, Ezra."

Grinning, Ezra strode to the GM. They clasped hands, and I wondered who the hell was cutting onions around here, because I wasn't tearing up over Ezra's visible gratitude and Darius's quiet pride. Definitely not.

Darius and Ezra murmured a quick, quiet exchange, and I didn't even try to listen. Only very recently had I realized they had a closer relationship than I'd ever guessed. Six years ago, Ezra had entrusted Darius with his secrets, his life, and his death, and in turn, the guild master had kept careful watch over his dangerous ward.

Squeezing Ezra's shoulder, Darius turned to me. "Shall we settle this once and for all?"

Nerves flared through my gut, but I managed to grin. Darius had me stash my backpack in a hidden compartment in the SUV's trunk—the same nook where his shovels lived, along with a small assortment of mystery bags and tools—then we climbed into the vehicle. I let Ezra have the roomy front seat and took the spot behind him.

The moment I was buckled in, I leaned over the center console. "Fill us in. What's been happening? How are Aaron and Kai holding up?"

Darius shifted into drive and the SUV rolled away from the warehouse. "Girard checked on them, and they're fine—though extremely displeased with the accommodations."

Yeah, I wouldn't expect a super-rich mage prodigy or a member of an international crime syndicate to enjoy imprisonment.

"I've been rather busy," Darius continued casually. "The MPD assigned an entire team of agents to apprehend me, which has proved inconvenient."

"Oh yes." I rolled my eyes. "Inconvenient."

"Aside from avoiding them, I've been connecting with the other GMs in the city, warning them the MPD is trampling their own protocols to discredit me, destroy my guild, and legally murder my guildeds."

"Did they try to turn you in?"

"None of them were that foolhardy." His humor faded. "They're seeing the warning signs as much as I am. All GMs are wary of the MPD's tendency to ignore their own rules when it suits them, but I've rarely seen MagiPol overstep this far."

"Could the Court have infiltrated the precinct?" Ezra asked dubiously.

"If that had happened, I'd expect a different sort of suspicious activity. I think this is something else." His hands tightened on the wheel. "I'm just not sure what."

I nervously bounced my knees. "So what's our plan for getting the bounty off Ezra, then?"

"There's an Arcana test for demonic presence. It's normally used to determine if an infernus contains or is linked to a demon, but it can identify demon mages as well. Our goal is to convince the MPD to test him."

Oh, that was handy. Well, *now* it was. Twelve hours ago, it would've been a disaster if anyone had tried it on Ezra.

As I tried to imagine what form this test might take, my relief faltered. Ezra had been demon-free for less than a day. What if the test detected something?

"When we arrive at the precinct, I'll appeal the charges, allege they're false, and insist you be tested immediately," Darius told Ezra. "And since you'll be standing right there, peacefully submitting to the test, they should have no reason to refuse."

"Should?" I muttered worriedly.

"On the chance they aren't cooperative, I intend to make this a very *public* appeal." He arched an eyebrow. "There's a reason we're doing this in the middle of the afternoon."

The MPD precinct, smack dab in the heart of downtown, stood out from the surrounding buildings in zero ways. Gray exterior, tinted windows, and one side that butted up against an even grayer concrete structure.

Darius turned toward the narrow parking garage entrance. The security arm automatically lifted, and he steered the SUV into the dimly lit passageway under the building. A sign overhead indicated a turn for "Intake," which Darius passed. A second sign directed "Deliveries" to turn, but Darius skipped that one too, following a third sign that read, "Visitor Parking."

Sunlight beckoned us onward, and the SUV emerged into a back lot open to the sky, surrounded by skyscrapers. Half the thirty or so spots were filled, but Darius was able to park near the double doors, unmarked except for the MPD logo. We climbed out of the car, and as I faced the plain but imposing building, my flimsy confidence withered.

Darius circled the vehicle to join us, carrying a simple blue folder. "Once we're inside, let me do the talking."

Ezra and I saluted in answer, and Darius smiled. "Then let's begin."

He led us to the precinct's door and swung it wide open, walking in like he owned the place. Ezra and I followed on his heels, and I could only hope I looked as confident as our GM.

A rectangular lobby greeted visitors, with a double row of back-to-back chairs down the center and a third row against the left wall. On the right, a service counter was set into the wall, the room behind it stuffed with filing cabinets and computers.

At the far end, directly ahead, a glass wall with another set of double doors separated the lobby from a bullpen office full of desks. Agents and analysts bustled about, oblivious to the coming drama.

A surprising number of mythic civilians waited in the lobby, most of them scattered among the chairs, with six lined up at the counter. Darius strode for the reception line, and the guy at the back of the queue glanced over. His gaze shifted past

Darius to Ezra—and his face went white. He grabbed the sleeve of the guy in front of him and backpedaled.

The rapid scuffle of their shoes drew the attention of the others in line, and an instant later, everyone was backing rapidly away as we approached the counter.

I remembered the pervasive dread of the unbound demon from last Halloween. This week's demon mage hunt must've created just as much of a fearful stir through Vancouver's mythic community. Ezra had become a celebrity—the infamous kind.

Darius walked to the reception desk and smiled at the white-faced woman sitting behind it. The two administrators at desks farther back in the records room were frozen in place.

"Good afternoon," he said pleasantly. "Darius King, GM of the Crow and Hammer, presenting myself as per summons MS-19-70493."

He wasn't speaking loudly, but just like in guild meetings, his confident voice carried to every ear in the room.

As he slid a paper from his folder and laid it on the receptionist's desk, he continued, "Accompanying me is Victoria Dawson and Ezra Rowe, guildeds of mine who are facing charges."

Whispers rippled through the watching mythics. The poor receptionist looked ready to faint.

"I also have appeals prepared for both of them," he concluded, adding two more sheets of paper. "Who's in charge of their cases?"

The receptionist just stared.

"Perhaps you should call them," he suggested gently.

She reached out with a trembling hand, picked up her phone, and fumbled with the ten thousand buttons on it.

Lifting the handset to her ear, she continued to stare between Darius and Ezra.

"A-A-Agent Harris," she stammered. "D-Darius King is here. He—he b-brought … Ezra Rowe."

Darius held his pleasant smile as she listened. Five seconds passed, then ten.

The glass doors to the bullpen flew open, and a swarm of agents burst through. Half were unarmed and half carried some sort of weapon. A disagreeably familiar face led them, his teeth bared and eyes wild behind thick-rimmed reading glasses.

Ah, Agent Brennan Harris. The supreme asshole who'd tried to coerce me into dishing dirt on the Crow and Hammer. He'd then thrown the hissy fit of all hissy fits when Darius had weaseled me out of murder charges by "proving" I was a mythic.

I swiftly scanned the other agents for faces I might recognize. Since becoming an official mythic, I'd encountered a few agents in brief doses—usually while submitting reports or evidence after one of our fun adventures, plus the occasional agent or two would stop at the guild to speak with Darius.

This time, I didn't recognize anyone besides Harris—though that might've been because they all wore expressions of shock, defensive anger, and fear.

Darius stepped in front of Ezra, shielding him from the oncoming force. The unlucky civilian visitors in the lobby pressed against the walls to get clear.

"Move, Darius!" Harris spat, pointing a silver wand at the GM's chest. "Protecting a demon mage is a capital crime and we're authorized to use lethal force!"

"You'd be entitled to do that," Darius agreed calmly, "*if* Ezra were a demon mage."

Harris's eyes bulged before he pulled himself together. He jerked a pair of handcuffs off his belt. "I'm placing you all under arrest."

He took a step closer, then froze as Darius's unyielding stare met his.

"As I was just telling your receptionist," the GM said in a quiet, dangerous way, "I'm here to appeal the charges against my guildeds—including Ezra. He's been falsely accused, and we will prove his innocence."

"He's already been convicted," Harris snarled, cuffs dangling from his hand. "We have irrefutable evidence that he—"

"What evidence is more irrefutable than the so-called demon mage presenting himself for the MPD's examination?" Darius raised a hand toward Ezra, still safely behind him. "Would a real demon mage be standing here peacefully?"

The agents behind Harris shifted uneasily. A few looked relieved that they weren't about to battle the most feared mythic out there.

"More bullshit, Darius." Harris dared to step closer, a crazed light in his eyes. "This is just another of your tricks, but we have video evidence of Rowe attacking a combat team with demon magic."

"And video footage has never, in all the history of cameras, ever been altered," Darius said with subtle but unmistakable sarcasm. "Nor is it exceptionally easy to do since magic records so poorly."

Harris hissed under his breath.

"Test him, Brennan. He isn't a demon mage."

"If he isn't a demon mage," the agent beside Harris asked, "why did you wait a week to bring him here?"

"We had no choice but to wait for the bloodlust to die down after the MPD issued a three-hundred-thousand-dollar DOD bounty without warning—skipping several lawfully required steps along the way, I might add."

"It was an emergency," Harris growled.

"Really? And how many murders has Ezra committed?"

"He—we have video evidence that he attacked—"

"Ah yes, the indisputable video. But I'm not here to discuss whether an emergency hearing to sentence him to death based on a single piece of questionable evidence was ethical or in any way justifiable."

A few more agents were looking uncomfortable.

"We're freely and peacefully presenting ourselves to see justice done, and with a young man's life in the balance, I require only that you *prove* he is a demon mage before executing him for a crime he isn't guilty of." Darius's voice hardened with command. "Call your Demonica expert to perform the test—or call someone with actual authority."

Harris's nostrils flared.

"You never change, Mr. King."

At the woman's voice, the battalion of agents parted, revealing the tall figure who'd just walked through a nearby door. A stack of folders tucked under her arm suggested she was an analyst, but she carried the dominating aura of a leader as blatantly as the other agents carried their weapons.

She strode through the group with a general's grimness and stopped a step ahead of Harris. With chin-length blond hair, model-worthy cheekbones, and probing eyes, she could've been thirty or fifty. I had no clue.

"Ah," Darius murmured. "Captain Blythe."

Her laser stare swept down Darius and back up. "Playing games again, are we?"

"I have never been more serious."

She snorted in an "I'll believe it when I see it" sort of way. "Then, as part of your peaceful surrender, your guildeds will be handcuffed."

"Of course."

At Darius's easy agreement, Harris shook with visible fury, which the GM completely ignored. Blythe gestured at two agents behind her—not Harris, despite the fact he still held his useless restraints. His face went even redder.

Trying not to stiffen defensively as the agents approached, I held my wrists out. The agent clipped a set of cuffs on me, the metal cold against my skin. Beside me, Ezra submitted to the restraints without changing expression. His poker face was as good as ever.

"This way, Mr. King." Turning, Blythe waved at the gathered agents and barked, "Back to work!"

They obediently hustled through the doors into the bullpen. Harris hesitated, his burning need to object written all over his face, but he stumped after the others without a word.

Blythe led us into a long hall, then opened the first door on the right. Stepping aside, she let Darius precede her into a small interview room with a table and four chairs. Ezra and I followed, and Blythe stepped in last, closing the door behind her.

Darius leaned against the table, assessing Blythe with surprisingly wary eyes. "This is unexpected, Aurelia."

I blinked bemusedly. Darius was on a first-name basis with Vancouver's precinct captain?

"I'm not complaining," he added, "but I fully expected you to jump on the chance to put me in handcuffs as well."

She stepped closer to him, her narrowed eyes raking over his face. "How many times have you done this, Darius?"

"Protected my guildeds? I'll do it as many times as needed."

"How many times have you exploited rules and bent laws to fit your ambitions?" Another step toward him. "How many fines and charges have you dodged by quoting my own laws back at me?"

"In this case, Aurelia, I'm saving an innocent life."

She slashed a look at Ezra, then took another step—which put her almost on Darius's toes. She glared into his face, their noses scarce inches apart, and I could've cut the tension with a knife.

Tension*s*, actually. Plural. Because there was a whole lot more than a battle of professional wills buzzing between those two. I was getting distinctly personal vibes, and I goggled at them in astonishment.

"You got overconfident once, Darius," she said in a low voice. "And it cost you your career."

"You're assuming I still wanted that career—and that losing it was unintentional."

Her eyes narrowed even more. "Then I hope *this* oversight was intentional too."

Darius's expression didn't change, but his fingers curled around the edge of the desk, knuckles turning white. "What oversight is that?"

"You assumed you could throw the book at me, and I'd cave because laws are laws." She stepped back. "But I'm not in charge here anymore."

His eyes widened.

Turning on her heel, she strode to the door and laid her hand on the knob. "And the one who is—he's not a 'play by the rules' man."

She shoved the door open and marched out. As the door began to swing shut, a hand caught it and pushed it wide open.

An agent stood in the threshold. Tall, wiry, dark brown hair, and a face like a fox. He smiled but the expression didn't touch his flat brown eyes. Gooseflesh ran up my arms.

"Darius King. Your reputation precedes you."

Another wave of gooseflesh shivered along my spine. The man's voice shared the same dead quality as his eyes.

"And you are?" Darius asked with cool poise.

"Agent Söze, Internal Affairs. We have a great deal to discuss." He stepped into the room, and more agents filled the doorway behind him, their faces cold and hard. "But first, it appears Captain Blythe neglected a fundamental safety measure."

Söze unhooked a pair of shiny silver cuffs from his belt, the chain jingling as he stepped toward Darius.

20

"GET YOUR HANDS OFF ME," I snarled, wrenching my arm.

My efforts earned me an eruption of stinging pain in my
wrists from the handcuffs and an annoyed huff from the agent
holding my elbow.

I knew resisting was pointless, but I couldn't stop myself.
Not while Darius was handcuffed to the table back in the
interview room. Not while four agents had led Ezra somewhere
deeper into the building. And not while two more agents were
steering me down a flight of stairs into the MPD's lower levels.

"Where'd they take Ezra?" I demanded as the lead agent
opened a security door. "He isn't a demon mage, and if anyone
hurts him …"

I trailed off, unable to finish the threat. My sketchy
knowledge of the MPD justice system included nothing about
any of this. I didn't even know how appeals worked.

The silent agents steered me through another set of security doors and into a cell block. Prison-like bars filled the left wall, the individual cells separated by thick concrete barriers.

I dug in my heels. "You can't just throw me in a cell! Don't you have to read me my rights or something?"

The mute duo dragged me along the tile floor, passing the first few cells.

"This is bullshit!" I squirmed against their hold. "It's tyranny! What kind of totalitarian secret police shit are you—"

"Tori?"

I jerked against the cuffs. In the cell ahead, a man in a gray prison jumpsuit stood at the bars, his copper hair rumpled and his jaw scruffed up by a short, unkempt beard.

My heart leaped. "*Aaron!*"

"Shut it!" one of my captors growled. He hauled me to the cell next to Aaron's, yanked the barred door open, and tossed me inside. The lock clacked loudly, and by the time I whirled around, the two agents were speed-walking back up the corridor.

"Assholes!" I bellowed. "Cowards! Corrupt bootlickers!"

The security door slammed shut behind them. The bang echoed down the hall, then eerie silence fell.

"Tori, where's Ezra?"

That voice belonged to Kai, and it came from my other side—one cell beyond mine.

I pressed my face to the bars. "He's in the building, but they took him somewhere else."

"What happened?" Aaron demanded.

"Everyone in here is dying to know," Kai added. His tone was dry, but I recognized the warning he was giving me: be careful what I said.

His remark was answered by an amused snort.

"Go on, entertain us," a man in another cell called, his voice hoarse like he hadn't spoken in a while. "Shit all to do in here."

"Yeah, go for it," someone else added.

Uh. Okay. Deciding to ignore our audience, I lowered my voice. "We came with Darius. Me and Ezra, I mean. Because …" I paused, ensuring my voice would stay steady. "Because Ezra is *not* a demon mage. As you both know."

Silence answered me. This wasn't how I'd imagined telling them that Ezra and I had successfully completed the mission we'd all begun together. They'd lived for years with the knowledge that they couldn't save him. They'd suffered and grieved, but against all odds, we'd reversed Ezra's fate. I wanted to cry and laugh and maybe scream, all while hugging them both until my arms broke.

Instead, I couldn't see them, let alone touch them, and they couldn't respond without giving away that Ezra not being a demon mage was a recent development.

"Darius is appealing all the charges against us," I continued, "and it was going okay, but then the captain, this Blythe person, said some other guy is in charge. Some 'internal affairs' guy?"

"Internal Affairs?" Aaron repeated, his voice thick with emotion he hadn't quite controlled yet. "That doesn't sound good."

"He's probably the same agent who wouldn't release Makiko," Kai revealed. He sounded even more businesslike than usual, which was how he coped with strong emotions. "Tori, are you okay?"

"Yeah … fine."

"Good. What about—" He cut himself off. "Get some rest, okay? Darius knows what he's doing."

He wanted to know more, but with so many ears listening in, we couldn't discuss anything.

I retreated from the bars and assessed my cell. A bunk bed was built against one wall, and there was a toilet in the corner with a tiny handwashing sink. That was it.

Gulping, I sat awkwardly on the lower bunk, my wrists handcuffed in front of me. I shivered, my limbs chilled. I wanted to see Aaron and Kai. I wanted to hug them. I wanted to go home with them and flop on their sofa, play a silly racing game, and drink beer until I passed out.

I wanted to know where Ezra was. What was happening to him. I wanted to drag him out of here and rush him straight home—or better yet, straight to Elisabetta. He'd had some healing, but he was nowhere near okay.

I wanted to hold him and kiss him and never let him go.

I just wanted this nightmare to be over, but I was locked in a cell, separated from everyone, and at the mercy of a man who wore the badge of a protector of justice but smiled like a tyrant.

AFTER SEVERAL HOURS of anxiety-filled boredom, an agent came through with dinner for the prisoners. I convinced him to unlock my cuffs, then shoveled down my meal, which resembled the cheapest microwave dinner I'd ever eaten, except worse. The mashed potatoes were made of blended cardboard and water. I was certain of it. Still, it was warm, and a semi-pleasant change from the granola bars and trail mix I'd been living off for the week prior.

Meal finished, I was again left with no distractions as another hour crawled past. Aaron and Kai weren't talking, and as much as I craved to hear their voices, I didn't start a conversation. Every word echoed in the concrete-and-tile corridor.

My thoughts returned to Ezra. What if Agent Söze had decided to ignore Darius's demand that they test Ezra and proceeded to carry out the death sentence? Would they murder Ezra right here in the precinct?

Terror flared and I dug my fingers into my knees, trying to contain my emotions. He couldn't die now, not when we'd finally, *finally* succeeded in saving him. Darius would protect him. I had to believe that.

With no better ideas on how to distract my brain, I started doing multiplication tables in my head. Yeah, I was that desperate.

I made it to sixteen times fourteen when the security door beeped and the handle clattered. Leaping off the bunk bed, I rushed to the bars, hoping to see Ezra, or even better, Darius coming to tell us everything was good now and we could leave.

Agent Söze walked into view, accompanied by two agent cronies. The Internal Affairs asshole held a clipboard, his lifeless stare sweeping across the cellblock.

"Aaron Sinclair, Kai Yamada, and Victoria Dawson," he intoned without emotion. "I'm here to inform you of the additional charges against you. As per regulation, these have already been presented to your guild master. With whom shall I begin?"

He flipped a page up. "Aaron Sinclair. On top of harboring a demon mage, your new charges include performing magic in front of a human, revealing mythic secrets to a human, involving a human in mythic affairs, conspiring to illegally induct a human into a guild, conspiring to falsify mythic registration documentation …"

As he spoke, Agent Söze's dead eyes drifted over me. My blood ran cold. The "human" in all those charges was *me*.

He turned the page. "We also have three counts of assault, three counts of assault with magic, and three counts of first-degree murder."

"*Murder?*" Aaron burst out in a snarl. "Who—"

"William Burke, Halil Demir, and Fenton Armstrong, members of the Utah-based guild, the Keys of Solomon. We have multiple witness accounts of confrontations between you and their team during the unbound demon hunt last Halloween." He ran a finger down his page. "Speaking of demons, your charges also include harboring a rogue Demonica contractor, participating in illegal Demonica magic, and abetting in … *numerous* murders."

"What?" Aaron snarled furiously.

Agent Söze observed Aaron's reaction with clinical indifference, then shifted his gaze toward Kai's cell. He began reading off the electramage's charges. They were similar to Aaron's, and the endless list turned to mush in my ears.

How did he know we'd killed three Keys contractors last Halloween? And the "rogue contractor"—was he talking about Robin?

Agent Söze finished Kai's list, focused on me, and began to speak again. My body chilled, limbs trembling, as he listed off my charges, which included most of the same ones as the mages, plus several new ones related to impersonating a mythic and lying to the MPD about it.

"It's very nearly impressive, the amount of criminal activity you three have racked up," he concluded dispassionately. "Between your crimes and Darius King's numerous infractions and evasions, this guild disbandment will be very straightforward."

He flipped the papers on his clipboard back into place. "Your charges will be finalized in the next twenty-four hours, and the Judiciary Council will convene shortly afterward to determine your sentencing."

"What about Ezra?" Kai asked, his voice low and terse.

"The MPD is duty-bound to pursue every avenue of investigation." Agent Söze tucked the clipboard under his arm. "However, none of our experts feel safe performing the Demonica detection test on a convicted demon mage."

"None?" Aaron spat. "You've got to be f—"

"The Judiciary Council will make the final decision."

With his two agents in tow, he walked away. The security doors clattered, then slammed shut. Silence fell over the cell block as I stared dazedly at the spot where Agent Söze had stood.

"That bastard," Aaron rasped, his voice thick with fury. "He's going to block anyone from testing Ezra and execute him anyway."

I didn't reply. My throat had closed, muscles locked. I could scarcely breathe, let alone make a sound. Stumbling, I retreated to my bunk and sat before my legs gave out.

All those charges against us. They couldn't possibly have hard evidence for most of them—but that didn't matter. Just like it didn't matter that Ezra had peacefully turned himself in to prove he wasn't a demon mage.

Aaron and Kai had gone quiet again, and the other prisoners stayed silent too. Maybe they felt sympathy for how completely screwed we were—or maybe they felt the same voice-muting powerlessness that this place radiated.

My thoughts twisted and boiled, consuming me entirely. I sat on the bunk, face buried in my hands, doing nothing but breathing and thinking. But no matter how I fit the pieces together or pulled them apart, no matter what wild idea I considered, I saw no way out of this. None.

I didn't know how much time had passed when, with an electronic click, my cell light dimmed to a faint glow. Blinking, I looked toward the hall, where the lights had dimmed as well. Bedtime for the prisoners?

I stared for a moment—then gasped.

An unfamiliar man stood outside my cell.

As I gawked, he smiled and pressed a finger to his lips, then crooked that finger in a "come here" gesture. Huh?

Cautiously, I pushed off the bunk and crossed to the bars.

"Hey there," he whispered. "Enjoying your stay at Hotel MagiPol?"

My forehead scrunched. "Who are you?"

"You don't recognize me? I remember *you*."

I squinted, taking in his youthful face. Early twenties, maybe? Short chocolate brown hair and the kind of blue eyes that made girls swoon—deep and penetrating but softened by an amused sparkle—accentuated his boy-next-door good looks.

"No clue," I muttered.

"Maybe our last encounter was more memorable for me than you. I was a forgettable rookie agent on his first field assignment at the time."

I recoiled. "Wait, you're an agen—"

"*Shh,*" he whispered, then stuck his hand through the bars. "Kit Morris—Agent Kit … uh, Agent *Morris.*" He grimaced. "Call me Kit."

Staring in bewilderment, I shook his hand. Weird time for a polite greeting, but why not.

He squeezed my fingers. "Ready to check out?"

"Huh?"

"Unless you *want* to face a rigged judiciary hearing, but I don't recommend it. I've been there and it sucks." He raised his other hand, a ring of keys hanging from one finger. "Personally, I'd like you out of the building before Agent Commodus gets *really* carried away. I think he's planning to display your head on a pike in the lobby, and that's just tacky, you know?"

When I merely gawked, he arched his eyebrows above those strangely perceptive blue eyes.

"Get on my page here, Tori. I'm breaking you out, and I don't have time to explain Joaquin Phoenix's filmography to you first."

21

"WHY ARE YOU, an MPD *agent*, breaking me out of lockup?"

Kit inserted a key into the door's bolt. "Why are *you*, doomed prisoner of the MPD, complaining?"

"I'm not complaining. I just want to know why."

He opened the cell door, careful to make as little noise as possible, and whispered, "Does a man *need* a reason to undertake his very own *Mission Impossible* heist? If there were an overhead vent in your cell, I'd be rappelling down from the ceiling right n—"

"Are we rescuing Aaron and Kai too?" I interrupted in a hiss.

Winking casually, he ambled over to Aaron's cell. The pyromage, sitting on his bunk with his shoulders hunched, looked up—and his jaw dropped. I shushed him before he could make any noise, and he silently rushed over as Kit unlocked the door.

"Agent Morris," he introduced himself in a whisper. "Professional film analyst and jailbreak consultant, at your service."

Stepping into the corridor, Aaron shot me a "who the hell is this guy and what the hell is going on?" look. All I could do was shake my head.

Kai, like Aaron, was sitting miserably on his bunk, and reacted with similar shock when we appeared in front of his cell. We repeated the shushing and door unlocking process, and in moments, Kai was free too.

I grabbed both mages' hands, squeezing hard and unreasonably moved by the feel of their warm, strong fingers gripping mine. Kai wore a jumpsuit too, and I was sad to see that not even the super-stud electramage could make prison garb look good.

"Okay," I whispered. "Now we need to find Ezra and Darius."

"My partner is taking care of them." Kit scowled like he'd been cheated out of his life savings. "My first chance to actually see the containment floor, but noooo, Lienna has to do it."

"The containment floor?" I repeated. "What's that?"

"No idea, but it's where they locked up your demon mage friend. Which, by the way, is both cool and terrifying. You're really friends with a demon mage?"

"He isn't a demon mage."

Eyebrows quirking skeptically, he faced the security doors. We'd have to pass three occupied cells to get to the exit, and if another prisoner saw us, they could ruin our escape.

"Let's see ..." Kit murmured. He tapped his chin thoughtfully. "Ah, I know."

I blinked at his back. A moment later, a frightened gasp echoed from one of the cells. Someone else squealed like a kid.

Waving at us to follow, Kit strolled down the corridor toward the doors. I followed him, glancing nervously at the nearest cell. Inside, a dimly lit man with thick arms and a greasy beard was halfway through scrambling up the side of his bunk bed like a scared monkey. He didn't notice us pass.

The next cell's inmate was staring at the floor with wide eyes, utterly fixated on the plain concrete. The third prisoner was hiding under his blanket, quivering.

What. The. Hell.

Kit tapped his security pass against the panel, then led us through the doors and up the stairs to the main level. He stopped on the landing and turned, surveying us critically.

"We're heading for the back door," he revealed. "All you have to do is follow me and I'll handle the rest."

Instant suspicion stiffened my back. "You want us to just walk out there?"

"Is this a stupid scheme to pin extra charges on us?" Aaron growled.

"Damn, you guessed it. The entire precinct got together and decided you three needed even *more* charges, even though you already have enough for several life sentences each." He sighed at our blank expressions. "That was a joke. Follow me."

Without waiting for us to argue, he opened the stairwell door and entered a hallway. Casual as could be, he ambled to the end, where he had two options: continue into the bullpen—visible through the door's small window—or turn left, which would lead us back to the comparatively safe lobby.

Kit put his hand on the bullpen door. "Oh, and if you see anything strange, just ignore it and stick with me."

"What do you mean by—"

He swung the door open and walked into the bullpen full of agents.

Gulping, I pushed my shoulders back and strode out after him. There was a *slight* chance I could slip through unnoticed since I was dressed more or less normally, but Aaron and Kai were wearing jumpsuits. No way the agents would ignore them.

We were three steps into the bullpen, its two dozen occupants beginning to glance our way, when a loud popping sound erupted.

A computer burst into flame.

Agents shouted and leaped to their feet as the guy sitting at the desk shoved back so hard his chair toppled over. Flames writhed, crackling merrily, and smoke billowed toward the ceiling.

Kit kept walking, circling wide around the desks. Every agent was focused on the fire—except for a nearby woman whose head spun toward us.

The burning computer exploded, grabbing her attention. Bits of flaming debris flew into the air, and people screamed. A man ran up with a fire extinguisher.

"Wait, no—" the owner of the desk exclaimed.

Wannabe Fireman blasted the extinguisher's white spray all over the desk. The monitor flipped over backward, papers flying everywhere. The flames rippled wildly but didn't go out.

"No!" the desk's owner bellowed. "Stop! *Stop*, damn it!"

Kit cackled under his breath as he opened the bullpen's back door. "After you."

I rushed through, Aaron and Kai right behind me, and as Kit stepped through last, the desk's owner shouted furiously, "It isn't real fire, you idiots! Where's Kit? *Kiiiit!*"

Snorting back laughter, Kit gestured at us to keep going. I shot him a wide-eyed look, then hastened down the hall. An emergency exit waited at the end, and I shoved through it.

We exited onto a quiet street illuminated by the orange glow of streetlamps, a few cars parked along the curb. I immediately understood why Kit had taken us out this way. If we'd fled through the lobby, we would've come out in the enclosed parking lot, which had no escape except the covered tunnel thing. Here, we could run in any direction.

"Thatta way," Kit instructed, pointing at an alley across the street.

Painfully aware of Aaron and Kai's prison garb, I trotted out into the road. The guys followed me, Kit bringing up the rear.

Just inside the alley, a black sedan idled with its taillights glowing. For a second, I thought it was a Miura vehicle and Makiko was here to provide another getaway car. But the person leaning against the driver's door was not the petite aeromage.

Zak looked over at the sound of our footsteps, his hood pulled up but his face illuminated by the cell phone he held. He slid it into his pocket and pushed off the vehicle.

I had about two seconds to panic over the fact that Zak was standing right there in plain view while an MPD agent walked down the alley toward him, then the druid spoke.

"Any trouble?"

"Who do you take me for?" Kit replied. "I might not be a wanted rogue with a million-dollar bounty, but I can handle one little felony."

Well, there went my hope that Kit wouldn't recognize Zak as the Ghost. My apprehension calmed as I realized Kit must be a criminal pal of Zak's and he wasn't a real agent after all. Talk about your smooth breakouts, seriously.

I opened my mouth to speak—then lunged to grab Aaron's arm as he surged toward the druid, his teeth bared furiously.

Right. Aaron and Kai didn't know Zak was back on our non-shit list.

"You bastard," Aaron snarled.

Zak shot the pyromage a cutting look, then asked Kit, "Did you get them out without anyone noticing?"

"More or less." Watching me yank on Aaron's arm, Kit canted his head curiously. "Is this a 'Captain America and Iron Man' thing or a 'Captain America and Red Skull' thing?"

Zak ignored that. "Let's get moving."

"Wait." I pinched Aaron's arm so he'd stop trying to shake me off. "Wait, wait, *wait*. What's going on? Why are you here? How do you know this skeevy agent guy? Where—"

"Skeevy?" Kit muttered in a hurt tone.

"—are Ezra and Darius?"

"I'll explain *in the car*. Get in."

Fuming with anxious irritation, I jerked the door open. We all climbed in—Kai, Aaron, and me in the backseat, Kit in the passenger seat, and Zak driving. He shifted into gear and peeled away aggressively.

"Where'd you get the car?" Kit asked conversationally.

"Stole it."

"Nice."

I leaned over the center console. "Explain. Now."

Kit twisted in his seat to peer at me. "Have you seen *The Untouchables*?"

"No."

He huffed with disappointment. "Fine, I'll explain the long way. It all started when Zak called me up and was like, 'Kit, I know I'm an unlovable jackass who claims not to care about anyone, but there's this *girl*—'"

The druid took a hand off the wheel and mashed his palm into Kit's face, shoving him sideways.

"Try again, Shakespeare."

Kit straightened, completely unruffled. "He called me up and was like, 'Kit, there's some weird shit going on in your precinct. Can you find out what's happening?'"

"Wait." Aaron leaned forward beside me. "You're *actually* an MPD agent?"

"No, I'm Batman."

"I called him when you didn't contact me after a few hours," Zak added grimly. "Clearly, your plan hadn't gone well."

Kit propped his arm on the console, and the teasing humor faded from his eyes. "My partner and I already knew something was off in our precinct, so Zak's call wasn't a surprise—except for the part where he actually called me. Söze is a real piece of work. He's usurped the entire precinct from Captain Blythe, and there's nothing she can do about it. Officially," he added under his breath.

"What does Söze want?" Kai asked. "How does he benefit from executing Ezra and disbanding the Crow and Hammer?"

"Everyone in our precinct hates your guild," Kit replied airily, "so that last part is a no-brainer. As for the rest, we're not sure yet, but you have bigger problems than Söze's private agenda."

That silenced my next question, and I pressed my lips together. He was right. Just because we were out of the precinct didn't erase all the charges against us—to which Agent Söze could now add "escaping custody."

Which begged the question of what we were supposed to do and/or where we should go. I was about to ask when I glanced out the window and recognized the street we were zooming along. This couldn't possibly be a smart idea, but I wasn't willing to suggest Zak change destinations.

He parked in front of the Crow and Hammer. The guild's windows glowed brightly despite the late hour, beckoning me inside. An illusion of safety, I knew, but I wanted it anyway. I wanted it *really* badly.

Right after Zak cut the engine, headlights glared through the car's rear window as another vehicle pulled up. I twisted around to look.

Darius's gunmetal-gray SUV had just parked behind us.

Aaron and Kai threw their doors open, and I scrambled out after them. The SUV's doors had opened too, and Ezra slid out and straightened, part of his face still covered in white bandages.

An instant later, Aaron and Kai reached him. Aaron grabbed Ezra's arm, and Kai stood unusually close, his gaze trained on Ezra's face. They bent their heads together, Ezra's lips moving as he spoke quietly. He grinned, then Kai gave up on composure entirely and clamped Ezra in a hug. Aaron's laugh rang out.

Despite everything else, happiness bubbled up inside me. This moment. This was what we'd all worked for. This was what we'd struggled and suffered for.

"How was the containment floor?"

At Kit's question, I tore my stare away from the guys. The young MPD agent had joined an unfamiliar young woman, slim and average height, who'd exited Darius's SUV. Her stern expression was at complete odds with her appearance—namely, the eclectic assortment of beads and charms hanging from her ponytail of thick black hair, the jumbled collection of necklaces resting on her slim chest, the mismatched bracelets jangling on her wrists, and the brown satchel slung casually over her shoulder, its strap decorated with even more random baubles.

"As expected," she replied in a voice that was soft but with a hint of exasperation. "How much chaos did you cause getting those three out?"

"Henry was *very* concerned when he saw a horde of adorable kittens stampeding through the archives. He really shouldn't have left the security hub unattended to investigate the kittens, though, don't you think? As for the rest"—he shrugged—"Vincent is used to my pranks."

She sighed. "Always Vincent. You're giving the poor guy a complex, Kit."

"He can take it." Kit peered at her. "How about *your* jailbreak attempt?"

"Remarkably easy once I freed Mr. King. He can *actually* make people invisible."

Kit's face scrunched into a sulk. "I can—"

"No way!"

Aaron's loud exclamation snapped my attention back to him, Kai, and Ezra. The pyromage was holding Sharpie, safely nestled in its sheath, with a look of utter shock.

"You guys got it back?" he asked disbelievingly, despite the fact he was literally holding the sword.

Darius shut the hatch on his SUV with a *thunk*. "Agent Shen was kind enough to make a short detour to recover it while collecting my car keys." He cast an amused look at the young woman beside Kit, then added, "Lingering in the open isn't wise right now. Agent Shen, Agent Morris, would you join us inside?"

"Of course," Agent Shen replied.

Zak, who stood a step behind me with his hood drawn up, shifted backward.

I grabbed his wrist before he could slip away. "Where're you going?"

"That invitation wasn't for me, Tori," he rumbled.

"You're coming in too."

"I'm not welcome, for obvious reasons."

Darius pivoted to face the druid. I tightened my grip on Zak's wrist, standing between him and the guild master but not tall enough to break their eye contact.

An unspoken challenge sizzled in the air between the rogue druid and the former assassin.

"People will close doors on you everywhere you turn," Darius said quietly. "Don't close them on yourself."

Zak blinked, but before he could respond, Darius was sweeping toward the guild. With Kit, Lienna, and the three mages following, he pushed the door open.

"Come on," I told Zak. When he started to protest again, I gave his wrist a hard tug. "If he didn't want you here, he would've said so."

He resisted for a moment longer, then gave in and let me drag him forward.

Noise rolled out of the guild—a swell of excited voices. Sounded like a decent portion of the membership was in there. Eagerness rushed through me, and I zoomed for the door.

I reached it just as Ezra stepped through, holding the door for me. I followed him in. Warmth, light, and sound engulfed me—and the overwhelming presence of people. There wasn't a mere *portion* of the guild present.

From our mini coven of witches, to our sorcerers and scholars, to our alchemists and healers, to our assorted psychics, to the wise and worldly officers, almost every guild member I knew and loved—or tolerated, in the case of a few—was crammed into the pub. The only faces missing were Robin and Amalia, their absence weighing on my mind.

A disorienting wave of voices—speaking, calling, shouting, exclaiming—left me reeling. Still gripping Zak's sleeve, I hooked my arm through Ezra's and braced my feet, trying to get my bearings.

"Everyone," Darius called, raising his voice over the competing conversations. "I'd hoped to return with good news, but I'm afraid our lockdown continues."

Somberness swept over the gathered mythics.

"We aren't giving up, and we've recruited new allies. Allow me to introduce Agent Shen and Agent Morris, who helped with our … exit from custody this evening."

Cautious gazes assessed the two agents.

"As well, a guest you may recognize—Zak, also known as the Crystal Druid and the Ghost."

The sober quiet turned downright icy. Hostility spread like an invisible miasma, every face turning to Zak and every gaze rejecting his presence.

He lifted his chin a little higher, defying their silent condemnation, his expression controlled and green eyes colder than anyone else's. I sighed. He'd apologized to me, but admitting fault to anyone else wasn't happening.

Darius stepped to the druid's side—and to everyone's shock, put his hand on Zak's shoulder.

"Many of you," the guild master said, "are only here today because someone gave you a second chance. This is a guild of second chances, lessons learned, and renewal." He leveled his steely gray gaze on the druid. "Trust is earned. You have a long way to go if you want it, but we'll give you that chance."

Zak returned the GM's stare, saying nothing.

Darius turned to Agent Shen. "Now. As we discussed on the way here, let's begin by proving Ezra's innocence."

22

EVERY MEMBER of the Crow and Hammer present—just under fifty—was crowded around the pub's perimeter. In the open center, cleared of all furniture except one table, Agent Shen had just finished drawing out an intricate array that spanned the tabletop.

Ezra stood across the table from her, patiently waiting.

Gazes darted nervously from him to the agent and back again. I wasn't quite sure how to parse their expressions. Concern from some. A nervous sort of amusement from others, as though they were *almost* certain this was a big joke. How could soft-spoken Ezra be a *demon mage*? It was preposterous.

A few faces gave off a different vibe, though. Girard and Alistair seemed expectant, while Sabrina's expression was carefully closed off—as was Bryce's.

I inspected the telepath where he stood between Drew and Lyndon. Should I be surprised that he knew or suspected more about Ezra than he'd ever let on? He could read minds, after all.

The only person in the guild who didn't seem bothered was Kit Morris, the bizarre agent who'd rescued us. He stood a few steps behind Agent Shen—or Lienna, as he called her—with his hands in his pockets, rocking on his heels as though he were bored.

"What's *with* him?" I muttered under my breath, watching the agent.

Beside me, Zak shifted his weight. Thanks to his presence, only Sin and Sabrina dared to stand near us. Aaron and Kai were positioned behind Ezra, and the sole reason I wasn't with them was a vague worry that Zak would disappear if I left him alone.

He followed my stare to its target. "Whoever made him an MPD agent is either a blind fool or a genius."

"What do you mean?"

His eyes, fixed on Kit, narrowed. "He might be the most terrifying mythic of our generation, and no one realizes it."

My heart skipped a beat.

"Including him," the druid added softly.

I pressed my fingertips to my sternum, encouraging my heart to toughen up already. "What kind of—"

"Who has the supplies I requested?" Lienna asked, stepping back from her newly drawn array.

Sylvia pushed through a cluster of guildeds, elbowing Darren in the kidney on her way past. Joining Lienna, she offered a handful of vials and a grape-sized glass crystal.

Lienna scrutinized the clear crystal, placed it at the bottom of her array, then gave the vials similar assessments. "You measured these precisely?"

"Of course," Sylvia sniffed in an insulted tone.

Uncorking a bottle, Lienna poured what looked like water over a rune. She poured a small pile of sand on another, then a few drops of liquid on a third.

"Fire, if you please," she said to Aaron.

He squinted at the liquid and it ignited with a puff of smoke. The small flame danced merrily.

"Ezra," Lienna instructed, "place your hand in the center of the circle."

He pressed his palm to the tabletop, with water, earth, and fire on three sides of his wrist. Everyone in the room, including me, collectively held their breath as Lienna referenced the small grimoire she'd produced from her satchel, then began to chant. No one else made a sound.

Ezra was no longer a demon mage—but after ten years of demonic possession, was he human enough to pass the test?

Her voice rose, smooth and confident. The puddle of water shimmered, then dissolved into a faint silver glow that lit the lines of the array. The pile of sand disintegrated, and the spell's radiance increased. The flame melted into the array. Once more the glow brightened.

"*Aqua et ignis, terra et ventus, revelate tenebras,*" Lienna intoned.

The silver luminescence swept over Ezra's hand. It rushed up his arm in a wave, passed over his head and shoulders, then whooshed down to his feet. Swirling back up his body, it flashed down his arm, over his hand, and into the circle. The pale light filled the clear glass crystal.

With a final flare, the light snuffed out. The crystal, sitting innocuously on the table, had turned ivory white.

Lienna smiled, the stern agency-ness of her face softening with relief. "The crystal is white. He has no Demonica contamination. Ezra Rowe is neither a demon mage nor a contractor."

"Of course he isn't!" Cameron shouted. "The MPD are idiots!"

"Is MagiPol going to drop the charges against our guild?" someone else called.

"Can we go home yet?" another voice—Alyssa, it sounded like—asked loudly.

"This is an important step," Darius answered, "but only the first. Our guild—and all of you—are not out of danger yet."

As he walked over to Lienna and began conferring with her in a low voice, buzzing conversations erupted around the room. Aaron, Kai, and Ezra had their heads bent together again, all three grinning despite the continued direness of our situation. I couldn't blame them.

"What are we supposed to do, though?" I said, more speaking my thoughts out loud than directing the question at anyone in particular. "It won't take the MPD long to figure out we're here."

"They probably already know," Sin answered, looking up from her phone. "Bounty hunters have been watching the guild day and night, waiting for someone to get reckless and leave."

My brow scrunched. "Leave?"

Sabrina folded her hands in front of her. "When the MPD came down on us a week ago, Darius told everyone that we could either flee right then or go to the guild. With all of us here, no bounty hunters have tried to get inside. As long as we're together, they can't capture us."

That made sense. Gather the troops, batten down the hatches, and pray MagiPol didn't attempt a siege. I imagined everyone was pretty damn sick of these four walls by now, though.

I squinted at Sabrina. "How did you get out, then?"

"Uh." She shuffled her feet. "Darius and a few others have been sneaking in and out, and he helped me."

Had he now.

"By the way," Sin added as she tucked her phone in her pocket, "you should call Justin. I just updated him, but he's been worried sick about you."

My squinty stare shifted to her. "You've been texting my brother?"

A flush spread through her cheeks. "Just … just, um, every day … mostly. He needed to know what was happening!"

I pursed my lips, then shook my head. "I'm glad you kept him in the loop. You told him to stay away from here, right?"

"Yes, he knows to steer clear."

"Good. The last thing I need is—"

"Tori!" Partway across the room, Aaron was waving at me to join him and Kai. "Come on!"

I swiftly scanned the room for Ezra. He was heading up the stairs, accompanied by Elisabetta and Miles. A follow-up healing, I was guessing.

Heading toward Aaron and Kai, I said over my shoulder, "Don't let Zak leave, 'kay?"

Sin and Sabrina looked alarmed by the instruction, while the druid scowled.

I joined the mage pair. "What's up?"

"Agent Shen and Agent Morris are heading back," Aaron explained. "As soon as we have word from them on what's happening at the precinct, I need to meet with Darius and the other officers, but we have some time to clean up."

"Clean up what?" I tugged on a scraggily lock of my hair. "Oh, you mean clean up *us*."

"Exactly."

As he and Kai turned toward the basement stairs, I threw my arms over their broad shoulders, needing the closeness after so much uncertainty and fear. When they each wrapped an arm around my waist, I bit the inside of my cheek against a renewed wave of dread.

We were out of custody, but nothing was fixed. Nothing was okay. We'd saved Ezra, but unless we could convince the MPD of our innocence, we were all doomed anyway.

And our fates now depended on Darius and two MPD agents we'd just met and didn't trust—at least, I didn't trust them. Hard to say how Darius felt.

Walking together, we headed into the hall behind the upper stairs, where the door to the lower level was hidden. There, we had to split up because we couldn't fit through the doorway in our current configuration.

In the quiet basement, the two mages turned toward me as though they'd rehearsed—but more likely, they just knew each other that well.

"You did it, Tori," Kai murmured. "You saved him."

A lump formed in my throat. "I couldn't have done it without you two."

"We were scared out of our minds," Aaron said roughly. "We had nothing to do but sit in those cells and worry."

"Zak saved us," I admitted. "He got us away from the Pandora Knights and arranged a secret location and performed the ritual. We never would've made it without him."

Aaron flexed his jaw as though debating whether he should complain about the druid's involvement.

Kai made a quiet noise in the back of his throat. "Let's shower first, then you can tell us everything that happened."

In the ladies' showers, I raided my locker for soap, shampoo, and clean clothes, and hustled into a shower stall. A minute later, I was standing under the hot water, washing away the sweat and grime of over a week as a wanted rogue.

After a luxuriously long time spent soaking, scrubbing, and shaving, I got out of the shower, dried off, and proceeded to apply product to my hair, moisturize my face, and floss and brush my teeth. *Thoroughly* brush my teeth. May I never go another day without a toothbrush.

Anxious butterflies fluttered in my gut, the unknown hanging over me, but I felt more human than I had in a week. I dressed in cotton yoga pants and a lavender tank top. The scent of clean clothing was like heaven. I finally exited the showers, carrying my jacket, a sweater, clean socks, and my not-so-clean shoes with one hand and my combat belt with the other, the back pouch weighed down by orb-Hoshi.

As I crossed the fitness room, the sound of running water filtered in from the men's showers. No way Aaron or Kai would take this long to clean up. They'd probably been in and out in ten minutes—five to shave, five to shower.

Swerving toward the room, I flipped my belt over my shoulder and rapped on the door. "Aaron? Kai?"

A muffled male voice answered me, and a moment later, the door opened. Ezra held it with one hand, and in the other was a toothbrush, its bristly end in his mouth.

He also wasn't wearing a shirt.

My gaze dropped, seeking out his injuries. Not only were the stab wounds healed, but the tearing of his scars caused by Eterran's exit from his body had transformed into pink lines. The scars would probably be thicker than before, but not by much.

Health assessment complete, I greedily drank in the sight of his jeans clinging to his lean hips, the black waistband of his boxers peeking out, before allowing my attention to return to his face. His pale eye had survived without any additional damage, the scar that ran down his forehead to the hollow of his cheek mostly unchanged.

He canted his head, inviting me into the shower room.

Eyebrows arching with bemusement, I set my things on a nearby weightlifting bench and walked barefoot onto the tile floor. The room was identical to the women's showers: a bank of sinks opposite a wall of lockers, with a bench in the middle. On the other side of the door, several shower stalls were hidden by heavy plastic curtains.

One of the curtains was open and steam floated out, the shower heating up before Ezra got in.

He hurried to the sink and spat out his mouthful of toothpaste. I waited patiently—I could wait patiently all night long with such a mouthwatering view of his thickly muscled arms.

"Sorry," he said after rinsing his mouth. "I just need a hand since you're here."

My eyebrows arched again. "What sort of hand?"

"I can't reach to wash this off." He turned around, showing me his back. Shiny silver lines dotted with runes ran down his spine, most of the array already wiped away.

Ah. Elisabetta's and Miles's work, I assumed. "Sure. Got a cloth?"

"I already put it in the shower. One sec."

He headed for the running shower, and I followed behind him. In the stall, he reached through the spray, water splashing over his arm, and grabbed a white washcloth from the little shelf under the taps where his soap and shampoo waited. He held the cloth under the spray to soak it, then handed it to me.

I bit my lower lip as he turned around. Pressing the cloth to his back, I scrubbed away the lines with slow precision. Very slow. Was I taking my sweet time? Oh yes, I was.

A memory flitted through my head—standing in the shower with Zak, washing dragon blood off his back. I'd been breathless over his appeal, but nothing I'd felt then compared to the way my heart drummed in my chest right now, each beat shuddering inside me.

I wanted to throw the cloth away and put my hands on him. I wanted to wrap my arms around him and never let go. I wanted to—

Realizing my hand had stopped moving, I lowered the washcloth. "Okay, you're good."

He swiveled to face me. "Thanks."

"Mm." Reaching out, I touched one of his scars where it crossed his hip. "How are you feeling?"

"Much better." He watched my hand as I traced the scar up to his sternum, then stretched out his arms to display the other, fainter scars that crisscrossed his bronze skin. "A lot of wear and tear, huh?"

"At least you're still in one piece." I looked up into his mismatched eyes. "So you're feeling good now?"

"Yes?"

"Healthy and hale again?"

"More or less."

"Not going to collapse or anything?"

"No."

"Good." I chucked the washcloth into the shower, not caring where it landed, then hooked my fingers over the back of his neck, pulled his head down, and kissed him.

His lips melded against mine and his hand sank into my damp hair. I pressed into him—and he stepped back, bumping the wall.

"I need to shower," he said, his smooth voice rumbling in a way I very much liked. "You're all clean and I'm—"

I dragged his mouth back to mine and kissed him again, tasting his minty toothpaste.

"Then get in the shower," I breathed against his lips. "I'm not stopping you."

He hesitated—and I opened my lips against his in invitation. His tongue slipped into my mouth and I moaned softly, fingers raking over his shoulders.

Two feet away, the shower pounded against the tile floor, steam drifting around us. I dragged my hands down his chest, over his tense, delicious abs, and found the waist of his jeans.

The breath rushed from his nose when I popped the button. His fly was down an instant later, and I shoved the jeans off his hips. As they slid down, he shifted back and stepped out of them.

In nothing but his boxers, he swept me into him and kissed me again. Wrapping my arms around his neck, I pushed my hips into his, a few thin layers of cotton separating our bodies.

He rumbled wordlessly, one hand sliding under the back of my tank top. His other palm ran up my side and over my breast.

His thumb stroked me through the thin fabric of my top and sports bra, and I arched into his touch, needing more. So much more.

Tearing away from him, I grabbed my shirt and yanked it up over my head. I was still dragging it off my arms when he pulled me back into him. His mouth covered mine, his hot hands running up my sides, over my breasts, then down to my hips.

I shoved my pants down my legs, then threw them and my shirt onto the small bench. Bra and underwear followed.

Ezra watched my every motion with ravenous intensity. His hands were on me before I'd gotten my underclothes safely on the bench, his fingers sliding over my skin. He kissed me, brief and hungry, before his mouth claimed the soft spot under my jaw.

I reached between our bodies. His breath caught when I wiggled my fingers under the waistband of his boxers. I took him in both hands, stroking and caressing until he was panting for air.

Then I pushed his boxers down. As the last piece of fabric between us disappeared, he swept me up off my feet. My bare legs clamped around his waist as he stepped under the shower's spray.

I gasped as the hot water hit us. It cascaded over our naked bodies, but its heat was nothing compared to the molten lava inside me.

I clutched Ezra. Kissing him. Touching him. My hands dragging across every muscle, every scar, every inch of his gorgeous bronze skin. His hands were occupied with holding me up, taking my weight with easy strength, but his mouth was busy—kissing down my neck, teeth grazing my collarbones.

He boosted me higher, one hand bracing my back, then his mouth was exploring my breasts with luscious, devoted attention. Lips and tongue. Tasting and sucking. I arched in his hold, quivering and breathless, hands in his hair, legs clamped tight around his waist.

When I couldn't take it anymore, when I was moments from flying into a million pieces, I squirmed my legs free and slid down him.

His hard length pressed between my thighs, and I moaned as I rubbed against him. He grabbed my hips and stopped my movement, breathing hard.

We stared at each other, his eyes burning and starved for more.

I seized the bar of soap. He continued to hold my hips as I lathered up my hands and pressed them to his chest.

He leaned down. As I ran my hands over his shoulders, rubbing the soap across his skin, he kissed me, slow and hot and consuming. I soaped down his arms, caressing every muscle, and when I pressed closer to run my hands over his back, his fingers tightened.

He pulled my hips into him, then guided them away. Back and forth, back and forth, the length of him sliding between my thighs, rubbing against me. Slow, erotic, unbelievably sensual. I whimpered breathlessly against his mouth but he held the slow, torturous, mind-melting pace.

Kissing with languid, flirting tongues. Hips moving in a slow, unhurried glide. Sweet torment that bordered on agony. We moved together, mouths locked, bodies pressed tight, and the steaming water rained down on us, washing away our fears and stress, our insecurities and doubts, the pain and struggle we'd endured to get here.

Then, as the teasing pleasure ramped higher and our mouths locked with growing urgency, he lifted me off the tiled floor. My shoulders met the cold shower wall as he braced me against it and slowly lowered me again. This time, instead of sliding between my thighs, he slid inside me.

My whole body quivered, muscles clenching, lungs gasping as hot pleasure swept through every nerve. I held him, legs hooked over his hips.

"Tori," he rumbled. His arms tightened as he pinned me against the shower wall, hands gripping my ass, fingers pressing hard into my skin. His muscles bunched, then his hips moved.

His strength supporting me, I could do nothing but hold him—and it was torture, it was bliss, it was pleasure and agony and everything I'd dreamed of and more than I'd ever imagined. Where I would've rushed with frenzied lust, he moved slow and steady and strong. So damn strong. Every thrust sent me spiraling, and I clung to him, pleasure building at a delicious pace.

Building higher. And higher. His mouth dragged at my throat as I panted and moaned. My legs shook. I couldn't take it.

"*Ezra*," I gasped.

His fingers dug into my ass—and he thrust hard into me. Faster. Stronger. I grabbed his hair, and then our mouths were locked, breath rushing, chests heaving. I was rising and falling and spinning out of control, my whole being consumed by the feel of him inside me.

A groan rasped from his throat, and he drove into me. Pleasure rose through me in a wave, sweeping out from my center and overtaking my entire body. I quaked, gasping, moaning, no idea what sort of noise I was making because I couldn't think, drowning in the tides of bliss flooding through me.

Finally, the waves of pleasure softened into a shivery warmth. Ezra leaned into me, half holding me, half pinning me to the wall as he caught his breath, his face pressed against the side of my neck.

I combed my fingers through his drenched hair. My hands were trembling.

"Holy shit," I gasped almost soundlessly.

He must've heard that even over the rushing noise of the shower because his shoulders moved with a silent laugh. He straightened and I let my feet drop to the floor. Too unsteady to take all my weight, I wrapped my arms around his neck, and he pulled me with him under the hot spray of the shower.

I brushed a curly lock off his forehead. "Ezra."

For an instant, just the barest instant, the words I wanted to say stuck in my throat. They'd always been so hard to utter out loud—but I'd never needed to say them more.

"I love you," I whispered.

His fingers traced the edge of my jaw. Leaning down, he softly pressed his lips to mine.

"I love you too," he murmured against my lips. "And I want to love you for the rest of my hopefully long life, if that's what you want."

A quiet tremor shook me. I'd never been good at planning for the future. I rarely knew what I wanted next week, let alone next year. My long-term goals had once consisted of "not getting fired," and more recently, "not dying." For most of my life, I hadn't had a clue what I wanted.

Closing my eyes, I kissed him hard, fingers tangling in his hair.

"Yes," I breathed. "That's exactly what I want."

23

EZRA HAD JUST pulled a clean pair of jeans over his new gray boxers when he froze, his expression locked with sudden chagrin.

Halfway into my tank top, I paused. "What's wrong?"

"Shit, Tori. I didn't even think about protection."

Relaxing, I tugged my shirt down. "It's okay. I have an IUD." I quirked an eyebrow in amusement. "And you've been celibate for, what … eight years? So you're clean, right?"

He opened his mouth, then closed it. "Yes, but I still should've asked you first. I'm sorry."

Warm affection fizzled through me, and I closed the distance between us. Rising on my toes, I pressed my mouth to his.

I'd intended to give him a reassuring peck, but as soon as my lips met his, the banked coals that had barely cooled sparked into full flames. I plastered myself against him, running my hands over his pecs and abs, then down to the front of his undone jeans. His breath caught as I caressed him through the soft fabric.

His tongue flirted with mine, one hand finding my breast for a return caress, then he shifted away with a reluctant sigh.

"If we take much longer, someone will come looking for us."

"Probably Aaron," I muttered. It would fit his track record for interrupting us. Not that it was his fault, but a girl could still be annoyed.

Ezra finished dressing, and I heaved my own sigh when his dark blue, long-sleeved shirt dropped down over his mouthwatering muscles. I could stroke his abs from now until my hundredth birthday and I wouldn't get tired of it.

A rush of warm, damp air escaped the shower room as I opened the door. Ezra followed me out, waiting as I sat on the bench to put on my socks and shoes. I pulled on my sweater too, needing the warmth.

Pausing, I stole one more kiss, then headed for the stairs. The rumble of voices trickled from the main level as we hastened up the steps and through the door.

The pub was as packed as before, and walking into the crowd was like submersing myself in a sea of tension. The relaxing effect of my showers—the first one and the second, more exciting one—evaporated as unease infused me all over again. For a few minutes, I'd forgotten that we were holed up in the guild because bounty hunters would pick us off the moment we left.

Though no one manned the bar, several members were clustered around the stools—including Sin, Sabrina, Kaveri, and Zak. The latter stood a couple long steps away from the women, arms crossed and expression stony, while Kaveri eyed him as though trying to work up the courage to start a conversation.

Sweeping over, I slapped him lightly on the arm. "If you keep scowling, your face'll get stuck like that."

Sharp green eyes swung to me. "You're back. Finally."

"I was overdue for a long-ass shower." I glanced around. "Where're Aaron and Kai?"

"They went upstairs," Sin revealed. "Girard and a few others went too."

"Did they—" I began.

I broke off as Sin pulled her phone out of her pocket, the screen lit with an incoming call. She lifted it to her ear.

"Hello? Yes, she's right here." She held the phone toward me. "It's Justin."

I took the phone. "Justin?"

"Tori," he said in a low, rushed tone. "I'm at work and we just received orders to evacuate eight square blocks of the Eastside. It's just like that demon thing on Halloween."

"They're evacuating?" I repeated blankly.

"Yeah, from Cambie Street to Princess Avenue—and you know what's dead center in the middle?"

The floor shifted unsteadily under my feet. "The Crow and Hammer. *We're* in the center of the evacuation zone."

Sin, Sabrina, and Kaveri stared at me with growing horror as they pieced it together. The only reason the MPD would go so far as to evacuate half the Downtown Eastside was because they expected mythic violence.

They were preparing for a showdown.

"How long?" I blurted into the phone. "How long will the evacuation take?"

"Around four hours. Do you know what's happening?"

"Not yet," I whispered. "I have to go. Sin will keep you updated."

Ending the call, I handed Sin her phone and jerked my head at Zak and Ezra. "Come on."

I didn't have to say more than that. Both men were already sweeping across the pub toward the stairs, and together we rushed up the steps. I glanced into the second-level workroom on the way by, unsurprised to find it empty—or rather, abandoned. Of people. It definitely wasn't empty. An inexplicable collection of boxes and crates had taken over the tables.

I tailed Ezra and Zak up the stairs to the third floor. The door to the offices was open, and a male voice rumbled out.

"… have to assume they've noticed we're not in our cells by now," Aaron was saying as we wheeled through the doorway one after another. "Depending on how they—"

He broke off, brows drawing down at our appearance—and obvious tension.

The room wasn't small, but it felt cramped with nine people in it. Along with Aaron and Kai, Girard, Alistair, Felix, and my favorite ice queen Tabitha were already scattered among the three desks.

"Where's Darius?" Ezra asked urgently.

The door to the GM's office opened in answer, and Darius swept out to join us with his cell phone in his hand.

"Is there a problem—an additional one?" he asked.

"Looks like it," I replied. "Justin, my brother—he's a cop— just called and told me the police are evacuating eight city blocks, and the Crow and Hammer is right in the middle of the evacuation zone."

Darius pressed his lips together, and I really didn't like the sight of our infallible GM's disquiet. Before he could reply, a phone chimed—his cell this time. He tapped the screen.

"Darius here. You're on speakerphone."

"Mr. King. It's Agent Shen."

I had to strain to hear Lienna's voice, not because the volume on Darius's phone was too low but because the agent was whispering so quietly.

"Are you safe?" Darius asked quickly.

"For the moment," she breathed. "Mr. King, you need to evacuate your guild immediately."

My fear turned icier.

"Söze's gone nuclear," a male voice added in a low growl. "I don't know what the hell he's thinking."

I had to assume that was Kit, but he didn't sound like a disarming jokester anymore.

"Shortly after we helped you escape," Lienna explained, still whispering, "a Keys of Solomon member arrived at the precinct to meet with Söze. After their meeting, he announced the MPD was ordering *Damnatio Memoriae* and assigning the Keys of Solomon as the prosecuting guild."

"Ordering what?" Darius asked.

"It means 'condemnation of memory.' It's an emergency provision dating back to ancient Rome that authorizes the complete eradication of the condemned, erasing them from existence and history. It allows the MPD to unconditionally sanction one or more guilds to use as much deadly force as necessary against the offenders."

No one moved. No one spoke.

"That ... that can't be real," Felix muttered, shaking his head. "The MPD isn't that barbaric."

"*Damnatio Memoriae* hasn't been enacted since the nineteenth century," Lienna replied. "It's a last resort for when all standard procedures have failed, and only for cases that risk publicly exposing magic—like mercenary mythics looting and burning villages."

"The Crow and Hammer isn't looting Vancouver!" Girard protested furiously.

"Söze claims most of your members are violent and your guild is preparing to attack the precinct en masse. He talked about your guild stockpiling weapons."

"We have been stockpiling weapons," Darius said. "In preparation for a battle with the Court of the Red Queen."

Ezra folded his arms. "We can probably assume the Court is in control of the Keys of Solomon now."

"That would explain why the Keys want to destroy us," Tabitha said, her eyes flashing. "But why does *Söze* want to destroy us? What's his stake in this?"

"Hell if we know," Kit interjected. "He's a slippery bastard. Before this, he was really subtle, and now he's behaving like Dr. Evil. I'm just waiting for the sharks with laser beams to show up."

I snapped straight. "Wait. The Keys of Solomon member he met with—was it a woman with black hair?"

"Yes, actually," Lienna answered in surprise. "Do you know her?"

"Xanthe," Ezra snarled. "She controls the Court."

Aaron frowned. "I thought Xever was the leader."

"He's the visionary, but Xanthe is the one running the show." Ezra looked at the phone. "Is she still in the precinct?"

"She was accompanying him earlier, but I'm not sure where she is now."

"If she's still around, she could be manipulating him," I said urgently. "The woman is a mentalist. She can make people do anything she wants as long as she can see them."

Kit's quiet curse filtered through the phone.

"I see," Lienna said quietly. "If she's still here, we'll deal with her—but that won't stop *Damnatio Memoriae*. The Keys of Solomon guild has brought in four teams and they're already moving into position around your guild. You need to evacuate now, before you're trapped."

Four teams of hardened combat mythics who specialized in dangerous kill bounties and thrived on violence? I didn't know how many men that equaled, but any number above zero was bad.

Darius stared down at his phone for several long seconds. "Do what you can, Agent Shen, Agent Morris. And stay safe."

"Safe?" Kit mused. "Not unless we plan to hide in this closet all night. It's kind of cozy, but—"

"We'll be in touch," Lienna interrupted, and the call clicked as she disconnected.

Darius slid his phone back into his pocket, and we all watched him, waiting for his response.

"Justin said it would take the police about four hours to clear the neighborhood," I revealed hesitantly. "If we assume the Keys won't move until that's complete, then we have time to evacuate the guild … right?"

"We aren't evacuating."

I twitched, wondering if I'd misheard him.

The GM surveyed us, then focused on his four officers. "There's no way to evacuate over forty mythics without the Keys following us, which would leave us in the same danger but in a less secure location. We could possibly sneak small groups past them, but then we'd be leaving those members with minimal protection."

"But if we can't evacuate," Tabitha whispered, her face white, "what will we do?"

Our guild master raised his hand, palm tilted toward the ceiling. Darkness plunged over the room, then the lights flickered back to life. Darius's gray eyes gleamed.

"We will defend our guild and the members we swore to protect."

I **LINGERED** near the bottom of the stairs, listening as Darius addressed his guild. The four officers, including Aaron, flanked him in silent solidarity. As the GM spoke, the expressions on his audience's faces slowly morphed from confusion to trepidation.

We were going to fight. We were going to defend our guild.

The Keys were professional killers, but we didn't have to defeat however many of them came after us. We just had to stand our ground. We would stand for justice—a word the MPD had forgotten.

And if we were lucky, Kit and Lienna might pull off a miracle and get Söze's orders revoked. But I wasn't counting on it.

My throat tightened, and I crept back up the stairs. I already knew the plan—Darius and the officers had hashed it out in the office upstairs—and I didn't want to listen to it again. I had enough anxiety and guilt to cope with already.

I'd provoked the cult, and the cult had engineered this. Had I saved Ezra's life only to be responsible for the deaths of my other guildmates?

Sucking in a deep, steadying breath, I hastened toward the open doorway into the second-floor workroom—only to pull up short at the sound of Ezra's voice just inside.

"Are you staying or going?"

I hesitated at his cool tone.

"Your guild is going to war with the Keys of Solomon," Zak replied, his tone even more arctic than Ezra's. "Shouldn't you be begging me to stay?"

"You don't care about our guild. You only care about Tori."

"Your point?" When Ezra didn't reply, Zak made a scoffing noise. "I'm trying to make things right with Tori. *That's* why I'm here, not to make friends with your little guild of misfits."

"So you'll let her guildmates die in front of her? I'm sure she'll appreciate that."

"Are you suggesting I single-handedly protect this guild? For a mythic who just lost most of his power, you've got a lot to say about what I should be doing with mine."

"I'm suggesting you be honest for once about what you intend to do."

"Maybe I'm not intending to do anything."

"Then why are you still here?"

I hastily stepped through the doorway before their argument could escalate. The two men turned toward me, Zak scowling irascibly while Ezra was … I wasn't sure. Calm, but in a grim sort of way.

He'd been freed from Eterran for less than twenty-four hours, and I didn't know yet how much he'd changed now that the demon wasn't influencing his mind, eroding his concentration, or requiring him to suppress his emotions.

"No one expects you to protect the guild, Zak," I told him. "Any way you're willing to help is fine."

His narrowed eyes flicked from me to Ezra and back.

"Seriously." I waved my hand. "You've already done enough."

Slipping between them, I peered across the workroom. One row of tables was covered in an assortment of weapons—from swords to spears to axes to guns. Another row held a display of artifacts—medallions, wands, tokens, and more, each marked with runes—and alchemic potions of every color and consistency in different-sized vials.

"Look at all this stuff," I muttered, squinting at a black sphere the size of a golf ball with gold runes etched into it. "Are we going to use all this stuff to fight the Keys?"

"The original plan was to use them against the Court." Ezra joined me at the table. "But they'll work just as well against the Keys."

"Is anything here unclaimed? What can I have?"

Zak appeared on my other side. "Carrying unfamiliar artifacts into battle is dangerous. It's difficult to remember more than one or two new incantations in high-adrenaline situations."

As I grimaced in reluctant agreement, he swung his backpack off his shoulder. It landed on the table with a thump. I watched bemusedly as he dug around inside it, then lifted out a tangle of leather ties. Hanging from the end of each one was a rough-cut crystal.

He fished out a ruby gemstone. "You know how to use the *decidas* spell already."

My eyes widened as he extended it toward me. My fingers, trembling slightly, closed around the cool crystal containing the same fall spell I'd lost.

"One won't be enough." Shaking the tangle of cords, he dragged out two more red crystals. "Here. Same spell."

I took those too, watching in amazement as the three gems clinked together. "These are …"

He contemplated the remaining crystals. After a moment's hesitation, he selected one and dropped the rest in his bag. Holding it up, he let the artifact—an elongated diamond shape two inches long, its violet depths veined with cerulean streaks— swing from its leather cord.

"This will be your one new spell. The incantation is *ori vis siderea*."

"*Ori vis siderea*," I repeated. "What does it do?"

"It's a rapid-fire artifact." At my blank look, he explained, "It can be used six times without recharge, but after that, it's done forever."

"Six times? Without needing to wait at all?"

"Exactly." Stepping away from the table, he grasped the crystal in his palm. "As for what it does … *ori vis siderea*."

The crystal flashed and a softball-sized orb of swirling blue and violet light appeared in his hand. Mini arcs of multicolored electricity crackled off it. My eyes bugged out. He was holding what looked like pure magical energy.

He cocked his arm back. "Ready?"

Alarm shot through my gut. "Wait, wh—"

He lobbed it into me.

The orb hit my right shoulder and burst. The detonation threw me back into Ezra, and as he caught me, I sagged weakly. Glowing purple and blue stains were splashed over me, as though the energy had turned into liquid. Wherever it glowed, my body had gone numb and weak. My right arm hung limply.

"Tori!" Ezra exclaimed.

"Three seconds," Zak said.

The magical stain over my shoulder fizzled away, and feeling returned to my skin. Muscles functioning again, I straightened and gave Zak my meanest glare.

He held the artifact out, the crystal swinging innocently.

"Now you know what it does," he said without the slightest hint of apology. "Five activations left."

I opened my mouth—then closed it again without berating him for attacking me and wasting one of the artifact's uses. Maybe he was right that I needed to understand its precise effects before taking it into battle.

"Thanks," I muttered, gripping the leather cord. As I dropped all four crystals over my head, I looked at him again. "Really. Thank you, Zak. You've done more than enough. If you want to go, that's fine. I won't hold it against you or anything."

Those green eyes fixed on me, boring through my skin. "You want me to leave?"

"Of course not, but this isn't your guild. You need to take care of yourself."

"And you won't care if I leave?"

"No. It won't change anything between us, promise."

A muscle in his jaw ticked as he studied me, lines of tension around his mouth. After a long moment, he gave a short nod. "Understood."

A strange zing of unease ran through me. "Zak—"

He caught my wrist and drew my hand up. Pulling something small from his pocket, he pressed it into my palm.

"You might need this too. Keep it this time."

The tight grip of his fingers disappeared from my wrist, then he turned, his long coat billowing out behind him as he swept toward the open doorway.

As he reached the threshold, he paused. "If you considered me a friend, would you have asked for my help instead of telling me to save my own skin?"

My eyes went wide and a wordless protest scraped my throat. "I didn't—I was just …"

He glanced back, taking in my guilty expression.

"That's what I thought."

Then he was through the doorway. His footsteps thumped quietly down the stairs, the sound quickly lost in the rumble of voices rising from the pub. Jaw hanging, I looked down at the object in my palm—a square of purple fabric, warm from his body heat and heavier than it looked.

The Carapace of Valdurna. His most valuable fae artifact.

I shot a disbelieving glance at Ezra, then vaulted toward the stairs. Taking them two at a time, I charged down the steps, but just before I reached the bottom, I spotted him across the crowded pub.

The pub door opened, and his dark form slipped into the darkness beyond. He didn't look back.

24

THE CROW AND HAMMER boasted twenty-five combat mythics—if you counted the half-trained apprentices. I wasn't sure I should be on the list, considering that, one, "half-trained" was too generous for my skills, and two, I was human.

Unfortunately, three members who did count as experienced and battle-capable were missing from our ranks. When shit hit the fan a week ago and Darius gave everyone the option of barricading together in the guild or running for it, Weldon, Zhi, and Ming had taken Option B. Good riddance to creepy old sorcerer Weldon, and the other two, young Arcana siblings, had never spent much time at the guild anyway.

The last member I would've loved to have standing beside me was Robin, not only because I was desperate to know she was safe, but also because her demon was scary-lethal and we needed all the help we could get.

But without them, that left twenty-two of us. Twenty-two men and women who would protect our guild from the Keys of Solomon bounty hunters while our non-combat guildmates hid inside.

The chilly night breeze smelled of coming rain. Each fitful gust nipped at my cheeks and tugged at my ponytail, a few stray strands dancing around my face.

Ezra stood beside me, his curls hidden under a black beanie. His bad-guy-smasher gloves ran up his arms, and in each hand, he held a short sword. Not his twin terrors, but similar in length and weight.

On my other side, Kai wore solid black, his combat vest loaded with small weapons. His two katana were sheathed at his hip. He wasn't a Crow and Hammer member on paper, but he belonged right here in every way that counted.

Arranged on the street with us were the rest of our combat mythics. Tabitha stood with Laetitia, Sylvia, Cameron, and Darren. Felix was teamed up with his wife Zora, Gwen, Drew, and Cearra. Andrew would lead Lyndon, Ramsey, Philip, and Venus—who was, it turned out, a combat alchemist.

Aaron stood just ahead of me, Ezra, and Kai. The three mages were powerhouses who could play off each other's strengths, and I'd act as their rearguard.

The last three members of our small army strode along the line like generals assessing their troops. Girard, artifacts clipped to his belt and two heavy pistols in shoulder holsters. Alistair, his white beard bristling and a thick, metal-capped staff in one hand.

Leading them was Darius. Dressed entirely in fitted black. Lots of leather. The four silver daggers hanging from his belt drew the most attention, but only a fool would miss the cuff-like bracelets gleaming around his wrists. He might be a rare luminamage, but Darius King wasn't a mythic who limited himself to a single type of weapon.

He reached the center of our line, halted, and glanced across the empty streets. The Crow & Hammer was situated on a corner, meaning enemies could approach from four directions.

"Ezra?" he murmured questioningly.

"I can't sense any movement yet."

Nodding, Darius faced the line of combat mythics, decked in gear, carrying as many weapons as they could wield.

"This is a situation I never thought we would face," he said, his voice carrying to every ear. "As your guild master, I am your guardian and defender. It's my duty and honor to stand between you and the MPD—whether their administrators, field agents, or a guild they've assigned power to.

"The Keys have the power, the temperament, and lawful permission to kill." His gaze swept down the line of mythics. "By myself, I can't protect you, but together, we can protect each other."

On my left, Ezra's swords shifted as he tightened his grip. On my right, Kai closed his gloved hand around the hilt of his longer katana. In front of us, Aaron drew Sharpie from its sheath, orange light from the streetlamp overhead gleaming across the faint, flame-like pattern that rippled down the blade.

My hand drifted to the paintball gun at my belt. Gone were my yellow sleep potions. Sin had given me two magazines. One was a "super" sleep potion, and she'd spent a solid five minutes warning me to stay at least ten feet away from my target before shooting because the stuff would put me in a coma for three days. In the second magazine was a potion she'd simply called "hellfire."

Each magazine held seven paintballs, totaling fourteen shots. Fourteen enemies I could potentially take down.

Zak's crystals hung around my neck. My force-amplifying brass knuckles were already on my fingers. My back pouch was empty—I'd left orb-Hoshi with Kaveri where she'd be safe—but I'd added the Carapace of Valdurna to my left pouch instead.

Ezra's head came up. His eyes half-lidded as he concentrated. "They're coming."

Nodding, Darius turned to the empty intersection. "Remember, we must hold this line. Protect the guild." He glanced back across us, a spark of bleak amusement in his eyes. "And don't die."

He made it sound so simple.

The chill breeze washed over us, its quiet rustle the only sound. Everything was still and empty, the police's neighborhood evacuation thorough and complete. Justin had been texting updates to Sin, and with his final "it's done" message fifteen minutes ago, we'd formed our line outside the guild.

A raindrop landed on my nose, cold and wet. Another plopped on my cheek. As the light rain fell, reflecting the glow of the streetlamps, shadows formed in the distant darkness.

They came from all four directions, striding confidently across the pavement. Nearly all male. Big, strong, muscular. Cold, hardened faces and hungry leers. Weapons of every kind. Mythics of every kind.

My stomach turned over with growing dread as more and more Keys men appeared. Fifteen mythics approached from the east, fifteen from the west. Fifteen more from the north, and yet fifteen more from the south.

Sixty. *Sixty.* That wasn't four *teams!* That was most of the guild split into four attack squads.

The rain increased from a light sprinkle to a steady patter as the four groups reached the intersection. Their lines combined into a single arc of men, weapons, and impending violence.

I sucked in rapid breaths, my head spinning with panic. We'd expected sixteen or twenty men. Instead, we were outnumbered three to one.

A man near the center of their line stepped forward—tall, heavily muscled, thick beard, and wide-set eyes. He carried a two-handed sword as long as he was tall.

"Darius," the man rumbled.

"Nicolas," Darius replied coolly. "You've moved up in the world since we last met."

"'Met,'" the Keys GM repeated, his tone thoughtful. "Is that how you describe murdering my predecessor in front of me?"

"Nothing personal. Business is business."

"As is this. Do understand that we can't accept the surrender of anyone from your guild, as demon mages could be hiding among your members."

My gaze darted over my shoulder, where a handful of familiar faces were visible in the pub's windows. Did the Keys intend to kill all our non-combat members sheltering inside too?

"There are no demon mages in my guild," Darius said.

"Men like you never change." Nicolas heaved the point of his sword off the ground, and his guildeds shifted with restless anticipation. "You shouldn't have sent your pets into my guild. Did you think you'd get away with murdering four of my men?"

"*Ha!*"

I didn't realize that sharp, humorless laugh had come from me until Nicolas's gaze snapped to my face.

"Something funny about the deaths of my men?"

Sixty murderous glares attempted to flay the flesh from my bones. Oops.

"Death is never funny," I called. "But it's funny that you think *we* murdered them. Can't you count?"

"Count?" the Keys GM growled.

"Yeah. You didn't notice the fifth guy? The total stranger killed by … wait, what was it?" I pretended to think. "Oh right. *Demon magic.* Just like Piotr, Anand, and Chay were killed with demon magic." I crossed my arms. "But no, go ahead and blame us."

Kai groaned almost inaudibly.

"Were you there, girl?" The GM bared his teeth. "You're one of the cowards who killed my men?"

Oh. Double oops. Now the entire guild would try to kill me first.

"Have you given any thought to what my guilded is saying, Nicolas?" Darius asked calmly. "Demon magic killed your men and killed the stranger in their midst, and you have no questions about that?"

"My only question is how you snuck your demon mage into my guild." Nicolas raised his fist in a wordless command, and every Keys member who didn't already have a weapon in hand drew one. Crimson power flashed over and over—two dozen demons taking form among the mythics.

Two *dozen* demons. They had more demons than we had fighters. I clenched my hands into fists to hide their trembling.

"I told you there are no demon mages in my guild," Darius said, his quiet voice rolling through the streets. "And you're about to take innocent lives at your enemy's bidding."

"I do no one's bidding, Darius."

Nicolas swung his arm down to signal the charge—and the earth trembled.

Behind the Keys' line, the pavement split open. A pillar of dirt and concrete shot upward, rising two stories and halting when it reached the top of a nearby building.

A man stood on the roof, glaring down at the gathered mythics. He stepped onto the pillar and it sank back into the earth, carrying him downward like an elevator. He thumped his wooden staff into the pillar's top and it went still, three feet above the road.

"Blake?" the Keys GM growled. "What—"

"Are you out of your mind, Nicolas?" The terramage yelled. "You're about to slaughter an innocent guild!"

Nicolas snorted. "You're the one out of his mind."

His gaze sweeping across the assembled Keys men, the terramage struck the earthy pedestal with his staff. "We faced Enright together. We fought a battle more horrific than anything we had ever seen, and we lost friends and comrades. It was worth it because we were stamping out an evil force before it could grow any larger—but that's not what happened. We *didn't* stamp out the cult."

"Shut up, Blake!" someone shouted. "You've lost it!"

"I was in there when Russel, Anand, Piotr, and Chay died," Blake roared. "They were part of the Enright cult! Russel had become a demon mage!"

A man laughed, the sound cruel and mocking.

"Get off that rock, Blake," Nicolas yelled. "You need medical attention."

"I needed medical attention after Russel blew a hole in my chest, not now." Blake pointed his staff at the GM. "Four weeks ago, a Crow and Hammer team showed up at Enright. They were investigating the possibility that the cult had survived, and we found an active sect in Portland. I called for backup. I got an assassin instead. The cult has infiltrated our guild, turned members, and is trying to discredit and kill me—and they're tricking you into destroying the only guild that knows the truth!"

The wet drum of rain on the pavement filled the quiet that answered him.

Nicolas chuffed. "A wild story without any evidence, Blake."

"You know what else you have no proof of?" Blake shouted. "That anyone in that guild is a demon mage!"

"The MPD has—" Nicolas began.

"You know the MPD plays its own games!" The terramage's deep voice rolled right over the GM's. "Everyone who was with me at Enright—you've all talked about the horrors of watching those families die. Women and children, damn it! And now you're going to commit the atrocity yourselves?"

Movement in the mass of combat mythics—scattered men shifting their weight or looking around as if to see what their comrades thought.

"Hell, Nicolas." The mythic beside the GM, a lean man pushing sixty with a wide, weathered face. "He's got a point. I thought this was a hardened combat guild about to go full rogue, not a bunch of misfits and kids."

Kids? We weren't *that* young—though, considering almost half our fighting force was under thirty, we probably looked pretty young to the grizzled veteran.

"The demon mages in Enright were kids too," Nicolas replied flatly.

"This isn't Enright." The man—probably an officer—shook his head and stepped out of the line. "If we're going to dismiss Blake's claims because he doesn't have hard evidence, then I'm not butchering a guild without hard evidence either."

"I've seen the evidence, Tyrone. I got it straight from the source. Now get in position."

"I want the evidence too."

"You calling me a liar?" Nicolas snarled.

Tyrone took another step back. "Why are you acting like this?"

I snapped to attention. Was Nicolas's behavior unusual?

Tyrone sheathed his short sword and pulled out a cell phone. "I'll decide for myself how much blood I want on my hands."

As he began to dial a number, I scanned the rooftops.

Nicolas snatched for Tyrone's phone but the officer twisted away, stepping farther into the no-man's-land between the two guilds. It rang on speaker.

I peered into the darkness behind the lines of Keys mythics, searching for a telltale shadow or glimpse of movement.

The line clicked.

"MPD Hotline," a bored female voice answered. "How may I assist you?"

"This is First Officer Tyrone Bartell of the Keys of Solomon. Get me Agent Söze and make it fast. This is an emergency."

"One moment please."

The line clicked again and a tinny elevator tune filled the street as cold rain peppered our heads. Twenty-two Crow and Hammer mythics, sixty Keys of Solomon bounty hunters, two dozen contracted demons, and one lone terramage stood in silence, waiting.

I surveyed the dense enemy line, three mythics deep, seeking the smallest, slimmest form among them. Kai and Ezra noticed what I was doing and began searching too.

A pop from the phone speaker as a line connected.

"First Officer Tyrone," a cold, commanding woman greeted.

Tyrone started. "Where's Agent Söze? I thought he—"

"Agent Söze is indisposed. You are speaking to Captain Blythe."

"Indisposed? We received orders from him less than—"

"He is unavailable," Blythe interrupted. "Has your guild engaged the Crow and Hammer yet?"

"No," Tyrone muttered. "We—"

"*Damnatio Memoriae* has been rescinded. Withdraw immediately."

Nicolas twitched strangely. "What?"

"I am ordering you to withdraw," Blythe repeated. "If you attack, you'll be charged with murder."

Nicolas went completely still, his face blank of emotion. "Fine. We will withdraw."

"Do so immediately and report to me."

"Yes."

Tyrone pressed his screen, ending the call. A restless shudder ran through the Keys mythics, and I could sense the relief in it. They might be remorseless killers when it came to rogue contractors and demon mages, but many of them were human enough to care if they were killing innocent people.

A similar wave of relief swept across our much smaller line of mythics, but my shoulders didn't sag like theirs. Instead, I rose on my tiptoes, neck craning as I scanned every face across from us.

"Well," Tyrone said, "it seems we—Nicolas?"

The GM's huge two-hand sword fell from his grasp. As it crashed to the pavement, he pulled a dagger from the sheath on his thigh.

"Watch out!" I screamed.

I expected the GM to lunge for his officer, but his feet didn't move. The blade in hand snapped up—and he plunged it into his own throat.

Blood spurted across the black pavement, and the tall man swayed. His mouth gaped, emotion contorting his face—confusion, then horror, then terror. The dagger dropped and he clutched his throat, trying to stop the bleeding.

Knees giving out, he collapsed on the street—and behind him, hidden by his broad form, was a tall, thin woman.

Xanthe smiled.

Right there. Right in the GM's shadow, controlling him. Blending in like always, dressed for combat with her raven hair tied into a high ponytail, her dark eyes glinting as they met mine.

With shocked cries, Tyrone and half a dozen Keys men rushed toward their fallen GM.

A shriek of terror.

My head snapped around. One of the Keys' demons, head and shoulders taller than the humans around it, lifted a man into the air by his neck. The demon's fist clenched, bone crunched, and the struggling man went limp.

Another roar of pain. A scream. A burst of white-hot flame among the Keys' men.

And chaos exploded among them.

Weapons clashed. Bodies surged. Magic flared. Screaming. Shouting.

I reeled backward and Ezra caught my arm. His face was pale, stare locked on the battle erupting in front of us. Keys attacking each other. Keys *killing* each other.

My horrified gaze caught on Xanthe and her smile widened before she disappeared among the struggling bodies.

Several Crow and Hammer members took uncertain steps forward, and Darius lifted a hand, silently commanding them to hold their positions. I craned my neck, trying to follow what was happening. This wasn't Xanthe's doing. It couldn't be. No way she could control this many people.

Men broke away from the tangle, stumbling backward toward us. Tyrone was shouting, rallying his men. Weapons flashed—then the earth heaved. With a crack louder than a cannon blast, a three-foot-wide fissure split the intersection.

In a frantic scramble, men leaped across the chasm, choosing one side or the other—joining their allies so they wouldn't be caught alone among enemies.

As the two forces separated, the violence quieted.

Twenty-five Keys mythics retreated toward our ranks, their backs to us. Tyrone headed the group, and beside him was Blake, who'd somehow crossed the chaos and created the narrow rift, drawing a literal line through the battlefield. He clutched his staff, breathing hard from the strain of the magic he'd unleashed.

He and his allies faced fifteen other Keys, who'd withdrawn to the far end of the intersection. Twelve were demon contractors, their powerful beasts lined up in front of them. The remaining twenty Keys mythics littered the pavement, victims of the sudden outbreak of violence.

Darius slowly slid two daggers from their sheaths, one in each hand.

Across the intersection, the group of Keys traitors parted down the center. A man wearing a black leather duster ambled leisurely toward the battle. He was too far to identify, but the winged demon following obediently on his heels was unmistakable: Nazhivēr.

Xever stopped—and Xanthe appeared from among the Keys' minions she'd corrupted to join him.

Side by side, the two cult leaders faced us.

25

"**READY**," Darius called quietly.

I tensed, my hand jumping to my holstered paintball gun.

"Who are you?" Tyrone shouted at Xever, his voice hoarse with rage.

"Enéas," Xever called. "Eight years ago, you left me no choice but to exterminate all of Enright."

Ezra went rigid beside me.

"Tonight, again due to your interference, we will exterminate your guild."

"And," Xanthe added, pushing her long ponytail off her shoulder, "we'll eliminate the Keys of Solomon. Controlling them has grown tedious since your friends murdered so many of my loyal officers."

Tyrone took half a step back, glancing at Blake. "This is this infiltration you were talking about?"

"We just thought you should know, Enéas," Xanthe taunted, "that you're to blame for all this death."

Ezra bared his teeth, his breath rushing through his nose—then he barked a sudden, quiet laugh. "She's trying to make me lose control in front of everyone."

My eyes widened. Lucky for us, Ezra losing control of his demonic magic was impossible now.

Tyrone shoved to the front of his Keys group. "You're dead—you and all your traitors!"

"Are you going to kill us?" Xever swept his hands out. "You and what army?"

Confusion bubbled through me. I wasn't the only one, and my anxious gaze darted from Ezra to Kai to Aaron's back.

Then I heard it. A raucous, pounding beat. Stone hitting stone, over and over.

Pinkish light glimmered down the avenue to the west. The strange glow grew closer—and the shapes grew clearer. A horde of stocky creatures stomped toward us. Short legs, long arms with claw-tipped fingers, and snarling snouts framed by a crest of horns.

Fiendish gargoyles, their faces identical to the sculptures that had guarded the Court's hidden lair in Enright. Every inch of their stone bodies was carved with runes that glowed pinkish white.

Golems. Animated golems.

As their crashing footfalls grew louder, a new sound reached my ears, low and insidious.

Snarls. Bestial, animal snarls.

I jerked around, facing the street to the north.

If not for the streetlamps, they would've been invisible. Moving with slow, skulking steps on silent paws. Raised hackles, matted fur, milky white eyes. Mutant werewolves with bulging muscles slunk along the pavement, foaming drool dripping from their bared teeth.

Terror screeched along my nerves, and I spun jerkily toward the avenue to the east.

Utterly silent shadows drifted through the night, visible only by the faint rings of red glowing in their eyes. One passed a bit too close to a streetlamp and the orange light illuminated a man—a man with inverted eyes, fingers elongated into claws, and a gaping mouth displaying two long fangs.

They could only be vampires. Lurking in the darkness, they were nearly impossible to see and I couldn't even guess how many prowled our way.

I turned to face the street to the south, the road from which Xever had approached. My mind reeled with panic, and a voice muttered that surely, *surely* there weren't more. Golems, werewolves, and vampires—already an unstoppable force, and they were likely enhanced with demon blood too. Xanthe and Xever couldn't have *more* overpowered forces to deploy, could they?

When I saw Xanthe's smile, I knew the answer.

The Court's final reinforcements didn't stomp or slink or prowl. They simply walked out of the darkness to join their leaders. Six young men, well built but not particularly impressive—except for their eyes.

Eyes sheened with crimson power.

Demon mages. Six of them.

My heart was in my throat, beating so hard and fast that I couldn't breathe around it. I reached out to either side and closed my fingers around Ezra's and Kai's arms, holding on tight.

"Keys!" Darius's voice cracked like a gunshot. "None of these enemies are what you know. They've all been enhanced—they're faster and stronger than you've ever seen."

Tyrone shot a disbelieving look over his shoulder, his jaw clenched and nostrils flared.

"Tyrone, deal with the contractors and demon mages. I'll run interference for you, and my teams will cover our flanks."

Nodding, the officer started barking commands at his diminished troops.

"Aaron, take the wolves," Darius ordered. "Tabitha, the golems. Conserve your strength—and watch out for the vampires when they make their move."

Aaron shot a quick look at Tabitha, then yelled, "Mages, to me! Drew, Philip, Zora, you too!"

"Sorcerers!" Tabitha called. "The goal is to knock them over. If you have an *impello* spell, get it ready! If you work best with a blade, get over to Aaron's team!"

Mythics ran in both directions, rearranging at top speed as the enemy forces approached the perimeter of the intersection.

"Tabitha!" I rushed over to her, digging into a belt pouch. "Here, use this."

I slapped a square of purple fabric into her hand. Her fine eyebrows scrunched in confusion.

"Unfold it and toss it over golems to drain their magic—but be careful, because it can drain your magic too."

Her eyes widened, but I didn't wait for her inevitable questions as I sped back toward the others.

Aaron was shooting off rapid instructions as his team got into position. "Kai, Laetitia, Zora, you're vanguard. Ezra and Drew, rear defense—"

"No." Ezra strode past Aaron, joining Kai at the front of their group, blades in hand. "I'm taking the lead this time."

Aaron recovered from his surprise in an instant. "Laetitia, take defense. Lyndon, you—"

I missed his order as Tyrone shouted at his men. The Keys had split into five teams of five and they faced the largest force, straight across the intersection—Xanthe and Xever, fifteen Keys of Solomon traitors, their twelve demons, six demon mages, and an unknown number of vampires.

How could twenty-five Keys mythics even slow that force down? The demon mages alone would obliterate them.

As I stood a few steps behind Darius, between the two Crow and Hammer teams and unsure where to go, Xanthe caught my eye. Her stare, roving across my guildmates, came to a halt on Darius.

No. She couldn't take control of him. She couldn't—

Darius raised his dagger into the air.

For a bare instant, everyone seemed to pause, all eyes turning to the GM. He swept the blade down to point at Xanthe and Xever.

Complete and utter blackness engulfed the enemy force—a perfect rectangle of ebony nothingness that popped over them like a light switch had been shut off. Shouts of alarm rang out from the darkness. The mythics inside it couldn't see.

Darius's lumina magic. He was blinding the enemy so they couldn't attack all at once.

Twelve demons barreled out of the darkness—and the Keys teams answered with enraged bellows as they ran to meet their first opponents, their own demons heading the charge.

"Cut off the werewolves!" Aaron roared. "Before they reach the intersection!"

I turned away from the exploding battle between Keys and demons as Aaron led his team toward the oncoming werewolf pack. Ezra and Kai flanked him, weapons in hand, and the others spread out away from them.

An instant later, I understood why.

The first wolf, a huge brute with dirty white fur, sprang for Aaron—and the pyromage's torso burst into flame. Rain evaporated in hissing clouds of steam as fire crawled over him, turning him into a flaming wraith. He slashed with Sharpie.

An inferno blasted from his blade and slammed into the attacking wolf. The pale blue blaze rocketed across the beast and rushed into the next three coming behind it.

A streetlamp exploded, glass raining down. Kai pointed his katana skyward as electricity leaped to the metal in a thick, twisting rope. He turned the sword counterclockwise.

Lighting burst over five wolves at once. The canines crumpled, limbs twitching.

And Ezra rushed in. As the shocked wolves clambered up again, he slashed downward with his blades. The air rippled— and a near-invisible wind-blade rushed away from him. It cut across three wolves, one after another. Blood sprayed.

Then the rest of the pack attacked.

I wrenched my paintball gun from its holster and sprinted to join my friends.

Our team crashed into the wolves, magic and magery flying. Aaron and Kai rained fire and lightning down on the wolves, and Ezra lunged in, using steel blades and air blades alike to cut the beasts down.

A scream—a wolf had leaped into Laetitia, knocking her to the pavement.

My gun swung around. As she kicked the wolf away, I shot at its back. The super sleep potion hit—and instead of a splatter of yellow liquid, it burst into a cloud of sparkling pink. The wolf's head snapped toward me, foaming fangs gaping.

The cloud of colorful mist condensed around the wolf, coating its fur like oil. The werewolf crumpled to the ground, tongue lolling out.

Holy shit. Sin hadn't been kidding that it was strong stuff.

Laetitia rolled to her feet, her *bo* staff spinning, and I darted behind her. As another wolf lunged out of the shadows, I fired into its face. The shot burst into mist, which the wolf lunged straight through. I backpedaled frantically, readying my brass-knuckled fist, but the moment before it reached me, the wolf plowed face-first into the pavement.

"Tori!" Laetitia cried.

I started to turn and a heavy weight crashed into my side.

Slamming into the ground, I shoved my gun up. The attacking wolf's jaws crunched on the metal barrel, and I flung my fist into its chest with all my strength. "*Ori amplifico!*"

The blow threw the wolf off me. It staggered, then braced to leap for my throat.

Ezra appeared. His blade plunged into its back, piercing its heart. He wrenched the steel out, lifting the heavy body before it slid off the sword. He grabbed my outstretched hand and hauled me up—then spun toward the wolf leaping for his blind side.

In midleap, a pale blue glow engulfed the wolf. It froze, hovering above the ground, legs outstretched and fangs bared. The glow brightened, then the wolf dropped to the pavement in a heap and didn't move.

A flash of light gray fur. An animal the size of a coyote hopped onto the fallen wolf. With a body like a weasel, the tail of a fox, and deer antlers, it was the weirdest thing I'd ever seen. Then it turned its head toward me, revealing pale blue eyes set in the face of a barn owl, framed by a thick, furry mane.

Now *that* was the weirdest thing I'd ever seen.

Philip ran out of the chaos, two tiny winged pixies zooming around him. He shot toward Drew, who was being overwhelmed by a pair of brown wolves, and the owl-faced fae leaped off its motionless victim to follow the witch.

I whipped around as Ezra knocked three wolves away with a single gust of wind.

I took aim. "Get back, Ezra!"

Three shots. Two hit but the third wolf ducked the paintball. As potion mist coated the first two wolves, Ezra ran the third one through.

But there were still more.

Ezra cut left to help Zora, and I backed away, allowing myself one second to glance across Aaron, wreathed in flame, and Kai, pulling endless streams of power from the streetlamps, then back toward the rest of the war.

Darius's pitch-black box still sat over the intersection's far end, but its walls were moving—he was shifting the darkness, keeping as many enemies inside its blinding effect as he could. The Keys teams were arranged around its perimeter, battling contracted demons and two of the demon mages who'd made it out.

Darius stood unmoving, shoulders rigid and attention wholly focused on the massive distortion of light he was manipulating. Girard and Alistair stood in front of him. The ground around them had split open, and glowing red lava bubbled in the gaps, black smoke coiling upward. Scattered around the sizzling lava pools were bodies—including two demons. The enemy had tried to take out our most powerful mythic, but they hadn't been able to get through his protectors.

I was about to return to the wolf battle when I caught a glimpse of movement—a streak of shadow, darting past Darius, Girard, and Alistair. Heading away from the battles.

Heading *for the guild.*

The creature slid to a stop a few feet from the Crow and Hammer's door—a tall, thin vampire with fingers that had elongated into stiff claws.

Another appeared beside the first. And another. And another. They gathered in front of the guild, mouths hanging open, fangs displayed. Two slammed into the door and two more grabbed the bars on the windows and wrenched.

Wood splintered. Metal groaned and snapped.

My heart lurched. Our guildmates were in there. Sin and Sabrina and Kaveri and all my friends who didn't have magic to fight demons and monsters.

A cacophony of alarmed shouts went up from the other side of the intersection, and I jolted, my attention drawn in two directions at once.

Darius's black rectangle had vanished. He'd turned away, a blade pointing at the bloodsucking fiends breaking down the guild door. The forces he'd been blinding charged into the Keys teams, and crimson power exploded.

I launched forward. A trick. A diversion. The enemy couldn't reach Darius so they were distracting him instead.

The vampires reeled back from the building, clutching their faces in confusion. Blinded by Darius's magic. I swung my gun up. Pink mist burst over a vamp. It shook its head. The mist hung in the air, then dissolved to nothing.

Shit. It didn't work on vampires? Not good!

I dropped the clip out and shoved the second one in. Taking aim, I fired a shot.

An orange paintball burst against the nearest vampire's chest—and fire exploded across it. A horrendous shriek of agony wrenched from its gaping jaw and it flailed at the flames. The fire stuck to its hands, spreading everywhere it touched. Staggering, it collapsed to the ground, writhing.

Whoa. Hellfire indeed.

I took aim and fired again—and every single vamp blurred with speed as it leaped aside. My shot flew past them all and hit Darius's SUV. Liquid fire splattered the hatch and a rear tire burst with a fizzing pop.

Even blinded, the vampires had heard the sound of the paintball gun and dodged.

Teeth gritted, I aimed into their group and pulled the trigger rapidly. Four shots flew out, striking two vampires as they tried to duck away. The flaming duo crumpled to the ground, screaming.

That left six blind but deadly undead monsters.

Holstering my gun, I yanked a crystal off my neck and rushed in. I slapped a crystal against one's shoulder.

"*Ori decid—*"

The vampire's arm snapped out, fast as Kai's lightning.

Its blow only grazed my shoulder—and the inhuman force sent me into a wild spin. I slammed into the wall, agony burning in my shoulder. I shoved off, fumbling with my remaining crystals, and grasped the blue-streaked violet one.

"*Ori vis siderea,*" I gasped.

My palm tingled. A sizzling orb of arcane power formed in my hand, and as I pulled it away from the crystal, the magic clung to my palm, insubstantial but somehow *real*, like an extra dense, static-charged bubble of … *something*.

Drawing my arm back, I hurled it into the vampire's chest.

The power exploded on impact, and the vampire tottered backward, stained with numbing violet magic.

I leaped after it, ruby artifact in hand. "*Ori decidas!*"

This time, I rammed the crystal into the vamp's throat, and it collapsed. Leaving the crystal sitting on the creature, I shot back up.

Claws hooked into my arm. A vampire wrenched me closer, fangs aimed for my throat.

Its head exploded.

The gunshot rang in my ears as I dropped back to my feet. Thirty yards away, Girard aimed his pistol at another vampire. A different vamp grabbed the back of my jacket, but I hardly noticed—because Darius and Girard had turned toward the guild to hold off the vampires. Alistair, a few steps away from them, had just melted another vamp into lava goo.

They didn't notice what was coming for them.

"*Behind you!*" I screamed.

They couldn't hear me—the cries, bangs, crashes, shouts, explosions of power were too deafening—but they must've read my lips. Darius and Girard whipped around.

Crimson power blazing up his arms, the winged demon Nazhivēr plunged out of the sky and slammed down on them, driving Girard and Darius into the ground.

I screamed—then screamed even more as the vampire who'd grabbed me crushed me against its chest. Its claws scraped my scalp as it wrenched my head sideways, and hot breath washed over my neck.

A low, vicious snarl.

A shaggy black wolf with ruby eyes vaulted out of nothingness, straight for me. Its gaping muzzle full of white fangs shot past my shoulder and the vampire toppled as the canine slammed us over backward. I wrenched free, leaped up, and darted away.

The varg rushed after me, leaving the vampire with its throat torn out.

I stumbled to a standstill, gawking at the fae wolf positioned beside me. With a shimmer, a second one appeared on my other side.

The vampires pivoted to face us—and I realized there were even more of them now than before. A full dozen. And—my gorge rose—the one with its throat torn up had just climbed onto its feet, blood drenching its front. The thirteen vampires focused their eerie stares on me.

The vargs snarled in warning.

Shadows writhed and danced in a way that was *very* not natural, and as one, the vampires looked up.

Phantom black wings outstretched and long feathers rippling, Zak dropped off the guild's roof. He landed in a crouch in the vampires' midst, rose to his full height, and swept both arms wide.

Black blades of shadow slashed out from his hands, tearing through the vampires. They screeched and hissed, scattering under the onslaught.

Zak's eyes met mine, and they shone with electric fae magic. Lallakai was back, concealed in his body and filling him with her power.

"I'll keep them out of the guild," he rumbled. "Help the others."

The vampires regrouped, their inverted black and white eyes fixed on the druid with ravenous hunger. Vampires were created by fae possession, and fae couldn't resist the lure of a druid's power.

"But—"

"Go!" he snarled, stretching his hand toward the nearest vampire.

My throat closed, and I spun on my heel, the two vargs still attached to my sides like well-trained German Shepherds.

Crimson power exploded far too close.

Debris pelted me, and I threw my arms over my face. When I lowered them, my chest seized with terror.

Girard was on the ground, unmoving. Alistair was on his knees, struggling to rise with blood coursing from a slashing wound across his chest. And Nazhivēr had just grabbed Darius by the throat, lifting the GM off his feet.

Darius thrust his dagger at the demon's face, but Nazhivēr caught his wrist. The demon bared his teeth in a vicious smile.

I wasn't close enough to help. No one was close enough to save Darius.

Nazhivēr paused. His head turned, glowing magma eyes narrowing as something else caught his attention.

In an empty gap between battles, thirty feet away, a man stood alone. Unmoving. Waiting. His garments were solid black and the hood of his combat-styled jacket was pulled up, hiding his face in shadows.

Nazhivēr opened his hand, letting Darius drop. He pivoted to face the stranger.

The man sank into a low defensive stance—and crimson light ignited over his hands. The power streaked up his arms, and six-inch phantom talons formed over his fingertips.

A demon mage?

Snarling, Nazhivēr summoned near-identical talons. His tail snapped, wings flaring. The mysterious demon mage waited a heartbeat more—then sprang forward.

Fast. Way faster than Ezra. Impossibly fast!

Nazhivēr lunged to meet his charge, and the man dove. He slid past the demon, launched off the ground, and slammed both sets of talons into Nazhivēr's lower back.

The demon roared furiously and snapped his tail up, shoving the man away. Demonic power blazed up the man's arms as he caught his balance, then leaped a full eight feet into the air from a standstill.

He caught one of Nazhivēr's long horns, wrenching his head to the side, and almost got his talons in the demon's throat before Nazhivēr snatched the man's leg and flung him off.

The man twisted in mid-air and landed on his feet a few yards away—and the streetlight's glow caught on movement directly behind him.

A thin, whip-like tail lashed back and forth behind the man.

And I realized he wasn't a man.

As Nazhivēr spread his wings, two more figures ran out of the darkness—a slim, petite one and a tall, willowy one, both dressed in similar black clothing with hoods drawn up. But I recognized that mismatched pair.

"Robin?" I shrieked. "Amalia?"

The shorter one glanced at me, the light catching on her pale face and large eyes, then she streaked toward Nazhivēr as the demon began a blazing crimson spell.

Darius was back on his feet, and his daggers gleamed as he circled around the furious demon. But he wasn't angling to join their fight. He was heading toward the other end of the intersection, where the most violent battle raged. The combatants had mixed, and he could no longer blind a large group of them.

Between one step and the next, he disappeared.

Assassin. The word whispered in my mind. He was going in there. Invisible, undetectable—and utterly lethal.

But alone, he wasn't enough. The full might of the Court's demons and demon mages were tearing through what remained of the Keys forces. They were being overwhelmed. They were dying.

And we were next.

"Stay with Zak," I told the two vargs, then sprinted toward the western avenue where Tabitha and her team fought the stone golems. They'd pushed—or lured—their enemies down the street, away from everyone else.

"Tabitha!" I shrieked.

I dashed into the chaos—the ground littered with motionless gargoyles and a few terrifyingly motionless human bodies that I didn't stop to identify. Up ahead, Tabitha and a handful of remaining mythics were dodging the swinging claws of the golems.

In her hand was the rippling purple fabric of the Carapace of Valdurna, its shimmering light dancing over the nearby buildings.

As a golem spun to attack Sylvia, Tabitha flung it over the creature. The fabric settled over its stone head and its glowing runes dimmed. The magic sucked out of it, and she swept the cloak off as the golem toppled.

"Tabitha!"

She spun to face me, eyes wide. "What's happening?"

"We need you!" I grabbed the fae artifact from her hand. "Leave the last few golems—we have bigger problems."

As I clutched the soft fabric, numbness tingled through my hand. I ignored it, running back toward the intersection, my feet pounding. I rushed back onto the battlefield.

Screaming, howling violence. I careened past the vampires ringed in front of the guild, their bodies marred by gory wounds and missing limbs that didn't affect them. Zak's dark form was like a bonfire of black shadows amidst them.

Praying he could handle the undead horde, I raced toward the northern street where the werewolf battle still raged, the beastly monsters almost as difficult to kill as vampires. Orange light flickered wildly—the buildings were on fire.

I squinted, searching for Aaron's fiery shape among the spreading flames.

"Tori!"

My head snapped in the other direction, and I veered off course. I didn't need to go get my three mages. They stood together, ready, waiting, as though they'd somehow known what I planned to do.

Aaron, his heat-resistant shirt burned away, blood streaking one arm from the tearing bite over his elbow. Sharpie was in his other hand, the blade steady.

Kai, smudged with soot, held his katana casually, his dark hair windswept and streaks of rain cutting through the blood running down his face.

And Ezra, a short sword in each hand, eyes burning with readiness. Of the three mages, he alone was unscathed.

As I sprinted to them, I yanked at my belt buckle. It gave way, and I shoved my brass knuckles into it. My remaining three crystals went into a pouch, then I tossed it. Ezra caught it out of the air.

"We're going after Xanthe and Xever," I yelled over the pandemonium, wasting no time on a tearful reunion. "I'll clear a path. Follow behind me as close as you can."

Whirling toward the horrific battle ahead, I flipped the Carapace open and swept it over my shoulders.

26

"TORI, TAKE THIS."

Numbness washed over my body, deadening my limbs, and it took me a second to look up.

Kai stood beside me, holding his shorter katana with the hilt extended toward me. I grasped the fabric-wrapped handle. He released the blade and hefted his long katana.

Ezra joined me on my other side, my combat belt hooked on an empty sword sheath at his hip. "Xanthe and Xever will be at the back, out of danger."

I nodded. "I think Darius is going for them too. We—"

Crimson magic exploded. Nazhivēr roared, silhouetted against the eerie glow with his wings spread.

The dark form of the mysterious man in black flew backward, thrown by the blast. He landed in a handstand and flipped neatly onto his feet. Sinking into a crouch, he set his feet and launched back toward his opponent, faster than any human. Red magic crawled over his arms, sparking off his shoulders.

Aaron's and Kai's jaws hung open. "Is that—"

"Yep. Leave Nazhivēr to them." I reached for the Carapace's hood. "Stick with me."

Three pairs of eyes locked on mine.

"We'll be with you," Ezra said.

I pulled the hood up and the world went quiet.

The cessation of sound pressed against my ears. With all my senses but vision muted, I faced the battle. My numbed limbs wouldn't stop me, nor the chill spreading through my core as the Carapace's magic sucked at my human body, attempting to drain my magic.

Except I had no magic. I was as human as could be, and the Carapace, instead of being a dangerous liability, was my best weapon.

As long as I wore it, I was impervious to any attack, physical or magical. I would clear the path.

I launched forward, and the three mages ran after me. The overwhelming violence of the battle hit hard as I closed in on it—silent explosions of magic and fire, flashes of light, writhing men, struggling enemies, brutal demons. Shattered concrete and flying debris.

And bodies. Unmoving bodies scattered over the ground.

The silence in my ears softened the effect, and I scanned for the best path. Seven demons still moved. Four demon mages. Dozens of men, and I couldn't tell friend and foe apart.

But there—where the south street met the intersection. Xanthe and Xever stood side by side, surrounded by three cultists, three wolves, and two vampires.

They were our goal.

Speeding up, I leaped across the crevice that divided the intersection in two. The cloak fluttered, clinging to my arms as the ends floated outward. I reached the edge of the melee.

Mythics whipped toward me. Shock, disbelief. Then a sorcerer hurled a spell in my direction.

The green light dissolved into sparkles, which the Carapace devoured. I swiped clumsily with Kai's katana and the man stumbled back. I shot past him—and orange light flared as Aaron dealt with the enemy.

All around me, magic dissolved and sucked into the fae cloak. Men jumped away, no idea what I was or what the cloak was doing. I plowed through, the guys right behind me, drawing ever closer to the cult leaders.

Then the demon mages noticed us.

Three of them peeled away from their opponents. Crimson magic blazed up over their hands, spells taking form. Terror weakened my knees as I flung my arms out. Ezra, Aaron, and Kai ducked behind the Carapace's outstretched fabric.

The demon mages' spells exploded from their hands. Screaming red power blasted toward me—and dissolved. The Carapace absorbed it all with a soft ripple of amethyst fabric.

As the demon mages' lips curled into furious sneers, the middlemost one jolted.

A flicker of movement, of light. For an instant, Darius appeared behind the demon mage, his dagger sliding smoothly into the man's jugular. The assassin pulled his blade free, and the demon mage clutched his throat, magma eyes blazing as the demon within realized his host was dying.

The luminamage vanished again, bending the light around his body.

I launched forward, brandishing my sword as the cloak billowed. The demon mages darted uncertainly away—and Ezra shot past my left side.

A blast of wind to throw a demon mage back. A slash of his sword, a blade of air. Blood sprayed. The demon mage flung out a fist and Ezra caught it with a boom of wind. His other sword plunged into the cultist's gut.

I whirled toward the last demon mage—just as the man erupted into flame. His mouth opened in a scream I couldn't hear. Then Kai pointed with his sword, and a thick bolt of electricity leaped for the man's chest. He arched, then buckled limply.

Aaron's lips moved with soundless words. *Go, Tori.*

I ran. They sprinted after me, the Carapace absorbing every attack that flew our way. Enemies fell back.

Then we broke free of the chaos and into the open space between the battle and its generals. I pushed the cloak's hood off as the mages spread out on my left. Three cultists, three werewolves, and two vampires to kill before we could reach the Court's leaders. And there was Xanthe's power to worry about.

Her cruel smile spread as she focused on Aaron.

"Darius!" I yelled at the top of my lungs. "Blind her!"

The GM didn't appear, but Xanthe started. She flung a hand out and grabbed Xever's arm.

Standing safely behind their lieutenants, Xever smirked. "You've shown remarkable restraint, Enéas. Still hoping to plead not guilty to the charges?"

Ezra spun his blades. "Is that what you think?"

Xever's eyes narrowed. He opened his mouth—

A vampire lieutenant's chest exploded.

The gunshot rang painfully in my ears as the vampire keeled over. With a shimmer of light, Girard appeared on my left, pistol still aimed at the vampire. Alistair rippled into view, his staff in hand and blood all over his shirt. And between the two, Darius appeared.

He no longer held his silver daggers. Instead, he gripped the long handle of a huge silver war hammer, the heavy end resting on the ground in front of him. But it wasn't just *any* war hammer—it was the one that normally hung above my bar.

When the hell had he gotten hold of that? Had Girard and Alistair brought it? I'd thought they were down for the count!

"Xanthe." Darius's voice cut like blades of ice. "Xever. When you decided to destroy my guild, you should've considered who you were challenging."

Even blinded, Xanthe curled her upper lip. "Is that so? You—"

Darius didn't wait for her to finish. He swung the hammer up and slammed it into the ground.

Grayish sparks burst from the point of impact and a wave of concussive force rocketed outward, hurling the enemy group off their feet.

Ezra, Aaron, and Kai charged for the fallen cultists. Darius heaved the war hammer to Alistair, who caught it one-handed, the thick muscles in his bare arms bunching. He dropped his staff, took a two-handed grip on the hammer's handle, and launched forward with Girard on his heels.

Darius drew his two backup daggers and vanished from sight.

I flipped the Carapace's hood up, adjusted my grip on my borrowed katana, and ran straight into the melee. Fire, wind, lightning, shaking earth, spewing lava. The silver hammer swung down and crushed a werewolf beneath it.

As their lieutenants fought and died, Xever backed away, Xanthe clinging to his arm.

Launching in front of a spell a cultist had fired at Kai, I rushed through the battling mythics and monsters. No one could touch me—or stop me—and I burst out the other side. Flipping the cloak open to free my arm, I pointed my katana at the two cult leaders.

Xever smiled coldly, and crimson light flashed on his chest. The infernus hanging around his neck glowed—and red power streaked from across the battlefield and struck the pendant. It filled the silver disc, then burst out again.

Nazhivēr took form in front of me.

On the plus side, he wasn't looking too great—bleeding gashes raked his limbs and one of his wings had a long tear in the membrane. On the downside, I was now facing a demon all by myself.

Clutching my sword, I lunged at the demon.

He slid aside with inhuman speed and swung at my head. His fist slowed as though he were trying to punch me through ever-thickening mud and came to a halt without ever touching me.

I slashed the sword down his immobile arm.

As thick demon blood splattered from the new wound, the demon's other hand snapped closed around my wrist—the one sticking out from the Carapace's folds and very much *not* invincible.

Nazhivēr wrenched me off my feet. The cloak flapped open, exposing me to attack.

Gasping, I grabbed the fluttering edge and threw it over the demon's head. Crimson sparkles whooshed out of Nazhivēr and sucked into the Carapace. His glowing eyes widened.

He flung me away.

The cloak tore free from my shoulders as I pitched backward, my head on a collision course with the pavement and limbs flailing. I plunged down—and landed on a thick cushion of nothingness.

The dense pillow of air beneath me deflated, and I thudded to the ground. Rolling over, I shot to my feet.

Ezra stood beside me, blades angled at the cult leaders and Nazhivēr.

The Carapace had caught on the demon's horns, and he ripped the artifact off, throwing it aside. I clutched my sword in both hands, knowing I couldn't reach the cloak without Nazhivēr killing me.

The demon's glowing stare raked Ezra. "Is Eterran too cowardly to …" His eyes narrowed to slits, and his expression froze. "Where is Eterran?"

"Good question," Ezra growled.

"I cannot sense him."

Ezra smiled.

Nazhivēr hissed furiously. "What did you do? How did you break the contract?"

"What?" Xever demanded from behind his demon. "A demon mage contract can never—"

With a flash of crimson, a dark shape leaped over the battling mythics behind us and landed with a thump ahead of Ezra. The newcomer straightened, chest heaving as he caught his breath. Dressed in black, hood drawn up, and a long, thin tail snapping behind him.

Robin clung to his back, her hood off and hair mussed into a wild tangle.

I saw the exact moment Xever realized the black-clad figure wasn't a man but a demon—Zylas, inexplicably dressed like the baddest of badass combat mythics.

"Robin and Zylas," he observed as he pushed up his sleeves, revealing rows of silver bands around his arms. "How kind of you to join us. Xanthe?"

His partner smiled, her confidence unruffled despite the fact that she was still blinded. "Go play with your toys, then, Xever, and I'll deal with the important matters, as I always do."

Smirking, he retreated, moving backward down the street to escape the impending violence. Nazhivēr moved in front of his master, wings spreading protectively.

A low, husky laugh rumbled from Zylas. Still carrying Robin on his back, he vaulted across the gap between him and his enemies, landing in a crouch a foot from Nazhivēr's knees.

"*Ori eruptum impello!*" Robin shouted.

A silver dome expanded around her, throwing the demon backward.

Leaving her and Zylas to it, I faced Xanthe. How did she think she could deal with us in that state?

She smiled and hooked a finger under the collar of her jacket. With a tug, she lifted out a jangling cluster of silver pendants. Three flat discs with jagged markings. Was each medallion an infernus?

She couldn't control multiple demons at once, could she?

Crimson flared across all three. Power leaped outward and hit the ground in three spots. It flowed upward, taller than Zylas—than Aaron—than Nazhivēr. At seven feet, the three demons solidified.

Glowing crimson eyes. Long, curved horns rising above hairless heads. Spines jutting from their elbows. Massive wings on thick shoulders. Long, powerful tails with bone-crushing plates on the end.

It was the near-indestructible unbound demon from Halloween—times three.

"First House demons?" Ezra whispered hoarsely. "*Three* of them? How?"

"In case you didn't know," Xanthe purred, "demons can see even in complete darkness. The luminamage can't blind them."

I tensed even more.

Xanthe waved a hand in our general direction. "Kill them all."

The three demons, in almost perfect unison, flexed their fingers. Crimson lit over their claws and veined up their thick arms. Jagged spell circles flared over the demons' wrists—a different spell for each of them. They lifted their arms, aiming the coming attacks at us.

I dove for the ground. Landing in a roll I'd practiced a hundred times on the mats in Aaron's basement, I snatched up the Carapace. I was still slinging it over my shoulders as I leaped in front of the demons' triple attack.

But the cloak wasn't properly in place around me.

Or maybe I'd pushed the fae artifact too far.

Or maybe the demons' combined magic was just too much.

"Tori!"

The next thing to register in my awareness was significant pain.

Arms were clutching me. I groaned. Why did everything hurt so goddamn much? And why were my eyes closed?

I wrenched them open. I hung in Ezra's grasp, Aaron flanking us on one side and Kai on the other. The three demons were straight ahead, and since everyone was basically in the same positions, I guessed I'd blacked out for only a few seconds.

The Carapace, though. It lay on the ground, a tangle of purple fabric that neither sparkled nor shimmered nor did anything remotely fantastical.

Ezra pushed me behind him, and I wavered unsteadily, unsure how or where I was injured. Everything hurt. How much of that blast had the Carapace absorbed and how much of the hit had I taken?

"Stay back, Tori," he ordered.

I realized he was about to attack. In the instant before he leaped forward, I snatched my combat belt off his sword sheath. Aaron swept after him, the flames on his sword doused but the blade dripping blood. On his heels, Kai darted toward the demons, electricity crackling over his limbs.

Movement flashed past my other side. Alistair, still wielding the war hammer. Girard, his pistols exchanged for handfuls of artifacts. And Darius, who wasn't bothering to hide himself when the demons could see him anyway.

Farther up the street, crimson power burst and crackled—Zylas and Nazhivēr battling. Zylas couldn't help us. He had his own deadly opponent.

How could the six mythics defeat three of the most powerful demons that existed?

A battle cry rang out behind me. I flung a glance over my shoulder—and my heart leaped.

Tabitha, Andrew, Laetitia, Lyndon, Ramsey, Gwen, and Drew cut through the debris, weapons at the ready. Bleeding, battered, but ready to join the final fight. They streamed past me and leaped into the chaos, Tabitha and Andrew shouting commands.

For any of them to survive this, we couldn't count on killing the demons. We had to stop the contractor—but it would take the combined efforts of everyone else just to keep the demons at bay.

Sucking in a deep breath, I scanned the raging battle—Ezra blasting a demon with air blades, Aaron lunging for its flank, Kai peppering it with throwing knives and sending bolts of electricity leaping for its body, each flash accompanied by a thunder-like crack.

Alistair slammed the war hammer into the ground and zigzagging fissures split the earth in every direction. Bubbling lava spewed from the cracks as, a few paces away, Tabitha cast a wave of ice across the legs of the middle demon, freezing its feet to the ground.

I picked my route—and ran into the howling violence.

Ducking Lyndon's mace as he swung it at Tabitha's frozen demon. Springing over a lava-filled crevice. Diving beneath a demon's sweeping wing as it vaulted skyward, crimson power rippling up its arm.

A sphere of red power exploded nearby, hurling me off my feet. I crashed to the ground, rolled, and sprang up again. With a final stumbling leap, I broke through on the other side.

Xanthe stood just ahead, her manic grin wide and gaze darting across the combatants. She could see again, and she was deciding who to take over with her mentalist powers.

Her attention landed on me, and I sprinted toward her, counting the seconds in my head. I had to reach her before she could get her psychic hooks in my brain. The distance between us shrank. Only a few more steps—

I slowed to a stop, four feet between us. I pulled my paintball gun from its holster, then reached for my belt buckle with my other hand. My fingers fumbled over the leather, and the belt dropped to the ground.

Turning the gun, I extended the handle toward her.

She took the weapon and, with a merciless smile, lifted the barrel to point at my face.

Crimson magic detonated nearby. A wave of pebbles and grit blasted over us, and Xanthe gasped, ducking her head and shielding her face. The instant her eyes left me, awareness exploded in my head. My lungs heaved, muscles spasming with adrenaline.

Jerking upright, Xanthe swung the gun loaded with a final shot of hellfire potion toward me. I swept my leg up in a roundhouse kick, and my boot hit the metal gun with a jarring thwack. It flew out of her hand, bounced off the pavement, and skittered away. Fire surged over it as the paintball broke from the impact.

As my foot came down, my fist veered toward her face. My knuckles hit her cheekbone and her head snapped back.

But Xanthe was a Keys of Solomon member, not an amateur combat apprentice.

She whacked my wrist aside, and her other fist drove into my sternum. As I stumbled, agony burning through my chest, her hand dipped down to her thigh where a long dagger was sheathed. She pulled the weapon.

I grabbed the violet crystal around my neck. "*Ori vis siderea!*"

A crackling, multi-hued sphere appeared in my hand and I hurled it at her as she lunged for me. It burst against her wrist, knocking her arm back. The weapon dropped from her numb, magic-stained hand.

"*Ori vis siderea!*"

A second orb manifested in my palm, and I chucked it at her face. It hit her in the forehead.

I yanked a fall spell from around my neck. "*Ori decidas!*"

As I leaped for her, crystal extended in my reaching arm, she threw herself back and kicked out. Her boot caught my hip, and my dive turned into an awkward fall. I crashed down on her legs.

She seized my wrist and slammed it on the pavement. The activated artifact flew out of my hand.

Desperate to keep her too busy to mind-control me, I threw myself into her.

We rolled across the ground. The hard parts of her body—fists, elbows, knees—were finding all the soft spots in mine, but I kept grabbing her, trying to pin her down. Her fist connected with my jaw and my vision went white. The world spun, and my chin hit the pavement, her knee driving into my back. She grabbed my right arm and wrenched it behind me.

I screamed as agony tore through my shoulder. Twisting away from her, I pushed up with one hand, shaking uncontrollably.

Her arm looped around my neck from behind and clamped tight.

As she pulled me into her, she caught my good wrist and bent my arm behind my back, locking me in place on my knees. My other arm hung limply, a nuclear inferno of agony burning through my shoulder.

"Look," she hissed in my ear.

Magic flashed and danced, the air rippling with the heat rising from Alistair's snaking lines of lava. The silver war hammer, splattered with blood, lay abandoned on the ground. Girard scrabbled at his belt for an artifact as he limped sideways, almost stepping in a molten fissure. Tabitha darted back and forth in front of a demon, flicking ice shards in its face.

Aaron had one arm around Kai's chest, the electramage sagging in his hold. He held a fistful of Drew's shirt in the other hand and was dragging the unconscious telekinetic away. Ezra, one of his swords missing the last few inches of the blade, faced a demon alone.

"They're all going to die," Xanthe crooned. "Just like everyone in Enright died. Xever was waiting in the underground temple. When the time was right, he had Nazhivēr slaughter them all like the brainless cattle they were."

I fought for air, my mouth gaping.

"These are First House demons. The most powerful of them all—except for a female demon, of course."

My lungs screamed for air. My head spun, sparks flashing behind my eyes.

"Stop fooling around," she called, "and finish them off!"

The three demons glanced at her, then faced their outmatched human foes once more.

Xanthe's constricting arm loosened enough for me to gasp in a tiny breath. "Don't die yet," she purred in my ear. "Watch your beloved die first."

I sucked in another wisp of air—then threw my head back, smashing my skull into her nose.

She gasped and jerked away. Wrenching my wrist free, I grabbed the purple crystal resting against my chest—and with my injured arm, I reached for her neck. Agony burst through my shoulder, blurring my vision, but I didn't stop.

"*Ori vis siderea!*" I gasped.

As my weak fingers scraped across her neck and caught on her infernus chains, I smashed the arcana orb into her sternum.

It exploded, throwing her backward—and I tore the demonic pendants over her head.

Her furious scream rang out as I whirled around. Her weight crashed into me from behind, and I slammed down. As she lunged for my wrist, I whipped my arm back—

And hurled the infernus pendants.

They arced through the air, crimson light creating a violent backdrop to their graceful flight, then plunged into a wide crack in the pavement where glowing lava bubbled.

The silver discs plopped into the lava, floating on top of the dense fluid. The metal edges charred, then the medallions melted into silver puddles.

27

THE THREE DEMONS went completely, unnaturally still. Their magma stares were blank, their bodies as motionless as flesh statues.

"N-no," Xanthe stammered. "*No!*"

Aaron leaped over a cooling lava fissure. Sharpie's blade glowed red with heat, flames licking the steel. He swung the weapon at the nearest demon's neck. The super-heated blade passed clean through flesh and bone.

The demon's headless body collapsed to the ground with a dull, heavy thud.

Xanthe's weight vanished from my back. Her shoes scuffed across the ground, then broke into a pounding run. I lurched up—and gagged as agony burned through my shoulder. Half blind with pain, I broke into a run, my blurred vision locked on her.

The gap between us widened. She was escaping.

She skidded to a halt. Her arms flew up, and she cringed backward. "No!"

Terror laced her high-pitched cry. My steps slowed, my gaze jolting over the dark, empty street for whatever was scaring her.

Then I saw them—the mob of combat-geared mythics streaming toward us.

For a terrifying instant, I thought they were cult reinforcements. Then I saw the woman at the head of the line, her long ponytail swinging with each step and a silver badge displayed on her chest.

Agent Lienna Shen. And the mythics with her—

"Pandora Knights!" she called. "Take the west side. Odin's Eye, take the east. SeaDevils, set up a triage immediately."

I stood in the center of the street, numb with disbelief as thirty mythics sprinted past me on either side, rushing toward the flashes of magic, booming bursts of power, and cries of pain that still echoed from the battlefield behind me.

They sped past, and then it was just me … and Xanthe. The cult leader cringed where she stood, hands gripping her head and fingers digging into her skull.

A footstep crunched, the sound almost lost in the weak patter of rain, and I realized there was one more mythic here.

Kit walked down the center of the street, his hands in his pockets and his badge hanging around his neck, the small shield gleaming. His stare was locked on Xanthe.

Choking on a terrified sob, she sank to her knees.

"Isn't it fun?" His voice was quiet, devoid of humor or snark. "Messing with people's minds."

"Stop it," she gasped, still clutching her head. "Make it stop. Please."

He halted six paces away from her. "Not so fun when it's happening to you, is it?"

"*Please*," she whimpered.

I pushed forward. As I lifted my last ruby artifact over my head, I murmured, "*Ori decidas.*"

I pressed the artifact against the back of her neck, and she crumpled bonelessly. As she thudded to the pavement, Kit pulled a pair of handcuffs from his belt. He snapped them around her wrists.

His blue eyes rose to mine. "You okay?"

I belatedly noticed I was trembling. "Um. More or less. Where did you come from?"

"The precinct?"

"Did you …" I squinted. "What happened with Agent Söze and the damnation order thing?"

He quirked an eyebrow. "Ignorance is bliss, my friend. You should go find a healer. I'll handle her."

"Oh … yeah, okay."

In too much pain to press him for answers, I left him with Xanthe and walked back toward the intersection. Sound filtered into my ears, gradually registering in my brain.

Gone were the blasts and screams. Instead, I heard raised voices calling to each other and the occasional clank of steel. No more magic flashed, and dark shapes moved about the intersection with purpose. The other guilds had subdued the last of the cultists.

Was it over? Really, truly over?

Xanthe's three winged demons lay on the ground, headless and macabre. The silver war hammer was still abandoned on the pavement, its crushing end splattered with rain-streaked blood.

My foot landed on something soft instead of the wet, crunchy grit that coated everything. Purple fabric.

Bending down, I picked up the Carapace. It hung from my fingers in a very mundane way, the fabric shimmery and soft like a blend between cotton and silk, but it didn't glow or sparkle or float eerily. Regret punctured my numb bubble and I spread the fabric out, my shoulder burning.

An almost indiscernible shimmer ran across the cloak, the faint sparkles dancing like midnight stars.

I lowered the Carapace—and blinked as a thick smear of shadows condensed in front of me.

Zak stepped out of the dark nothingness. His leather jacket was tattered, tears in the fabric wet with blood. His face was pale but his eyes glowed with fierce fae power.

Alarm pricked me. "MPD agents are here. You need to leave."

"I know," he said in a low rasp. "I just had to make sure you weren't dead."

"I'm not dead."

"Yes, I noticed." His eyes flicked over my face. "I'll see you again."

It wasn't quite a question, but his inflection lifted on the last syllable, revealing his uncertainty.

I wanted to ask him what he'd offered Lallakai in exchange for the power to defend my guild. I wanted to demand that she release his body and soul from her heartless talons this very moment. I wanted to beg him to cut ties with the toxic fae forever.

But not only did I have no time to broach those questions, but his problems weren't mine to solve. As much as I wanted to help him, some burdens couldn't be shared. Lallakai was deeply entrenched in his life, his past, and his magic, and he was the only one who could change that.

I swept the draping fabric of the Carapace together and rapidly folded it. It compacted into an unnaturally small, heavy square like it usually did.

Grabbing his wrist, I pressed the fae artifact into his palm. "I know you told me to keep this, but you need it more."

"I already told you I can't use it without sacrificing—"

I tightened my grip on his wrist. "The day is coming when you'll need it, Zak."

His eyes narrowed, and I wondered if I was imagining the flash of anger in them that could only belong to Lallakai. He considered me for a moment longer, then curled his fingers over the artifact.

Releasing his wrist, I threw my arms around him, ignoring the flare of pain in my injured shoulder.

"Thank you," I whispered. "Thank you for protecting my friends."

His arms wrapped around me and, for two long heartbeats, he crushed me to his chest.

"Come visit me soon," I added, my throat tight. "Hoshi and I will need a new familiar bond and I want you to do it this time."

"All right," he murmured.

I stepped back, a hand on his shoulder as I stared up at his face, hoping Lallakai would hear my next words. "If you need help, I'm always here."

He nodded. The shadows swirled around him, and Lallakai's transparent wings lifted off his arms. They swept around him and he vanished.

I gulped my heart down, my hand curled around the purple crystal resting on my chest. I needed to find my ruby fall spells—but first, I needed to locate my three mages.

I turned—and there they were. Ezra, striding toward me through the smoke and rain. Aaron followed him, Kai's arm over his shoulder as the electramage limped. Scorched, scuffed, bloody, hurting, exhausted. But alive.

My knees weakened with relief. I stumbled forward.

Ezra caught me, sweeping me into him. I buried my face in his shoulder, shaking. Aaron and Kai joined us, standing close, and none of us spoke. We didn't need to.

We were alive. We were together. That's all that mattered right now.

A quiet disorder filled the intersection. Bits of debris crumbled off the surrounding buildings, their windows shattered, walls smashed, and burst pipes spewing water onto the already drenched streets. The light rain continued to pepper everything, keeping the merrily dancing flames of many small infernos in check.

Mythics from the Pandora Knights, Odin's Eye, and the SeaDevils hurried among the injured and fallen, calling for healers or helping battered combatants clamber painfully to their feet. Among the rubble, a handful of Crow and Hammer members who'd waited out the battle inside the guild assisted them.

The surviving Keys clustered up, and small groups moved among their fallen, searching for survivors. Another group sat along a cracked, scorched wall, their arms bound and weapons confiscated. Blake and Tyrone stood side by side in front of the captured men, conferring together and calling orders.

Reluctantly, I lifted my cheek from Ezra's shoulder. As much as I wanted to collapse in a corner somewhere and pass out for ten or twelve hours, we had one more loose end to sort out: Xever.

We split up. Ezra, whose stamina had yet to recover after his recent injuries, supported Kai, who was limping even worse, and together they headed back toward the guild. Aaron and I briefly scoured the intersection, then ventured down the street where I'd last seen Zylas chasing Nazhivēr.

My tired feet dragged as we headed farther from the intersection, the noise and bustle of people fading until the only sound was the falling rain. There was no doubt we were heading the right way. Fissures split the pavement. Shattered walls. Gaping holes in buildings. The battle between demons had been intense and violent.

"Up ahead," Aaron murmured.

Squinting, I spotted them. Two figures stood beside a third who seemed to be sitting on the ground, hunched over.

As Aaron and I approached, one of the upright mythics—Amalia—turned toward us. Beside her was Zora, the petite blond sorceress smudged with blood and two huge swords sheathed in an X on her back.

Their comrade on the ground pushed to his feet, and I realized it wasn't one person but two: Zylas with Robin cradled in his arms, her face tucked against the side of his hood.

"You're alive," Amalia observed as Aaron and I walked into earshot.

"For the most part," I agreed, my gaze flicking across Zylas and Robin. "Is she okay?"

Robin lifted her head from the demon's shoulder. "I'm fine. Just … unsteady."

Zylas lowered her feet to the ground and she leaned against him, one hand hooked on his shoulder. The hood of his black jacket-like top shadowed his face, his telltale magma eyes dimmer than usual.

"Xever and Nazhivēr?" I asked quietly.

Robin pushed her tangled hair off her forehead, her eyes even larger without her glasses. "Escaped. Nazhivēr flew off with him."

My jaw clenched with dismay.

"They are not the hunters any longer." Zylas's husky growl sent a shiver down my spine. "Now I will hunt them."

Robin's hand tightened on his shoulder, her gaze rising to his face. "*We* will hunt them."

The demon's lips curved in a savage smile that revealed his predatory canines. She slid her hand down his arm and took his hand. Turning, she glanced back at me—and her stare was almost as fierce as her demon's smile.

"Leave Xever to us."

With Amalia on one side and Zylas on the other, she walked away. Zora arched an eyebrow at me and Aaron, completely unruffled by Zylas's obvious free will, then turned and followed the trio.

I watched them go, my heart pounding in my throat. How they would find Xever and his demon, I didn't know.

But I had no doubt they would.

THE GOOD NEWS: by some inexplicable miracle, no one from the Crow and Hammer had died yet. I wasn't celebrating—the list of injuries was terrifying, from broken bones to concussions to lacerations to burns to internal bleeding—but the outlook was decent, especially with extra healers on loan from other guilds.

The bad news: we were back in the MPD precinct.

I would've been delighted to never set foot in a precinct again, but that wasn't possible—not when I'd been charged with serious crimes, taken into custody, charged with a dozen more crimes, then mysteriously vanished from lockup.

Standing between Aaron and Kai, I observed in silence.

A long, plain table filled one end of the long, plain room. Four elderly men and women in suits sat behind it, as did a not-quite-elderly man with shoulder-length auburn hair tied back in a ponytail and an ancient woman who wore a patterned knit sweater instead of a suit. They also observed wordlessly.

Across the table from them, Ezra held his hand against a carefully drawn sorcery circle as a wave of pale light rushed over his body and infused the crystal placed in the array. The portly sorcerer who'd prepared the ritual picked up the now ivory-white gem and held it close to his nose, examining it carefully.

"Negative," he announced in a nasal voice. "No demonic contamination."

Ezra lifted his hand off the spell. "Am I cleared of charges?"

The elderly man in the middle nodded slowly and made a note on a paper. "Cleared of demon magery, but your behavior merits further investigation."

Ponytail Man leaned back in his chair. "Based on what, Everett? He was fleeing for his life with a DOD bounty on his head—a bounty *you* authorized."

"We can examine him more closely after we investigate the circumstances of the indictments and sentencing procedure,"

Sweater Woman added serenely, hands folded on the table as though she missed her knitting needles.

The centermost man frowned at his paper. "In that case … Ezra Rowe, all charges against you are dismissed. You're free to go."

The aeromage didn't show any relief, but he also didn't waste any time striding over to me, Aaron, and Kai and joining our line.

"Excellent," Darius murmured. "*All* charges against my guild are dismissed, then?"

I flicked a hopeful glance at the GM, who stood at one end of the table beside the sternly beautiful Captain Blythe.

"Hm," the old man croaked, glancing at his outspoken colleagues. At a glacial pace, he riffled through the papers on his desk. "That may be … ah … but …"

I shifted my feet, resisting the urge to shout at him to hurry. It'd been just over eight hours since our guild had nearly been obliterated. I was aching, exhausted, and my abused shoulder burned fiercely despite my arm resting in a sling.

Unfortunately, shouting at the MPD's Emergency Judiciary Council would be counterproductive to my goal of leaving ASAP.

"The only charges remaining," the wrinkled old relic wheezed, "are those against Miss Robin Page. The accusations of an illegal contract are serious, very serious."

"And lack any proof aside from unreliable witness accounts," Darius interjected smoothly. "As we determined already, the charges against my guildeds stemmed entirely from the Court of the Red Queen's attempt to discredit and destroy my guild before I could uncover their secret operations."

"Exactly so," Sweater Woman agreed, as though nothing in Darius's statement was at all alarming. Not that we hadn't been over it already in this meeting, but it was still shocking to *me*, so why not her?

The center council member hesitated over his papers.

A slight cough from the far corner of the room.

"Sorry to interrupt." Agent Lienna Shen stepped forward. "I'd like to add that our investigation into the attack on the Crow and Hammer so far indicates that Robin was present, but no one reported seeing her demon."

Nope. And no one *would* report seeing her demon, because all anyone had seen was a mysterious "demon mage" running around in all black clothing and a hood. Who even knew which side the unknown demon mage had been on?

"Thank you, Agent Shen." Ponytail Man nodded firmly. "Charges dismissed, and we'll leave the rest to you, Captain Blythe. We expect a full report on this week's events, and if further investigation is required, notify us immediately."

"Of course." Blythe cast a flinty look across Darius. "You're free to go … for now."

Darius's smile was faint, but judging by Blythe's suddenly clenched jaw, she hadn't missed it.

Stifling a victorious grin, I hustled after Darius and the guys as they headed for the exit. As we filed through the door, I caught a pair of mischievous blue eyes—Agent Kit Morris, standing in the corner with his partner, Lienna. He smiled crookedly as I passed him.

Darius knew where he was going and led us unerringly to the staircase. As he started down, the guys following eagerly on his heels, the strangest thing happened.

The word "WAIT" appeared in front of my face, glowing like a neon sign.

I jerked to a halt, wondering what the hell was wrong with me. Was I hallucinating? Did I need medical attention?

The commanding vision vanished and a voice called my name.

I turned around to find Kit striding down the hall toward me.

He grinned. "Don't look so freaked out. That was me, not you."

Him? He was the reason I'd just seen a disembodied word?

My eyes narrowed. "What sort of mythic are you?"

"I've been told I'm quite charming."

"Huh?"

"I'm a charming sort of mythic, obviously." He held out his hand, fingers curled loosely around a small object. "You should take this."

Brow furrowing, I held up my palm. He dropped a grape-sized white crystal into my hand—the gem that had proved Ezra was Demonica-free.

"I convinced the gremlins that, after all he went through, Ezra should get a souvenir for his trouble. Since they'd already witnessed the test results, they agreed."

Gremlins? Oh, he meant the Judiciary Council. I peered at the crystal. "So why're you giving it to *me*?"

His humor faded. "Take a closer look."

I pushed the crystal with my thumb, rolling it across my palm. The fluorescent lights overhead shone across the glossy white surface. I flipped the gem over.

On the bottom, a crimson starburst marred the white surface.

"Lienna noticed a similar marking after the first test, too," Kit explained quietly. "She said if Ezra were a demon mage, the crystal would be solid red. If he were a demon contractor, it'd be marbled with red. She can only guess what the starburst means."

My pulse fluttered in my throat. It could only mean there was still a little bit of Eterran in Ezra.

My fingers closed tightly over the crystal. "You hid that mark from the Council, didn't you? Why would you do that?"

"Petty revenge."

"Huh? Seriously?"

"Yep." He pressed a finger to his lips. "So don't tell on me, 'kay?"

Snorting, I pocketed the crystal and turned toward the stairwell. "Later, Agent Morris."

"Later, barkeep."

I hurried through the door and down the stairs. Darius and the guys were waiting for me, and I merely shrugged my good shoulder when Kai asked what had kept me. On another day, they would've pestered me until I answered, but we were all way too tired for that.

As Darius guided us through the precinct's main level toward the exit, I slipped my hand into my pocket and touched the crystal. That crimson starburst ...

Whether it was a remnant lingering in Ezra's body or in his soul, a tiny piece of Eterran had survived. His strength lived on in Ezra, and I knew the aeromage wouldn't waste whatever the demon had, knowingly or unknowingly, passed on to him.

Pulling my hand from my pocket, I rushed to catch up as Darius threw open the precinct's front door. Early morning sunlight blazed over us in a wash of amber and gold, the sky a beautiful, clear blue.

As we stepped across the threshold, I caught Ezra's hand and entwined our fingers. He looked down at me, a soft smile on his lips, one eye as warm and sweet as melted chocolate, the other pale as snow and a touch icy.

Would that hint of steely, ruthless power someday fade? Or was it as much a part of him as his aero magic, his scars, and the violent past that had shaped him into who he was?

Only time would tell—and I was more than ready for that journey to begin.

EPILOGUE

FOUR MONTHS LATER

I SLEEPILY RAN MY HAND across warm, smooth skin. Bare, delicious skin enveloping the second-most beautiful abs I'd ever laid eyes on. *The* most beautiful set belonged to a demon and I wasn't touching *them* with a ten-foot pole, so I was one hundred percent content with these most beautiful human abs.

My fingertips ran across hard-edged scars as I caressed my way across firm pectorals and the inexplicably mouthwatering lines of his collarbones. Why did I want to chew on his collarbones? It made no sense … but the world was full of nonsensical things. Why fight it?

Following that thought, I pushed up on one elbow, leaned over, and grazed my teeth across Ezra's collarbone. A drowsy inhalation lifted his chest, and I resumed my exploration of his physique as I breathed in his mouthwatering scent. Moving my mouth to the side of his neck, I did the teeth grazing thing to the underside of his jaw.

Another sleepy breath. "Are you chewing on me?"

"Complaining?"

He turned his head until our noses touched and studied me with grave sobriety.

My lips twitched.

Without warning, he rolled on top of me. The blankets tumbled off the bed as his mouth closed over mine. He kissed me slow and deep. I wrapped my arms around him—and, for good measure, I wrapped my legs around him too.

He rumbled against my mouth and pushed me into the bed with his hips. I moaned in answer. I loved sleeping naked. It made mornings so much more fun. And lucky for me, it'd taken exactly one morning together for Ezra to come around to my way of thinking.

Tearing my mouth away from his, I craned my neck to check the alarm clock glowing on my nightstand. Whoops. We'd slept in too long.

I rocked my hips against his. "We don't have much time."

His lips nuzzled down my throat. "Do we need that much time?"

I grinned. No, we did not. I could feel how ready he was.

We made it out of the bed not long after, sweaty and breathing hard. I stretched my arms over my head, arching my back. "How is it so hot? I was hoping for a cooler June."

He kissed my shoulder on his way by, heading for the bedroom door. "We could talk Aaron into installing air conditioning and spend the summer with him."

I wrinkled my nose. "No thanks."

Ezra glanced back as he pulled my bedroom door open. "He only teased you a little, Tori."

"He needs to grow up."

Which wasn't an entirely fair assessment, since Aaron had only started teasing me after he'd walked in on Ezra and I making out like horny teenagers in various rooms of his house about six times in two days.

"Speaking of Aaron," Ezra added, "when is he arriving?"

"Fifteen minutes."

"Oh, shit."

As he hastened for the bathroom, I grabbed my lightweight housecoat and pulled it over my naked body. I didn't strictly need to cover up in my own apartment, but I never knew where Twiggy might be lurking.

I hopped in the shower first while Ezra shaved. He'd made the switch from a scruffy jaw to clean-shaven shortly after Eterran's exorcism. I wasn't sure why he'd decided on the change and I hadn't pestered him to explain.

Lots of things about Ezra had changed, some small and some big—but at his core, he was the same man I'd fallen in love with.

He wasn't quite as cool-headed as he used to be—though not because he'd suddenly gotten temperamental. Not even close. He was as steady as ever, but he'd gradually become more opinionated. When he didn't like something, he let us know. When we annoyed him, we *definitely* got to hear about it.

And I loved it—because after ten years of suppressing every spike of negative emotion, Ezra was letting himself feel again.

He wasn't merely indulging in occasional grumpiness, though. His smile was brighter. His laugh was louder. His happiness was bolder. And his protectiveness of his friends was fiercer than before.

He was still soft-spoken. Still perceptive and kind. Still a little shy. But he was also evolving, growing, discovering who he was—and I was with him every step of the way.

We switched places in the shower, and I massaged hair product into my long curls while we discussed my training session tomorrow. Aaron was refusing to start me on a real weapon until I'd mastered my brass knuckles, which was completely unfair. I wanted a giant-ass sword like his because *hell yes.*

I opened the bathroom door, letting a wave of cold air inside. Wrapped in a towel, I hurried across the hall.

"Tori?"

I came up short. Twiggy had appeared near my legs, his prickly head tilted back as he peered intently at my face. See? This was why I didn't walk around naked.

"Yes?" I inquired cautiously, knowing that the spinning-gears expression on his green face meant nothing good.

"Are you having a baby?"

I almost dropped my towel. Clutching it against my chest, I squeaked, "What? No!"

His waxy skin crinkled with his frown. "Then who's your baby daddy?"

"*What?*"

"Is Ezra your—"

"No! I don't have a baby or a baby daddy, Twiggy! What the hell?"

He continued to frown, then walked over to the bathroom, pushed the door open, and asked loudly, "Ezra, are you Tori's baby daddy?"

"*What?*"

"Or is Aaron Tori's baby daddy?"

"*WHAT.*"

As the shower abruptly shut off, a loud knock sounded at the other end of the house. Saved from trying to explain the idiot faery's latest brainwave, I rushed down the hall and up the stairs to the back entryway.

Aaron's eyebrows shot halfway to his hairline when I flung the door open. He gave my towel-clad self a swift once over, then sighed. "I even waited an extra five minutes in my car to be sure you weren't naked when I got here."

I rolled my eyes. "Yeah, yeah, Tori likes to bone her hot boyfriend, so funny."

"Maybe I should get me one of those."

"A hot boyfriend?"

"Or the girl variety."

"Well, what's stopping you?"

"Good ones are all taken."

I snorted. "The problem is *you're* too good, Aaron. The average girl can't keep up with a guy like you."

"I *think* that was a compliment?"

I waved a hand dismissively. "You know the drill?"

"Yep. I'll keep him hostage while I try on every piece of combat gear available."

I snickered. Poor Ezra. "He should be just about ready. I'll let him know you're here."

"And I'll wait in my car, just in case you lose your towel between now and him making it up the stairs."

"Har har."

He pushed through the screen door, and I hastened back down the stairs, already cringing over explaining Twiggy's baby questions.

Ezra stood in the hall with a towel wrapped around his waist, but he didn't seem to be waiting for me. He was gazing into the living room where a loud voice exclaimed something with overly dramatic intensity.

I stopped beside him. Together, we watched the TV show's host pace across a set made to look like a cozy living room while he somberly explained how, in just a few minutes, he would reveal Sara's infant son's paternity test results, determining once and for all whether her husband or her husband's *best friend*—cue audience gasp—was the real father.

Twiggy sat three inches from the screen, enraptured by the talk-show host.

Groaning, I slapped my hand against my forehead. "Why do I have a faery roommate?"

Ezra laughed. Looping an arm around my waist, he drew me into the bedroom and pushed the door shut with his foot. An instant later, his hot mouth was against mine, and I plastered myself against him without thought, hands stroking down his damp chest.

And there went my towel. Damn it, Aaron had been right.

Ezra slid his hands down my sides, over my hips, then back up to my waist. He pulled me close and his mouth brushed over my ear.

"Someday, do you think?" he murmured.

"Huh?"

He chuckled, the husky sound diving straight to my core, then stepped back from me with a final caressing touch. "I'm going to be late."

"You're already late. And someday, what?"

"Nothing."

"What?" I growled, annoyed.

His eyes sparked with mirth but he didn't reply as he opened the closet and slid a pair of jeans out.

I forgot my annoyance at the sight of his clothes hanging in my closet. Why did his belongings mixed with mine stoke that fire in my belly even hotter? I wanted to drag him back into bed and have my way with him for a few *hours* before releasing him to Aaron.

But that would ruin a lot of careful planning, so I banked my desire for later.

As Ezra dressed, I glanced at the stack of his combat gear peeking out from the top shelf of my closet. Short, black leather cords hung from beneath them—the ties of Eterran's bracer. Ezra had begun wearing the bracer on jobs, keeping it hidden under his long, metal-studded gloves.

In the months since he and Eterran had separated, Ezra's enhanced strength had faded from "impossibly strong" to "impressively strong" and was holding steady there. His reflexes weren't blindingly fast anymore, but they continued to be above average.

That spark of demonic essence would live on in him, maybe for the rest of his life.

Oblivious to the direction of my thoughts, Ezra swept over for a goodbye kiss that left me weak in the knees, then hurried into the hallway. I listened for the door.

The moment it banged shut, I dove for my closet, dug into the very back, and pulled out a dress bag from the darkest corner. Little did he know I wasn't spending the next several hours lounging around eating cereal and fighting Twiggy for the TV remote. And if I didn't hurry, I'd be late too.

Fifty-three minutes later, I came flying out of the bathroom, awkwardly clasping a small seashell pendant around my neck—a spontaneous gift from Ezra after the whale-watching tour we'd gone on last month.

"Twiggy," I called, "have you seen my purse?"

The faery barely glanced up as I rushed into the living room and peered over the sofa. Shit. Where had I left it?

A shimmer of orange and green danced in my head, then a scaled silver body swept over to me. My purse hung from Hoshi's small paws, fuchsia eyes bright.

"Ah! Perfect. Thank you, Hoshi." I hitched my purse over my shoulder and gave her head an affectionate rub. "Keep Twiggy calm while I'm away."

Her tail flicked, a sunny swirl of yellow telling me she was amused.

Grinning, I sped up the stairs, and a minute later, I was standing on the front sidewalk, catching my breath but ready to go—and looking damn good. My vibrant cobalt dress featured a plunging halter neckline offset with a playful tiered skirt that fluttered around my knees. My hair, still slightly damp, was piled up on my head, and I'd spent a painstaking fifteen minutes on my makeup. A pair of dangly earrings and strappy white sandals finished my outfit.

Ezra wouldn't be able to keep his eyes off me, and I was already itching for him to slowly peel off my dress when we got back to my place tonight.

You'd think, after four months, my libido would've calmed down a bit, but nope. I mean, how could it? The man was ripped, tireless, and deliciously eager to make up for lost time.

I indulged in two minutes of inappropriate reminiscing before a dark blue Dodge Challenger pulled up at the curb.

The passenger door flew open and Sin leaped out, arms already reaching for a hug.

I grabbed her, squeezed the air from her lungs, then stepped back to take in her outfit. Her little black number with a strappy back was sexy as hell, her dark makeup enhancing the sultry look. Her hair color of choice this month was a deep, shimmering violet that made her skin look like porcelain.

"Hot," I announced. "You told her that, right, Justin?"

My brother leaned across the center console. "Repeatedly."

"Good."

Sin laughed, a faint flush in her cheeks. "I actually wore this dress for our three-month anniversary dinner, so I've been complimented about twenty times."

I almost teased her about celebrating a three-month dating anniversary, but she was glowing with happiness and I just couldn't do it. They were such a ridiculously cute couple that I'd hardly teased them at all.

Sin flipped the passenger seat up so I could climb into the back. She got back in, and then we were off, the Challenger's V8 engine rumbling aggressively.

"Does Ezra suspect anything?" she asked, her voice high with excitement.

"He doesn't have a clue," I confirmed gleefully. "Do you have the decorations?"

"In the trunk." She clapped her hands in determination. "The pub won't be recognizable when we're done with it."

"Perfect."

As Justin turned onto Powell Street, heading into Gastown, she twisted to look back at me. "Did Justin tell you?"

"Sin," he complained. "Save it for—"

"He quit his job!"

I choked on saliva. "What? You quit the force, Justin?"

He cast a look of smitten exasperation at Sin. "I was going to tell her later when she wasn't so busy."

"*Pff*, she can handle it. Tell her!"

"Yeah," I added with heavy emphasis. "Tell your sister the big news. I didn't even know you were thinking of quitting!"

"I got hired at Huginn & Muninn Investigations."

"At … what?"

"Huginn & Muninn!" Sin exclaimed. "Don't you know about it? It's a PI firm that partners with Odin's Eye. They collaborate on bounties and investigations that cross between mythic and human jurisdictions."

My eyes popped. "Whoa. Really? I didn't know that sort of thing existed!"

"Me neither," Justin laughed. "Lyndon mentioned it to me, and I asked Izzah the next time she was at the pub. She passed on my résumé, and I went in to interview last week."

"No way!"

"Yeah. I have to get my PI license before I can start any real work, but once I do, they're partnering me with their most experienced investigator."

Excitement buzzed through me. "I can't believe you didn't tell me about all this right away!"

"You were busy planning the surprise party of the century," he teased as he executed a smooth parallel park outside a familiar bakery.

He waited in the car while Sin and I went into confectionary heaven to pick up my massive order of cupcakes. We added them to the trunk, which already contained half a dozen bags of streamers, balloons, banners, and colorful tablecloths.

The drive to the guild took only a few minutes. As the car zoomed through the intersection where the guild sat, seeing repaved asphalt and repaired buildings reminded me what the spot had looked like four months ago.

The search to uncover the Court of the Red Queen's final sects was ongoing, but with Xanthe in custody, it was steadily progressing. Darius had reported last month that they'd weeded the cult's remnants out of Vancouver, and guilds from Seattle to San Francisco were hunting for hidden "circles" in their cities. It might take another few months, but the cult was going down for good.

Justin parked in the tiny back lot, and I put all that out of my mind as we carried our haul in through the kitchen.

"You're here!" The cheery cry came from Sabrina as she rushed around the bar, her pink dress fluttering and her chin-length blond hair styled with salon-perfect beach waves. She helped us stack the cupcakes on the counter, then gave me and Sin hugs, gushing over how pretty we looked.

Kaveri followed more sedately. The witch wore an earthy brown dress that brought out the golden tones in her skin.

"Ready to make this place festive?" she asked me.

"Let's do it!"

We got to work. Standing on tables, Kaveri and Sin hung blue and white streamers from the ceiling beams while Sabrina arranged the matching tablecloths. Justin sat in the corner, red in the face as he inflated an entire bag of balloons.

I pulled out a shiny banner and, climbing onto the back counter, attached it to the wall so it looped beneath the massive silver war hammer where it rested on its heavy hooks. Jumping down, I checked my work.

"Happy 24th Birthday," the sign read.

My throat constricted. Twenty-four. The birthday Ezra was never supposed to have. If we hadn't changed his fate, he would never have survived to this day. Together, we'd saved him.

"Tori?"

I started, then realized tears were about to spill from my eyes. I tilted my head back, blinking furiously before the moisture ruined my makeup.

"You okay?" Sabrina asked softly.

Makeup saved, I examined her concerned expression. "Did you see it coming, Sabrina? Everything that happened?"

"Not even the greatest prophet can see everything," she replied lightly. "My mother once told me, 'Most people in this world are carried by the current, but beware the rare few who create waves with every step they take.'"

My forehead crinkled.

"You're a wave-maker, Tori, and waves are difficult to predict—so maybe you could just coast along for a bit so my tarot cards behave?"

"Uh … I'll try?" I hesitated. "Your cards were wrong, though, weren't they? They predicted Ezra would sacrifice himself. The Hanged Man and the Death card, remember? But he didn't die."

"The cards weren't wrong." She pressed her hands together. "The Death card doesn't mean literal death. Just like the Devil card doesn't mean a literal demon … usually."

My eyes widened.

"The reversed Devil—redemption," she said softly. "The Hanged Man—sacrifice. Death—endings *and* beginnings. Do you see?"

Oh.

Yes, I could see it now. The fortune she'd seen had never been about Ezra alone. It'd been about Ezra … and Eterran.

Sabrina watched that sink in, then offered me a hesitant smile. "By the way, are you sure you don't want a rabbit?"

"A rabbit?"

Her eyes lit up with devoted fervor. "Cinnabunny's babies are *so* cute. Rabbits make wonderful pets, you know. Really!"

"I'm good," I said quickly, shaking off my shock. "Twiggy and Hoshi are enough trouble for me."

A cheerful jingle rang through the pub, and I spun toward the door, half petrified that Aaron had blown it and Ezra was walking in. But nope—not unless Ezra had developed a new love for leather in the last couple of hours.

A sexy hunk and equally sexy hunkette walked in, both clad in motorcycle leathers with helmets tucked under their arms. Kai's hair was mussed while Izzah's raven locks were beautifully wind-swept in a way my curls could never achieve.

"You're early!" I trotted over for an electramage hug. It was a hug sort of day. "I thought you had a big meeting."

"Cancelled," Kai revealed. "Makiko called me ten minutes before I left explaining how the VP we were supposed to meet with got run over by a golf cart during his morning round on the course."

"How does one get run over by a golf cart?"

"That's what I asked." Izzah shrugged airily. "We can only guess."

"He was probably drunk," I decided.

Kai set his helmet on a nearby table. "Speaking of drinks, who's manning the bar today?"

"The big man upstairs volunteered."

"Darius?"

"Who else?"

Kai arched a dark eyebrow. "I'm telling him you called him the big man upstairs."

Alarm shot through me. "Uh—"

"You'll do better tonight, *eh leng chai*?" Izzah asked, planting a hand on her cocked hip. "You overdid it a bit last time, hm?"

"I was celebrating," Kai muttered. "And Aaron kept bringing me shots."

"It's fiiine," I sang, throwing my arm around his leather-clad shoulders. "It's not every day he can celebrate joining his first guild—again."

Izzah's stern expression softened into a sparkling smile. "No, but try-*lah* not to throw up in the cab on the way home this time."

"Whoa, you threw up?" I gasped.

Kai scowled darkly, then walked off with a low mutter about getting changed. Izzah sashayed after him, a predatory spark in her eyes. She had him on the run, and she'd keep teasing him until he exploded—by which I meant, until he pinned her to a wall somewhere and kissed her into speechlessness.

I watched them disappear in the direction of the stairs, beaming happily. Things weren't perfect, but they were heading in the right direction.

Kai couldn't change his family, but turning himself in to the MPD to save Makiko's life had produced an unexpected side effect: it won him the support of her father. It'd taken months of careful maneuvering, but Mr. Miura had helped Kai respectfully end his engagement to Makiko, move into a business role in MiraCo, and, barely a week ago, transfer back into the Crow and Hammer.

Even splitting his time between MiraCo and his guild, Kai still got to chill at the pub, hang out at Aaron's place, and do all the bounty runs that Aaron's bad-guy-busting heart desired—

when he wasn't out with Izzah, that was. Thank goodness she'd given him one more chance.

I tapped my chin. The text message I'd sent her a week after Kai officially became single probably helped. It'd said something like, "Kai was an asshole because his family was gonna kill you. Tell him to tell you everything."

Smirking, I got back to work on the party decorations. We spent a ridiculously long hour hanging balloons—with no small amount of time wasted by literally all of us static-charging ourselves with the balloons and trying to shock Kai—and just as we finished, Clara and Ramsey breezed in, both loaded down with bulging grocery bags.

"The food is here!" I cheered.

"Are we late?" Clara fretted. "The line at the store was a nightmare."

I glanced at the clock. "You're good. We have just enough time."

We all piled on the groceries, separating the snacks from the hors d'oeuvres. Sin, Sabrina, and Kaveri emptied bags of chips into big silver bowls while I arranged the million cupcakes on the tiered dessert tray I'd last used for a long-ago Halloween party. Kai and Izzah reappeared to help, the former wearing slacks and a dress shirt, while the latter had changed into a strapless emerald dress.

As I nervously rearranged the napkins and plates stacked beside the dessert tree, guests began to arrive. The bell over the door rang every minute, voices called out excited greetings, and conversation swelled through the room. I zipped into the back to throw the cupcake containers in the recycling bin, and when I returned, Kai and Izzah were standing at the bar with petite, dark-haired Makiko.

The young MiraCo GM looked like a million bucks in a silver, knee-length sheath dress, her hair coiled into an updo. A Japanese man around her age stood beside her, and my eyebrows shot up. A casual plus-one or a special someone?

"Makiko!" I called brightly as I swung around the bar to join them. "How are you?"

"I'd be better if my most important meeting of this quarter wasn't indefinitely postponed," she huffed.

"The VP broke his tailbone in the golf cart accident," Kai informed me. "He won't be back to work for weeks."

Makiko sighed.

"I'm sure it'll work out," I replied brightly, not in the mood to worry about random drunk VPs. "Or if you want a less stressful work environment, transfer to our guild!"

A small smile curved her lips. "We made it work for Kai, but my father needs me."

I tapped my lower lip. "How *did* you make it work?"

"There are certain advantages to keeping his association with MiraCo unofficial. As a … consultant … he can get away with things a guild member can't."

"That was our spin on it, at least," Kai added dryly. "My grandfather's allowing it because I'm not a complete embarrassment for once."

He said the last part with a spark of humor he wouldn't have felt before, and I hid a sigh of relief. Kai was no longer running from his past. He'd found new confidence in dealing with his family, and he had a more relaxed air about him than I remembered.

Or maybe it was Izzah's influence. Who knew.

The clock ticked closer to 2:45, and I did a swift headcount on the guests who'd arrived so far. If even one person was late,

I would smack them into next Christmas for ruining my party.

The guild door swung open again and Darius stepped inside, dressed smartly in a black bowtie over a baby blue button-down shirt that made his gray eyes pop even more intensely than usual. A bunch of guildeds called out greetings as the GM headed toward me.

"Good afternoon," he said. "I see everything is prepared."

"Yep!" Clara chirped, sweeping over to us with Sabrina and Sin on her heels, grinning proudly. "We're ready to go."

"Excellent. Tori, I'd like a word in my office please."

My eyes widened. An invite to Darius's office almost always meant someone was in trouble. "Someone" being me.

"It'll only take a few minutes," he assured me before I could protest.

I hesitated, then nodded. Not like I had a choice.

He led me up two flights of stairs, past the officers' desks, and into his office. As I sank nervously onto the chair in front of his large desk, he circled around it and took his seat.

I peered from the bookshelves to the stacks of papers on the desktop. It looked just like it had the first time I'd sat here.

"Tori." Darius steepled his fingers. "You've come far since you first wandered into this guild."

Oh. Uh … okay. I bobbed my head. Did he really need to drag me away from my about-to-begin party to tell me that?

"Clara mentioned that you recently finished final exams for your college term. How did they go?"

"Not bad." Especially considering how many classes I'd missed in January and February. "Pretty sure I passed everything. My Associate's Degree is in the bag, and if I complete another two years, I can get the full degree."

"Have you decided if you'll pursue your full degree?"

"Um … not really. I haven't decided anything." I squinted at him. "Why do you ask?"

He smiled seriously. "While updating me on your exam progress, Clara also informed me that she's utterly fed up with trying to run a guild and a business at the same time, and I need to hurry up and promote you to pub manager."

"M-manager?" I stammered.

"If you accept, your responsibilities will include ordering, accounting, scheduling, staffing, licenses, maintenance, and so on. Clara will oversee all your training, and once you're ready, she'll withdraw entirely from the pub side of the guild to focus on her AGM duties."

My mouth hung open.

"You'll also have more schedule flexibility should you choose to pursue bounty work on the side," he added. "Felix indicated in his last evaluation that you're ready to apply for your bounty license."

"He did?" I blurted.

"For your first year, you'll need an officer's approval for every case you take on—which won't be difficult to obtain, I imagine."

Yeah, because any bounty I wanted to take on that was too difficult, Aaron the Fourth Officer would just go with me. "I— I'm not sure … what I … I mean …"

Darius assessed my stunned expression with an understanding twinkle in his eyes. "Take your time and think about it."

As I nodded, he circled the desk and held out his hand. After a moment of confusion, I placed my hand in his. He drew me to my feet, smiling warmly.

"Before your new career options distract you too much, we should return to the party. I have a bar to prep."

Right. The party.

Darius and I returned to the main floor, and with a panicked look at the clock, I shouted for everyone to quiet down and get in position. They all scooted toward the pub entrance, leaving an empty half circle around the door. I squeezed through to stand at the front of the group, wringing my hands nervously.

Behind the bar, Darius waved casually, and the room went pitch black. In the eerie silence, the seconds ticked into minutes.

"How long do we have to wait?" Cameron whispered from near the back.

"*Shh!*"

Another minute ticked past, then I heard it: Aaron's familiar voice, chatting exuberantly about something, drawing closer. Footsteps scuffled outside, then the door swung open.

Ezra stood in the threshold, lit by the streetlamp outside, his amusement at whatever Aaron had said flickering into confusion when he saw the pub's dark interior.

The lights popped back on, and right on cue, a deafening shout blasted through the room:

"*SURPRISE!*"

My voice rang the loudest, and Ezra reeled back into Aaron, shock all over his face. Laughter and cheers broke out, and I ran forward, arms outstretched. The rest of the guild crowded in behind me.

As Aaron nudged Ezra across the threshold, I grabbed him in a hug. He gawked at me.

"What—is this—*Tori!*" he complained, half laughing.

I beamed. "Happy birthday!"

His astonishment softened, and he dipped his head for a swift kiss.

Half the guild wolf-whistled, and Ezra quickly straightened, rolling his eyes. Kai appeared from the group, snagged the aeromage's arm, and pushed him into the crowd for birthday hugs and well wishes.

I nudged Aaron. "Perfect timing!"

"Of course." He preened. "I'm a pro at this stuff."

"Really?" Kai replied with a snort. "What about Ezra seeing my text about picking up his gift? I had to pretend it was a present for Izzah."

"I was showing him a funny video! How was I supposed to know you'd text me right at that moment?"

Ignoring their banter, I watched Ezra receive a dozen birthday hugs before deciding the length of the room was too much distance between us. As I set out to join him, someone started music. Darius, behind the bar with his sleeves rolled up his forearms, was pouring drinks with a level of finesse I'd need another twenty years of practice to reach.

I wove through the gathered mythics, stopping to hug people, laughing, teasing. All familiar faces. All friends—no, family. Some closer than others, some nicer than others, but they were all my family now.

Justin tagged after Sin, grinning like a lovestruck idiot as she bounced from friend to friend, telling everyone about his new job. Cameron, Darren, Cearra, Alyssa, Riley, and Liam had started a drinking game. Lyndon, Bryce, and Drew had stationed themselves at the cupcake tray and were methodically eating their way through the sweet desserts.

Our witches Kaveri, Kier, Delta, Philip. Our officers Girard, Felix, Tabitha. Our healers Elisabetta, Miles, and Sanjana. And our newest member, who was in earnest discussion with Alistair: Blake, formerly of the Keys of Solomon.

The Keys of Solomon guild was no more. Too many members had betrayed them and too many had died, and the guild had quietly disbanded once the MPD's investigation into their actions had closed. I was openly delighted to have Blake as part of our crew—and secretly happy that he'd finally let go of Enright to find a fresh start in a new city and at a new guild.

Not every face I longed to see was present, but that was okay. Almost everyone was here, and happiness swelled in my heart until it felt like it would burst.

Music pounding and voices raised in boisterous conversation, the party swirled around me. Finally, I made it over to Ezra at the end of the bar, and a moment later, I was tucked against his side, his arm around my waist as he laughed at the story Andrew was telling him—something involving a fae he'd mistaken for a were-fox.

Drunk on joy, I beamed at everyone until Ezra nudged me with his hip. He nodded toward the other end of the room

I spotted Kai and Izzah first. She was leaning into his chest, her arms around his waist and—I grinned—her hands tucked in his back pockets. He was listening to her, focused entirely on her face, and I wish I had my phone out to snap a picture of his gooey expression. He was melted ice cream in her expert hands.

Then I spotted the other, far more unexpected couple only a few paces away. Aaron had his head bent toward Sabrina as she explained something animatedly. Eyes widening, she threw her arms up—and he tossed his head back in a laugh.

My eyebrows rose—then shot ever higher as he leaned toward her and said something that made her burst into peals of laughter too.

Were my eyes deceiving me, or were those two *flirting?* And even more shocking—Sabrina hadn't pulled out her phone for a round of bunny photos.

"Interesting," I purred. "Very interesting."

Ezra chuckled, his chest vibrating with the sound. "Don't get too excited. Aaron's dating history is against him."

"Oh, come on. Sabrina is adorable. His parents will love her." Laughing at his dubious expression, I slid away from Ezra's warm arm, circled behind the bar, and ducked beneath the counter.

Reappearing with a silver gift bag topped with white tissue paper, I held it out to him. "Happy birthday, Ezra!"

His eyes lit up, and he slid the bag closer. He hesitated, the tissue paper pinched between two fingers. Then he plucked the paper out, reached inside, and withdrew his gift.

It was a photo album, the leather cover patterned with musical notation. He flipped it open and blinked to find the first page empty.

"Next page," I suggested.

He turned it to the following page and blinked again at the two tickets tucked behind the protective plastic.

"The album is for photos of all the concerts we're going to go see," I told him, inexplicably nervous as I watched his unreadable poker face. "And those are tickets to our first one—the biggest folk music festival in the country!"

He carefully set the album down on the counter. Then he leaned across it, wrapped his hand around the back of my neck, and pulled our mouths together. His kiss was everything I'd ever wanted—fiery passion, sweet promise, and a helluva lot of heat.

Was the party over yet? Because I wanted my man back in my bed, like, *now*.

Sinking my hand into his hair, I deepened our kiss, my tongue flirting with his—and a loud cheer went up, swiftly spreading through the entire pub. Reluctantly, I straightened as my guildmates whooped and catcalled us.

"Hey, you're doing gifts without us!" Aaron zoomed to Ezra's side, digging in his pocket. "Happy birthday, man."

He dropped a white envelope on the open photo album, the "gift" decorated with a slightly crumpled gold bow. Ezra opened the top and slid out a packet of plane tickets.

"First class!" Aaron boasted. "Round trip for your music festival."

"What?" I gasped. "No way! Thank you, Aaron."

"Don't forget my gift." Kai slid into the spot on Ezra's other side and handed the aeromage a folded piece of paper. He hadn't bothered with a bow. "Hotel reservations."

Aaron rolled his eyes. "You're supposed to let him open it, Kai, not just tell him what it is."

"It's a hotel reservation printout. Not very glamorous." He canted a look at me—his smoldering, woman-melting look. "But your room will be very glamorous, I promise."

I grinned so broadly my cheeks hurt. "Thank you, guys. This is the best gift ever."

"It's not your gift, Tori." Aaron gave me a stern stare. "It's Ezra's. And it's totally up to him who he brings as his plus-one."

My gaze swung to Ezra. He thoughtfully tapped the plane tickets back into the envelope.

"Choices, choices," he murmured.

"*Ezra*," I growled.

His grin flashed, and he leaned across the bar again to plant a kiss on my scowl. "Of course I'm bringing you."

"Of course." I stuck my tongue out at Aaron.

He stuck his tongue out back at me, then pointed behind the bar. "You got the rest of his gift?"

"Oh, right!"

Ezra watched bemusedly as I dove through the saloon doors and reappeared a second later with a three-foot-long black case. I heaved it up on the counter beside the photo album and turned it toward him.

"Ta-da!" I said.

A grin was already spreading over Ezra's face. He didn't need to open it to know what was inside, but he flipped the thick clasps up and lifted the lid anyway. Nestled in black foam, a pair of short swords with equal length silver blades and black hilts shone under the overhead lights, the two weapons designed to fit together into a two-foot-long baton or a four-foot-long double-bladed staff.

"Are these from your blacksmith, Aaron?" Ezra asked with awed disbelief. "The one in Tennessee?"

"Yep. He makes weapons for half the Sinclair Academy mages. No offense to the deceased Twin Terrors, but these are superior blades. They won't break."

Ezra ran his hands along the hilts, then closed the lid. Turning to Aaron and Kai with an eager fire in his eyes, he asked, "Tomorrow morning?"

"Afternoon," Aaron corrected. "I'm not doing a live-blade practice with you while hungover."

"I suppose."

Snorting, the pyromage swiveled toward me. "Okay, last gift."

Panic fizzed through my chest. Another gift? I didn't know about any other gifts for Ezra! Had I forgotten something? Had *he* forgotten? What—

"*Your* gift," he added.

"Wait, mine? Why am I getting a gift?"

Aaron, Ezra, and Kai exchanged gleefully wicked looks.

"Well, you see …" Aaron began.

"This is actually an important day for you too," Kai continued.

"Because it's your guild anniversary," Ezra finished.

I stared at them. "No, it's not."

"It is!" Ezra insisted. "It's your one-year, one-month, one-week anniversary from your first shift here. Remember?"

Aaron tapped the counter. "I'll jog your memory: you threw a drink at us."

I ignored that. "You can't be serious."

"We are," Kai said. "We even got you a—"

Someone screamed.

I whipped toward the sound as mythics surged backward, opening a gap in the middle of the room—and revealing the shaggy black wolf padding across the floor toward us, scarlet eyes shining eerily. A tiny brown paper bag hung from its teeth.

All conversation fell silent as everyone nervously watched the varg. I fully expected it to approach my spot at the bar—but it walked right by and stopped before Kai.

He took the bag. "Thanks."

The wolf stared at him, turned and stared at me, then disappeared in a swirl of shadow right where it stood.

Zak's vargs were as melodramatic with their exits as he was.

Kai waved a casual hand at everyone watching us. "Just a druid delivery. As you were."

With much chuckling and head shaking, they resumed their eating, drinking, and talking.

"Why is a varg delivering something to you?" I asked Kai suspiciously.

"Since I stole Zak's number out of your phone so I could pick his brain on a certain … project." He slid the tiny paper bag to me. "He sent you this."

I opened the top and peered inside.

"Finally!" I lifted out a violet-and-blue crystal—the long overdue replacement for my new favorite artifact. "He was supposed to send this last month."

"He'd planned to show up today and surprise you with it, but he canceled last minute due to a dragon-chimera duel."

I looked up, jaw hanging. "A what?"

"He had to referee. Couldn't wait, apparently."

I continued to stare, trying to imagine what a fae duel—and refereeing one—would entail, then dropped the leather cord over my head. The crystal settled beside my seashell necklace.

Ezra cleared his throat. "As we were saying, we have a gift for you."

"An *anniversary* gift." Dubiousness dripped from my voice. "For a one-year, one-month, one-week anniversary."

They grinned, then Kai reached into his pocket and withdrew another envelope, this one folded in half. "This is from me, Ezra, and Aaron—with some help from Zak and Darius."

"Zak?" Blinking, I glanced along the bar, where the GM was busy with the blender. "And Darius? What kind of *help*?"

Kai held it out. "You'll see."

Nearly vibrating with anticipation, I unfolded the envelope, bent the top open, and slid its contents out.

Three playing cards, worn and yellowed with age. The hand-painted King of Hearts sat regally, a crown perched on his head and an eyepatch covering one eye. The dangerous Jack of Clubs wore all black, two daggers crossed in front of him. And the Joker, dressed in black and red, grinned mischievously as he held a deadly sword at a cocky angle.

"The Queen of Spades can never be replaced," Ezra said softly, "but these cards are from the same deck. The sorcerer who created the Queen made these too."

I stared at the three cards.

"We aren't sure about their spells yet." Aaron rubbed his jaw. "We've got consultations with a few experts lined up. We'll get it figured out."

"Their spells?" I whispered.

"The incantations aren't just written on the backs," Kai pointed out. "And since the deck's original creator passed away thirty years ago—and the cards' previous owners weren't forthcoming about how to use them—we need to do some Arcana detective work."

My eyebrows shot up, but he just shrugged mysteriously. My gaze slid to Ezra, smiling serenely, then to Aaron's broad grin.

I fanned the cards out. The dark, enigmatic Jack. The one-eyed King. The laughing Joker.

Tears spilled down my cheeks, and I didn't even care about my makeup. I set the cards on top of the photo album, planted my hands on the bar, and vaulted across it. I landed in Ezra's arms, then I was hugging all three of my mages, crying all over them while they laughed and patted my shoulders.

"Guildeds!"

I lifted my face from Ezra's chest at Darius's loud call. Clara had joined him behind the bar, and the two of them were lining up an assortment of glassware, from rocks glasses to wide-mouth snifters.

Everyone swept toward the bar, and after tucking my cards in the photo album, Aaron and Kai hustled me and Ezra to the spot right in front of the GM. Our guildmates crammed in all around us.

"It's time for a toast," Darius announced. "And we'll be drinking my secret sparkling strawberry sangria."

Loud *oohs* and *ahhs* filled the pub. I laughed, tears still streaking my cheeks.

He picked up a pitcher of candy-red sangria, and Clara lifted the other. As they filled each glass, Aaron and Kai started passing them out. I grabbed two glasses, and when I turned to hand them off, I found Justin and Sin behind me. Sabrina and Kaveri beside them. Izzah at Kai's side. Makiko behind them with her plus-one.

We handed out drinks to everyone, and with a cold wine glass in my hand, I turned back to Darius. Ezra slid his arm around my waist, warm against my side.

The GM's piercing gray stare touched on me, then Ezra, then Aaron and Kai. He lifted his gaze to the rest of the guild and picked up his glass of sangria.

Silence fell, every mythic—and two humans neck-deep in mythicness—listening intently.

"I could make a long, heartfelt speech about family, loyalty, love, and bravery," he mused, "but really, there's only one thing to be said."

My breath caught.

He raised his glass into the air. "Don't hit first—"

"—*but always hit back!*" we shouted at the top of our lungs.

Laughter and cheers rang out, and as one, we brought our glasses to our lips and drank.

DISCOVER MORE GUILD CODEX BOOKS AT
www.guildcodex.ca

ACKNOWLEDGEMENTS

The first person I must thank, without whom the Guild Codex world would be vastly different (and not nearly as awesome) is my husband, Jacob. He's been my sounding board from day one, a creative kickstart any time I got stuck, the voice of reason when I got crazy (bad) ideas, the first reader and then the final reader of every book before publication, and my rock whenever things got hard and the deadlines got bad and I got exhausted. Thank you.

Thank you to Elizabeth, my amazing editor, whose ability to keep on schedule simultaneously leaves me in awe and ensures I never screw up my own deadlines too badly (because I never want to release a book that hasn't passed through your hands first).

Thank you to Breanna, for dropping everything on far too many weekends to read each book and provide invaluable feedback.

Thank you to Amber, for also dropping everything when I needed you and for catching the little (and not so little) things.

Thank you to Jax, for your support, feedback, and fantastic character essays.

Thank you to Erich Merkel, master of Latin and Ancient Greek, who freely offered his time and expertise on every book and never got fed up with my "by the way, I need this tomorrow, I'm so sorry, thank you thank you thank you" emails. The Guild Codex world wouldn't be nearly as cool without your input.

Thank you to Cris Dukehart, who not only brought Tori, Robin, and the entire Guild Codex gang to life with her amazing narration, but also showed more passion and dedication for the series than I ever could've asked of a narrator.

Thank you to Kara and the team at Tantor, for bringing Cris on board and making the audiobooks happen, no matter the obstacles.

Thank you to Rob Jacobsen, for jumping onto the Guild Codex ship without a second thought, for unreservedly immersing yourself in my particular crazy, and for contributing your astonishing imagination to this world.

Thank you to Uma, for sharing so much to help bring Izzah to life and add such a fun, badass character to the series.

Thank you to Liz and Christina, for contributing your exceptional medical knowledge and experience so I could horribly wound my characters in the most realistic ways possible.

Thank you to Ashleigh, for allowing me to see my characters in a way I'd never imagined.

Thank you to Erich Orris of Fudo Forge, who enabled me to check a box on my author bucket list that I didn't know existed until his first email landed in my inbox. Sharpie is breathtaking!

Thank you to my author besties, for keeping me sane, commiserating, congratulating, and making me laugh when I most need it.

An extra special thank you to my ARC Team, for your enthusiasm, support, and dedication to making every release the best it can be. I don't know what I'd do without you.

And lastly, a huge thank you to my readers. Thank you for joining me on this wild ride, for reviewing and recommending the series, for cheering on each release, and for loving the Guild Codex crew as much as I do. I hope you'll join me for the next romp in their world.

ABOUT THE AUTHOR

Annette Marie is the author of YA urban fantasy series *Steel & Stone*, its prequel trilogy *Spell Weaver*, and romantic fantasy trilogy *Red Winter*.

Her first love is fantasy, but fast-paced adventures, bold heroines, and tantalizing forbidden romances are her guilty pleasures. She proudly admits she has a thing for dragons, and her editor has politely inquired as to whether she intends to include them in every book.

Annette lives in the frozen winter wasteland of Alberta, Canada (okay, it's not quite that bad) and shares her life with her husband and their furry minion of darkness—sorry, cat—Caesar. When not writing, she can be found elbow-deep in one art project or another while blissfully ignoring all adult responsibilities.

www.annettemarie.ca

THE
GUILD CODEX
DEMONIZED

Robin Page: outcast sorceress, mythic history buff, unapologetic
bookworm, and the last person you'd expect to command the rarest
demon in the long history of summoning. Though she holds his
leash, this demon can't be controlled.

But can he be tamed?

DISCOVER MORE BOOKS AT
www.guildcodex.ca

THE
GUILD CODEX
WARPED

The MPD has three roles: keep magic hidden, keep mythics under control, and don't screw up the first two.

Kit Morris is the wrong guy for the job on all counts—but for better or worse, this mind-warping psychic is the MPD's newest and most unlikely agent.

DISCOVER MORE BOOKS AT
www.guildcodex.ca

THE
GUILD CODEX
UNVEILED

Powerful druid.
Deadly alchemist.
Notorious rogue.

The Crystal Druid's identity has been unveiled—and
now his true story begins.

STEEL & STONE

When everyone wants you dead, good help is hard to find.

The first rule for an apprentice Consul is *don't trust daemons*. But when Piper is framed for the theft of the deadly Sahar Stone, she ends up with two troublesome daemons as her only allies: Lyre, a hotter-than-hell incubus who isn't as harmless as he seems, and Ash, a draconian mercenary with a seriously bad reputation. Trusting them might be her biggest mistake yet.

SPELL WEAVER

The only thing more dangerous than the denizens of the Underworld ... is stealing from them.

As a daemon living in exile among humans, Clio has picked up some unique skills. But pilfering magic from the Underworld's deadliest spell weavers? Not so much. Unfortunately, that's exactly what she has to do to earn a ticket home.

GET THE COMPLETE TRILOGY
www.annettemarie.ca/spellweaver

Red Winter

A destiny written by the gods. A fate forged by lies.

If Emi is sure of anything, it's that *kami*—the gods—are good, and *yokai*—the earth spirits—are evil. But when she saves the life of a fox shapeshifter, the truths of her world start to crumble. And the treachery of the gods runs deep.

This stunning trilogy features 30 full-page illustrations.